Specific Intent

Specific Intent

STAN POLLACK

To order additional copies of this book, contact:
Xlibris Corporation
1-888-795-4274
www.Xlibris.com
Orders@Xlibris.com
38117

PROLOGUE

Copenhagen, Denmark, 2007

I WAS A blonde, a blonde to make a bishop kick a hole through a stained glass window. In Italy a woman can have a face like a train wreck as long as she's a blonde. However, I'm from Denmark where the competition is keener. It's not that gentlemen prefer blondes it's just that we look dumb. So, I'm not certain of the attraction he had for me, but we became lovers.

In Denmark I called him Charles. When I visited with him in America where he lived, I called him Dr. Feelgood, sometimes even in bed. This was our little joke, our subterfuge to the outside world. Charles was a well known and respected surgeon, married to a wealthy wife, Sophia, heiress to a family fortune. No, not steel mills or railroads, but rather designer coats and dresses. Charles called them shmottes (rags). He used the same word to describe her family members.

I would visit America four to six times a year, timed for out of town physicians conventions. My son Hans and my daughter Susan, then seven and five, often accompanied me. Why not? These were his children too! The good doctor was effective at reconnoitering his life and his wife. After all, he could find his way through the maze of an open stomach with his eyes closed.

The time we spent together was short and so each day became precious. One realizes the full importance of time only when there is little of it left. We lived our lives as we would climb a mountain. We took occasional glances towards the summit to keep our goal in mind. Many beautiful scenes were observed from each new vantage point. We climbed slowly, and steadily. Each passing moment was enjoyed to its fullest. Finally, the view from the summit served as a fitting climax for the journey. We counted each day in this manner as if it would be the last.

However, change is inevitable. Everyone gets their share of difficult times. No one gets a free ride. Some days you tame the tiger, and some days the tiger eats you for lunch. In the case of Charles, the tiger was present for dinner as well. This is his story, and in a sense, mine as well. Me? My name is Harriet Leeds. Some might remember the name, for I was headline news some twenty five years ago.

CHAPTER 1

June 18th 1977

I PUSHED THROUGH the double swinging doors of the surgical lounge and yanked off the mask which hung limply on my chest, dangling by its elastic. Tossing it into the waste receptacle I felt relief after breathing through the blasted thing for the past six hours. The area was abuzz with staff members coming on the evening shift. The changing of the guard inevitably created momentary chaos. As usual I ignored all this commotion and headed down the main corridor towards the locker room. The loud speaker and its annoying bells continually rang out calling the flock for this and for that. Suddenly it caught my attention.

"Dr. Feelgood, Dr. Feelgood, please call the operator." Then the bells began ringing. They were my bells, three long and two short. I guess I did not call the operator quick enough to suit her, for she hit the bell button within seconds. "Why can't they ever give me a minute to breathe?"

"Hello, this is Dr. Feelgood – yes operator, I know an Anna – put her on. Yes Anna what's the problem. (pause) Did you see Sophia leaving the house this morning? (pause) I'm certain that you just missed her. She told me that she planned to go shopping for most of the day. Anyway Anna, don't worry, they always return for dinner. (pause) Yes, of course, just a joke. I'll tell you what you can do. If you missed her leaving the house then perhaps you missed her as well coming in. Why don't you check the bedroom? If she is napping, it's OK to wake her up. I should be leaving the hospital shortly. Let's plan for dinner at nine o'clock. (pause) That's OK Anna, it was all right to call me here."

"Is everything OK Doc? You look pale. Don't you feel good? No pun intended."

"Nurse Brown, you are getting too proficient at determining who looks good and who does not. I always thought this was a doctors' domain. All kidding aside, I'm OK. My housekeeper is just a worry wart. I guess it rubbed off on me now. I'm only human you know!"

We moved down the hallway in different directions. The locker room was empty. I sat down on a bench, grateful that the day was over for me in the hospital but apprehensive of the hours ahead. I threw off my scrubs and entered the shower, quickly dressed into civies and retraced my steps back towards my office. The name plate on the door identified its occupant – DR. CHARLES FEELGOOD, CHIEF OF SURGERY – . I thought about the perils of getting what you wish for. I slid the key into the lock and entered the room.

I sat down behind my desk piled up with papers and a scattering of framed photos. A family picture was directly illuminated as I flipped on the desk light. There I stood next to Sophia and our two adult children. I began to induce myself into an hypnotic trance staring at the photograph longer than I would usually do. This was a talent I had acquired as a young intern working sixteen hours a day and needing a way to prompt sleep into a standby mode at an opportune moment when there was a break in the action. I called it a haze. Sophia called it a shmooze. That was the wrong word but I never corrected her.

Within minutes the four images on the family color photo faded away as I began to doze off and reappeared clearly in my haze as a black and white photo of myself and Sophia in our early twenties sitting on the steps of a library at a university. Yes, she was there during the schmoozing times. We were two young Jews on the campus of Harvard University who should have known two things, – one was suffering and the other was where to find great Chinese food. We struck out on both. Sophia was rich and I was Orthodox.

At first we were just good friends. For whatever strange reason, we loved each other's company. Then worlds collided. We came to the conclusion that platonic love was just love from the neck up – so we quickly got married at an early urge! The only class we shared together was Latin. It was a course all pre-med students took. Sophia, who was a pre-housewife student bitched that when a subject becomes totally obsolete Harvard makes it a required course. The fact that she found herself at this prestigious university in the first place was due to her father's generosity as a major contributor of mostly money to this institution. He was a man who would say things like, "whom are you" so as to remind the listener that he had attended night school, his Alma Mater!

Almost all married couples fight, although many are ashamed to admit it. Actually, a marriage in which no quarreling at all takes place may well be one that is dead or dying from emotional undernourishment. If you care you probably fight. And fight we did, but unfortunately, we went way, way over the top in this regard. Many years passed in this status quo situation. As a student of Latin I translated these words to mean, "what a mess I'm in!" At some point in time I began to ask myself, "so, Doc, what have you learned about marriage?"

Well, I learned too late that the success of our marriage was dependent upon avoiding the unforgivable. Leaving about three or four things a day unsaid is a good rule to follow. Medically speaking, it's best to catch a cold early, so I would advise people never to confuse I love you with I want to marry you!

My bad marriage was taking its toll upon me physically as well as mentally. After living with death for many years as a physician I concluded that one only lives once. For me it would be better to rent, as I no longer could mate in captivity. There of course, was the social stigma surrounding adultery. However, I decided that this would not deter me. I merely looked at it as another first. I was the first person in my family to graduate from college, and now the first to commit adultery – although I couldn't swear for my uncle Henry. I've always tried to find the silver lining in life, so I can offer one positive thing in favor of adultery. Out of the deceitfulness and selfishness flow love and joy and peace beyond anything that can be imagined.

I was pleased that the thoughts I was experiencing during my hypnotic spell were giving me such good feelings of inner peace. I did not want these moments to end. A soft knocking at the door confused me. Was I still in a haze or back in the real world? As the knocking became more persistent, the call of the wild began. "Dr. Feelgood, Dr. Feelgood, are you there?"

"Yes I'm here," I shouted out, "I'm on the phone."

"Sorry, not important," apologized the voice on the other side of the door.

"Not important," I muttered to myself. They have been hounding me since I was twenty two years old. It's either not important or panic important, never anything in between.

On the days I would operate it was my practice to visit my patient before leaving the hospital for the day. Tonight, however, I was pre-occupied with what was lying ahead for me at my home. As I was going through the routine of closing up my office I thought of the patient now in the recovery room. So no matter what was going on, I had one more stop to make, and headed to his bed. The head nurse walked towards me as I was making my way down the hallway.

"Where have you been, Dr. Feelgood?" she barked.

I wondered if she was just an underling or my wife growling!

"The operator told me that you might be on your way home. I sent an orderly to check to see if you might still be in your office or not. He came back a few minutes ago and told us that you were on the phone. With all due respect, Dr. Feelgood, we have an emergency on our hands!"

"Hold your horses, just wait a minute," I said angrily. "Whoever was at my office door told me 'no problem', when I called out from my desk that I was on the phone. That did not sound like an emergency to me – does it sound that way to you? Anyway all this is beside the point. What's the problem?"

The nurse tossed me a large gown to put over my street clothing and a pair of cotton overshoes.

"Your patient is in cardiac arrest!"

I was shocked. "Cardiac arrest? I can't believe that." I asserted.

"The nurse on duty claims that you never gave her instructions to monitor his blood pressure before you left the operating room."

"But that's normal care!" I protested.

"Yes, normal care," she shot back, "but it always has to be reviewed by the surgeon with the first nurse on duty and then signed off in writing by that nurse and passed onto subsequent relief nurses. Why wasn't this hospital rule followed?"

"With all due respect to hospital rules," I lectured, "normal care is normal care. I'm sure you can agree to that?"

"No!" she berated.

I felt that I had my wife standing in front of me, and so there was no sense continuing this conversation. I began to put on the gown, but was stopped by the nurse.

"Look doctor, you're not scrubbed, and Dr. Frank is inside with the anesthesiologist."

At that moment my colleague, Dr. Frank, swung open the door and put his hand on my shoulder.

"Don't worry," he assured me, "your patient is sleeping comfortably, hopefully till morning."

He urged me to go home. I guess I didn't look too good to him either. I checked my watch. It was after nine o'clock already. I headed out the front door of the hospital.

My home was about thirty minutes away, in an area named Kennsington. Living up to its British name, we occupied an eighteenth century country home, dotted with gardens of wild flowers and surrounded by three heavily wooded acres. An active stream meandered about until it disappeared into the ground. The road to the property was almost a half mile long. It was winding, unpaved, and tree lined, just as God intended. Family, friends, and even strangers described the house as a mini-mansion. As far as I was concerned, it was a question of compared to what. Compared to our studio apartment at Harvard, it was. Compared to my father-in-laws place, it wasn't.

As I swung my car around the final curve I was blinded by the silent spinning lights on the top of the roof of a hospital ambulance. This emergency vehicle I might add, came from my hospital. The driveway was also blocked by two police cars. I stopped my car and parked at the side of the road about one hundred feet away. I began to feel cold, and short of breath. I felt momentarily dizzy. "Stay cool," I said to myself. My thoughts now turned to how I could best approach the police. With only a short way to walk, I began to organize the questions I might ask while presenting a good persona.

One of the policemen on the top of the hill started to approach me with his flashlight focused on my face. We met about half way.

"What's going on here?" I inquired. I did not give him a chance to respond, for I planned to get in two more questions in rapid succession. "What's the ambulance doing here?" The next question was intended to throw him off a little. "Who got hurt? Is it serious?"

The cop didn't know where to begin answering me. After all he was trained to do the asking, not to sort my questions out. So, he reverted to police academy class 101, – "How to secure information in the field."

"Who are you? Why are you here sir?"

I answered him in seven words, calling him officer only because he called me sir. "Officer, I'm Dr. Feelgood, I live here."

He set his flashlight onto the ground to help lead the way towards the house. I felt that we were on the same wavelength. He, a professional cop, and me, a professional doc. This feeling was verified when we reached his partner leaning against one of their cars.

"John, it's OK, this is Dr. Feelgood. He lives here," he reported.

"My words exactly," I thought.

John put his hand out to shake mine. I was very pleased, for within minutes we had become a threesome.

The cop who had met me on the road spoke up. "Look Doc, why don't you go inside the house and talk to the medics." Then John half bowed his head and whispered, "God bless you sir." My first condolence was from Inspector Clouseau.

I moved swiftly around the ambulance and ran up several steps to the front door. Just as I was reaching for the handle, the door opened. Two medics were on either side of a stretcher.

"Can you open the door wider and hold it open for us?" one medic requested.

"Sure," I responded.

In the stretcher was the outline of a person covered from head to toe with a white sheet.

"I'm Dr. Feelgood," I said. Who's this?"

"We know who you are," the other medic answered. "We all work in the same place, Doc."

Now I had four new friends. I followed the stretcher to the ambulance and watched them maneuver the body inside and close the doors.

"Is this Anna?" I speculated, not having received an answer to my question.

"Didn't the policemen tell you? It's your wife. We're sorry, but it was just too late when we arrived."

At that moment Anna, dressed in her maid's uniform, came to the front door. She was crying softly. I walked back, met her at the bottom of the steps and clutched her hand.

"Why did she die? Why? I called you back at the hospital. They told me that you may be on your way home. I tried to wake her just as you told me to do. She would not wake up. I looked at the time to see if you would be home soon. I was so nervous that I knocked the clock off the night table to the floor."

I felt a tinge of apprehension, but I had to ask her if she also knocked over a bottle of pills as well.

"Just the clock," she replied. "I don't remember any bottle of pills."

Because she seemed a bit confused I decided not to pursue this line of questioning. I was also anxious to get to the bedroom.

As I made my way up the staircase I thought about how the two policemen were so laid back. Surely, they would never be promoted to detective. Then again, why should I care about that. The bedroom door was wide open. All the lights were lit. The bedding was disturbed. I closed the door behind me and clicked the lock shut. My hand began to shake as I removed a small medicine bottle from my inside jacket pocket. I glanced at the label on the bottle just to make sure. It read "Demerol." I shook the bottle upside down just to make sure. It was empty. I did not want to think that I was losing confidence. I knew what the label read and I knew that the bottle was empty, so, I told myself that it was only my training to always double check everything that was in play.

I placed the bottle on the night table. I glanced at the clock which was knocked over by Anna. The fact that she did not remember seeing a medicine bottle raised some concern. However, I dismissed it in my mind. After all, I could not begin to worry about things that could only remotely develop. Having accomplished my task during these critical seconds, I walked over to unlock the door.

"Is that you, Doc?" The voice came from the other side of the door.

I opened the door. It was John, the cop. I stepped aside to allow him to enter the room. He looked around in silence, moving about in slow motion.

"Officer," I said, "by the way, I noticed that bottle of medicine on the night table."

I walked over towards the table and picked up the bottle to show to him. The cap was off, and I shook it upside down.

"Empty!" I mumbled. "You may want to take it."

John briefly hesitated. I thought, "jerko, now I'm certain you'll never make detective." He pulled out a plastic zip lock bag from his pocket and held it open for me. I dropped the bottle in and he sealed the bag up.

"This is how they like me to bring things back," he proudly proclaimed.

John stared at the bag for a few seconds. Then it seemed to me that he suddenly put two and two together. While nobody else was in the room with us, he approached me and whispered, "maybe a suicide."

I nodded my head in sort of agreement. He gently patted my shoulder. "I'm sorry sir," he added.

"Thank you John," I replied. I guess the back pain was just too much for her."

At that moment, I had some concern that believing he was a dumb cop he might tell his superior that I suggested that he bring back the empty bottle. So, I decided to compliment him for deciding that it might be important to do so. I told him that he was a real smart cop for doing this. I hoped that this sort of conversation would in fact make him truly believe that it was his idea in the first place. I was convinced that I had pegged John perfectly. This feeling only lasted a few seconds more as he pushed the plastic bag into his pocket and headed for the door. He suddenly turned around, pulled the bag out of his pocket and, in "Columbo style," began to wave it in my direction. In an authoritative manner, with a tone of voice I had not heard before asserted, "too bad you picked up the bottle Doc. It muddied the fingerprint evidence."

"You're right, how stupid of me, sorry about that," I apologized.

John turned back towards the door and whirled around again. "By the way sir, one more thing. I've been wondering why you assumed that someone had been hurt when you arrived home?"

I did not answer. He wasn't waiting for an answer. As he left the bedroom he closed the door a little harder than expected. It was close to a slam. I stood stunned by the fact that I only asked his partner that question way down on the road. They must have discussed it. I now pondered whether John was really a dumb cop after all, or a Columbo. I tilted towards Columbo!

I did not bother to fully undress, even though I was exhausted. I flipped two sleeping pills into my mouth and stretched out in the bed. I must have fallen asleep in a deep state, for at first the ringing of the phone seemed to be coming from my dream. Now awake, I picked up the receiver.

"Yes."

"Is this Dr. Feelgood?"

"Yes."

"Sorry to wake you. This is Dr. Green at the hospital. I'm part time on the night shift. I'm calling to tell you that your patient in the recovery room passed away about thirty minutes ago."

CHAPTER 2

June 19th

T HE PLAQUE ON the desk read, "CHIEF MEDICAL EXAMINER, NASSAU COUNTY, N.Y." A man in his late fifties sat behind a large desk. He was dressed in a physician's white smock, an appropriate uniform, for a pathologist, and a renowned one at that. The desk held two sizes of microscopes. Glass slides were scattered about like fallen dominos. Dr. Paul Sales was the medical examiner with a past history of similar positions in San Francisco and Boston. His claim to fame was his role in the famous Boston strangler case. He came to New York at the time of the headlined Alice Crimmins murder trial.

The knock on the door began softly at short intervals and then picked up speed.

"Come in," called out the doctor. "You win, I always give into persistence."

A woman in her mid-twenties entered the room. She held a few sheets of paper in her hand and began to wave them in the air as she approached the desk.

"I see them Beth. It looks as if whatever you got there is burning a hole in your hand."

"It's the Feelgood autopsy report."

"What about it? Any problems?"

"Yes, well perhaps."

"Sit down Beth. What's up?"

"Well, we determined that the cause of death was from a massive overdose of Demerol."

"OK, but we knew this for certain going in."

"That's true, and, in fact, the autopsy confirmed that."

"So, what's the problem?"

"Well, here is the dilemma. The blood test report indicates that some of the properties of Demerol are those only found in its liquid form administered by injection. Yet, the police officer on the scene turned in an empty capsule bottle of Demerol taken from the bedroom where the doctor's wife was found. Just as an aside, he reported to his superior that he was uncomfortable with his discussions with Dr. Feelgood."

"That's very interesting, Beth. Are you certain about the accuracy of the results?"

"Yes, I asked the lab to test a second time. The results were the same."

"I see. Leave the report with me for now. Let me think about it. I'll return it to you later in the day."

The hands of the clock were poised exactly at noon. I had not slept as late in years. The sleeping pills coupled with the exhausting past twenty four hours played havoc with my normal daily routine. I began to think of the happenings of yesterday and I felt that all had pretty much gone according to plan. Yes, there had been several glitches. John, the cop, was one for example. I figured that they may have performed an autopsy last night or maybe this morning. I could have challenged it on religious grounds, but because of the circumstances, the authorities would have brought the matter into court. It seemed prudent to do nothing. I didn't want some little bureaucrat raising his eyebrows because I would object to an autopsy.

I instinctively became aware that for a period of time I would have to play the role of a grieving husband. I planned to minimize talking to or meeting people. However, there were several telephone calls I had to make. Sophia's mother had passed away some years ago. I knew her father had to be notified, but I could not contemplate calling him and hear him answer, "whom is calling?" I would have my son contact him as he always was patient with his grandfather.

The first order of business was to notify the hospital. This was a call I hated to make. I placed the call directly to the administrator's office. Gary and I never saw eye to eye with each other. That dumb bastard must have graduated from some kind of school like The Mary Poppins Institute of Business and Accounting. He often got his jollies by challenging my decisions, often not in his domain. At some point he stopped talking to me. What luck! This was another body off my back. I explained to his secretary what had happened and that I would be out for perhaps a week. She was very sympathetic and all, but went on to tell me that her boss needed to talk with me. She asked me to please call back later as Gary would be in all day meetings. I told her that I would and hung up the phone.

"Meetings all day?" I thought, "What can that jerk be meeting about all day?"

I recalled the phone call I received from the night shift doctor at the hospital about the passing away of my patient. Perhaps this was the reason the administrator needed to speak with me.

I had made a decision to cremate Sophia even though my orthodox religious beliefs prohibited this. I knew the manager of the local crematorium and placed my next unpleasant call to him. He offered his condolences, words he knew by heart which he also mastered in Spanish for when the occasion called for it. I told him that my wife either was autopsied last night, or possibly today. I asked him to take care of all the details towards a quick cremation. He assured me that he would keep me advised.

I spent the next twenty minutes or so talking with my children. My daughter happened to be far away in some third world country. To my surprise I was able to reach her without any difficulty. I told her of my cremation plans. She knew my views here, so she may have thought that I had lost it. However, she did not question the decision. Actually, she may have agreed because we often had disagreements about my "silly religion", as she would term it, when she was losing the argument. Anyway, I suggested that there was no need for her to rush home as there would be no funeral. I also suggested that we could schedule a memorial service at a later date. One thing I knew for sure was that she would be back for the reading of the will.

Before I tried to reach my son, the phone rang. It was the man at the crematorium informing me that the autopsy had been completed last night but the medical examiner's office placed a hold on her release. They would not give him the reason. He asked me if I knew anything. Of course, I didn't. I suggested that he check back with them later in the day.

My son lived on the West Coast. I caught him at home just as he was leaving for work. He took the news very hard and was dismayed that I planned to cremate his mother. I explained that while I am personally against cremation, it had always been her wishes. He argued that he had never heard his mother express such a desire. I assured him that this is what she had told me. I mentioned the memorial service, an idea that had just sprung up when I was talking with my daughter. My son asserted something to the effect that he never heard of such a thing in Hebrew school. It was best to let this conversation end. However, I asked him to do me a favor and contact his grandfather because I did not have the heart to do so.

I was now anxious to go through Sophia's papers, particularly the financial ones. My first inkling that things were not going well were bits and pieces of clues that stocks, bonds, and other investments, which she owned from her family's holdings, were taken out of the estate and entrusted directly to our children. This must have been executed after one of our rip-roaring arguments.

In the early years we had privy to each other's wills. Each left everything to the other. Although, in all fairness, the everything was not equal. Eventually, I changed my will and now wondered if and when she had done likewise. Her will alluded me in my search. I was certain that her lawyer held the original, but most people keep a copy for themselves. I finally found it hidden in a shoe box under a pair of sandals. After reading through all the legal bla, bla, bla, the bottom line reflected what I had guessed. Under New York State law one third of the estate went to me. The balance at her option was divided between our children and some charities. However, the catch twenty two hung its ugly head for me. The entire estate, which had been fluid, appeared to have been shifted away to the ownership of our children. I would not know the full extent of this until the reading of the will. It may very well turn out that my legal share would be worth "bubkis." That's my word for what my father-in-law learned in night school as Zippo!

It was getting late in the day, and I remembered that I had promised to call the hospital administrator back. I dialed up his direct line.

"This is Dr. Feelgood returning your call."

I really wasn't returning his call, but I said it anyway. He thanked me and muttered through some words of condolence. Then he got right to the point. I don't remember his exact words, but the essence is ingrained in my brain to this day. Basically, it went something like this:

The family of my patient, who had passed away early this morning, was at the hospital at the time of death. A talkative nurse trying to protect herself began some damage control. She told them of my failure to leave specific care instructions according to hospital rules. The family remained at the hospital awaiting their attorney, and demanded a meeting with the hospital administrator. All they talked about was, "How can the hospital allow this to happen?" They had no choice but to contemplate a malpractice law suit. It seemed that they had the will and the means to see it through.

As a reaction to this threat, the hospital's board and their lawyers decided to minimize their liability as best they could. The best way they decided was to suspend me. This was the lowest point of my professional career. Their action, under the circumstances, seemed unreasonably vicious. It certainly was not the kind of support or vote of confidence I would have expected. I thought of taking legal action myself against the hospital for their unwarranted act, but decided to sit tight, for this would be better resolved in my favor after the malpractice suit failed. Surely, the wisdom of the courts would see the family as just another litigator who sues anybody with deep pockets whether the evidence is strong or not. In any event, as it stood then, I was positioned to take the first heat. I did not find fault with Gary. After all, he was just the messenger.

I decided to turn the answering machine on. Every conversation today amounted to zippo. Just then the phone rang again.

"What now?"

It was the manager of the crematorium calling me back. Another inquiry had been made to the medical examiner's office. There was no release authorization available as yet. In fact, they advised him that the situation would be the same the next day. I thanked him for following up and told him that I would get involved myself the first thing in the morning.

Finally, I turned on the answering machine. I needed some uninterrupted time to consider a new issue. The real possibility of a law suit now tied into Sophia's will. Malpractice insurance costs had always been expensive and crept up over the years. Because of Sophia's financial position it made sense for us to self-insure. Hundreds of thousands of dollars were saved in insurance monies. I panicked at the thought of possibly not being able to cover myself now. I flipped through my telephone directory and placed a call to my insurance agent. It was now after five o'clock and his office was closed. I left a detailed message and asked him to please call me back in the morning.

I was not much of a drinker, but I knew it was necessary to pour myself a large glass of scotch whiskey. I had spent the entire day in the bedroom and had not eaten at all. The drink began to make me hungry. I found Anna scrubbing down the kitchen. I guess it was her way of coping with the stress. I asked her if she could prepare a fruit salad for me. Anna was happy to do so and got busy pulling cottage cheese and fruits out of the refrigerator.

The front door bell rang. I told Anna to continue preparing the salad and that I would answer the bell. Perhaps flowers were beginning to arrive. The floral arrangement turned out to be two young men, dressed in business suits who identified themselves as assistant DA's. One handed me a sealed envelope.

"What is this, a subpoena?"

"No it's not," the other young man answered. "It's an informal request for you to meet with the District Attorney of Nassau County briefly tomorrow to clear up some problems that have arisen surrounding the death of your wife."

"What's the problem?" I responded.

"We have no idea sir. It may well be only some simple details. Honestly, we have no idea."

Trying to hang on to a thread of positive information, I replied back, "Well, I'm sure that you are right, just some simple details."

I opened the envelope while we all stood together at the door. A brief note reflected what these men said it was. The notice was written on official stationary with an assigned reference number in the left hand corner of the paper. They did not say goodbye, only nodded, and headed back to where they had parked their car. I stared at the auto's rear red lights until they disappeared along the first curve in the road. Anna came to the door to tell me that my supper was on the table. I thanked her, but the hunger I felt earlier suddenly disappeared. I did manage to finish the entire salad, only to please Anna.

I returned to the bedroom. It had been a very long and tiring day to say the least. I sat down in my favorite chair to think and try to put everything that happened so far into perspective. It became obvious that things were unraveling fast in all directions. My training as a physician taught me to write things down in an orderly way in order to arrive at some sort of workable decisions. I took out a legal pad from the desk drawer and began to organize the trouble spots.

JOHN THE COP – read him wrong – I can live with that – no real damage.

ANNA – claims not to have seen bottle of pills on the night table – too upset to be absolutely certain.

MY SON – skeptical about my cremation plans – so what!

MEDICAL EXAMINER'S OFFICE – delaying release of Sophia – not unusual, just normal snafu from municipal government.

I felt as if I had covered the "B" list. The "A" list was more troublesome.

SUSPENSION AND POSSIBLE LAW SUIT – need to talk with my insurance agent.

FINANCES – certainly problematic – did I say "bubkis?"

DA'S INVITATION – just an informal chat – sounds like foreplay to me.

Now I had the entire picture in front of me. In total, things did not look very good, better yet, even scary. However, until the uncertainties actually happen, I remained confident that I could come through this mess unscathed.

I had one final call to make before I could even think of sleep. First, I placed my pad on the night table so as to read my entries under a good light. They didn't look any better there, so I slipped the whole pad in the under drawer. I picked up the phone. I asked the overseas operator to connect me with Copenhagen, Denmark. The phone on the other end rang about six times. I didn't expect anybody to pick up as it was three o'clock in the morning there. The answering machine clicked on. A female voice known to me as Harriet requested first in Danish, then in English, that a message be left at the beep. My message was short and to the point.

"Hello darling, it is done. There are some minor glitches. They are simple details at the most. However, they will delay my trip for a few days. Let's plan for you to meet me at the airport on Saturday instead of Thursday. I'll be on the same flight at the same time. Give the kids a big hug and kiss for me. I love you."

It was time for another scotch. I poured the drink into a larger glass than I had used before. I deserved it!

CHAPTER 3

June 20th

M Y INSURANCE AGENT woke me up around ten o'clock this morning. I was glad to hear from him. He was a nice fellow. However, we had little contact with him. While his company covered all our insurance needs, they did not have the privilege of collecting high malpractice insurance premiums. This would have given my agent commissions that could buy him a new car every few years. As such, I was not on his preferred client's list. I had left him a message that sort of explained the situation, but now he needed the specifics to do what he does.

He first questioned my need for malpractice insurance at this time. I told him about Sophia's death. I also explained that we had self-insured depending on her own private funds which may no longer be available to me because of personal family reasons. I added that there is a possibility that the hospital I worked for might be sued over an issue that I was involved in.

He listened politely and then responded. "Well to be perfectly honest, I have bad news and bad news!"

"What's the first bad news?" I replied.

"In the first place, malpractice insurance only covers future events. So, whatever may or may not occur in possible litigation now would not be insured. So, if you are still interested in a policy on this basis I can develop quotes and send them off to you."

"What's the other bad news?" I continued, without responding to my interest in a policy.

"Well, I checked your insurance records this morning before I called and found that your wife has a life insurance policy in effect with you as the beneficiary."

"Thank you for telling me. I was totally unaware of this."

"Before you thank me Dr. Feelgood, there is a major problem here for sure."

I was becoming anxious. "What's the problem?" I shot back.

"Well, your message to me yesterday said that your wife committed suicide."

"So!" I asserted

"I'm sure that you are aware that this cause of death voids the policy."

I was beside myself. "What's the value of the policy?" I pursued.

He responded in as few words as humanly possible.

"Five mil!"

"What if it was accidental?" I explored.

"Well, that would have to be proven, probably in a court of law, without any reasonable doubt. By the way, how did she die anyway?"

"She swallowed a full bottle of Demerol tablets."

"Look, I'm not a lawyer, but I can't see the accident here, can you?"

I did not respond. I had said too much already. He may not be a lawyer but he was sure sounding like one. I asked him to send the quotes and a copy of the insurance policy. He promised to send them by overnight mail. He then went on to tell me how sorry he was and apologized for being the bearer of bad news on several fronts. I took my pad out from the night table drawer and made a note of our conversation under the "A" list. It was close to eleven o'clock already, and I decided to visit with the DA before he went to lunch. I grabbed my "invitation," shoved it into my jacket pocket, and told Anna that I'd be back late in the afternoon and headed for my car.

The DA's office was housed on the tenth floor of a large building that was part of many other government business sites. As I exited the elevator a cheerful receptionist asked if she could help me. Unhappy to be here, I just reached into my pocket and handed her my "invitation." Everything she needs to know was now at her disposal. She glanced at it, picked up the phone and after a brief conversation with someone, directed me down a corridor. At the end of the narrow hallway a policeman sat at a desk in front of a set of high double doors. As he saw me approach, he got up, took a key out of the desk's drawer and snapped open the lock behind him. I entered into a small space where several women were typing away furiously. I thought they may be knocking out informal request forms. Thinking this way made me feel good, knowing that hundreds of others were in the same boat as I am. One typist, keeping in the spirit of bureaucratic government, finally lifted her head and reluctantly volunteered to show me the way to the DA's office. I thought the stroll down the hallway would be a welcome break for her, but her demeanor showed it to be an interruption. She knocked on the frosted glass door which was etched with the words, DISTRICT ATTORNEY, NASSAU COUNTY, NEW YORK. The name of the DA was stenciled in a less permanent print even though he held the job for ten years. We heard a voice on the other side of the door call out that we should come in. The woman held the door open for me and left without saying a word.

"I'm Dennis Dillard. Thanks for coming in Dr. Feelgood. I know that you must be very busy now so I'll try to make your visit as brief as possible."

I told him that it was no problem to be here and that I would be happy to answer any questions he had. I then added that the young men who visited with me at my home assured me that it's only a matter of some simple details. The DA seemed surprised to hear this.

"Well, it's even easier then that. I'm only concerned with one simple detail."

He went on to explain that he had received a call from the chief medical examiner advising him that they verified that the cause of my wife's death was indeed an overdose of Demerol. There was every reason to think it was a suicide because the policeman on the scene found an empty bottle of the drug in the bedroom. They were just getting ready to release her body to a proper party when a glitch developed.

The DA then stood up, and said to me in a firm voice, "this is the simple detail I need to clear up."

I volunteered again that I would try to help him satisfy whatever was bothersome to everyone. However, so far I had no clue as to what he wanted to know. There was definitely foreplay going on here or he was keeping me in the twilight zone.

At this point he finally threw the left hook with a scenario that went something like this:

Blood tests were taken as part of the autopsy to measure the level of Demerol in the body. The lab technician noted that some very minor properties found in liquid Demerol were present here. As there had been no mention of injected Demerol in the initial report, the technician underlined this fact on the final report.

The DA sat down again and in an almost inaudible voice asked me that as a physician what I thought about this. I told him that it was absolutely ridiculous. I asserted in a raised voice that I had been dealing with almost every drug on the market for more than twenty years and never heard of such a thing.

He countered my argument by explaining that he was aware that generally any physician had no reason to care about such a thing as there is no consequence to knowing or not knowing. This is just some oddity seen at testing labs in their routine work. The technician would have not considered this except for the circumstances, he pointed out to me again.

I assured him that as a person that has dealt with labs, I know from experience that they make more mistakes and come up with more wrongful conclusions than you can throw a bedpan at.

He acknowledged that he has had bad experiences with labs from his vantage point, and so he ordered a private company to conduct the same test. He then pointed to a piece of paper on his desk and said, "Would you like to read their report."

When I showed no inclination to participate in his set-up, he put the report aside and told me in no uncertain terms that we both have the right to disagree with each other and that others will eventually have to decide on whose position is right or wrong. He then advised me to secure an attorney, and added that as far as he was concerned his initial investigation was complete and so the crematorium could pick up Sophia's body today.

Apparently we both had nothing more to say to each other. I stood up and headed for the door. The DA must have pushed some kind of button, for when I opened the door the woman that escorted me in was there to lead me back.

I reached the lobby of the building and searched for a public telephone. I found a whole bank of them. I selected one that had a seat. I flipped through some business cards which were stored in my wallet and pulled out one which read "BARRY HODGES, ATTORNEY AT LAW." I dialed the number, and recognized the voice that answered.

"I'm surprised that you picked up directly. This is Dr. Feelgood, Barry."

"Hi Doc," he replied, and then went on to explain that it's lunchtime and his entire staff is out so it's his job now to answer the phones and take messages.

I was not in the mood for any humor, so I cut to the chase. I told him that I needed his help as several unfortunate situations have come up all at once. He asked me to tell him what was going on.

"I guess I should start with the death of my wife."

"Your wife! Sophia is dead! What happened? When? Where?"

"A few days ago. It was awful. She had been suffering from severe back pains on and off for some time. Lately the condition worsened. The Demerol which helped in the past was less effective now. I would leave her two tablets every morning. In my rush to leave for the hospital the other morning, I left the entire full bottle on the night table. I will never forgive myself, never."

"So, what happened?"

"What happened? She swallowed all twenty capsules. That's what happened!"

"Oh, my God, that's terrible. So, what can I do for you?"

"Well, the Nassau County DA has been investigating the suicide. In fact, I just left his office."

"You spoke to that son-of-a-bitch without a lawyer!"

"Yes I did. I was assured that he only wanted to clear up a few simple details."

"So, I assume you helped him clear them up. I bet then he advised you to seek a lawyer."

"Exactly!"

"Simple details, my foot. Cops never want to discuss simple details. Look, we have to continue this conversation at my office. I've got to take proper notes, and I . . ."

I interrupted him at this point because I had much more to tell him and I wanted him to see the entire picture in one shot.

"There is something else you should know, Barry."

"I'm listening."

"I've been suspended from the hospital."

"Suspended! Why? What happened?"

"For a minor infraction of the rules."

"Sounds harsh to me considering that you have practiced there for many years."

"True, but I had a patient that died after an operation, and the family is contemplating a malpractice lawsuit.

"Well, at least your malpractice insurance will cover you."

"I don't have any!"

"I don't understand?"

"We decided many years ago to self-insure. It actually paid off as we saved perhaps many thousands of dollars in premium costs."

"So, why is your plan not working for you now?"

"Well, the funds that were slated to cover an incident would come from Sophia's private money or if necessary from her family."

"What's changed then? I'm sure your share of her estate will take care of this."

"Not exactly. As I see it now the estate ranges from five million dollars to bubkis. That means nothing! I'm certain about the nothing, claiming the five million is what I need you for."

"I'm listening."

"I spoke to the insurance agent today, and to my great surprise he informed me that my wife left a life policy in this amount and I am the beneficiary."

"Now wait a minute Doc. You just told me that she committed suicide, right."

"Right."

"Let me put it in three words – suicides don't count!"

"What about accidental suicides?"

"They count. Sometimes accidents count for double."

"I think it was an accident."

"Charles, I'm beginning to think that way as well."

"Good!"

"Look, as I said before, we have to continue all this at my office."

"Barry, there is just one more thing. Then, I'll let you go."

"I'm listening."

"You see, I have this very special relationship with this woman."

"What woman?"

"First of all she lives in Copenhagen."

"A mistress, eh?"

"More than a mistress. She is the mother of my two young children."

Barry did not respond. At first I thought that the phone went dead.

"Barry? Barry, are you there?"

"I'm here. What a fucking mess!"

"Do you really think so?"

"Not really. I say things like that to clients just to jack up my fees, but you managed to jack them up all by yourself. Let me ask you one question? From everything you have told me, what worries you the most?"

"To tell the truth, I'm more concerned with getting my passport pulled than getting indicted."

"Now look, whatever you do, do not, I repeat, do not leave the country now. Leaving would not be something in your favor down the road."

"I'm not talking about fleeing, I'm only talking about a few days away."

"I repeat for the last time, do not do it!"

I decided that I would think about his advice. After all, he offered it for free so it may not be worth much.

"So Barry, for all these problems I will need your services. Are you on?"

"As I look at it, you come forward as five clients. I can only manage one problem at a time, so there is a need to prioritize."

"What's first as far as you are concerned?"

"That's an easy one, Doc. As far as I'm concerned, your wife's insurance policy reigns tall. Without a successful challenge you will not be able to afford me to handle this entire case."

"Well, that is very discouraging to hear," I added.

"Not really, there are good and decent hard working public defenders out there. In fact they are the best plea bargainers."

When he told me this I got the feeling that deep down he thought at some point I might have to plea bargain. However, Barry was the type of a lawyer who would do his best as long as the money was there. Yes, as with everything else, it always comes down to money. Barry asked that I make an appointment with his secretary as quickly as possible.

I had parked in the building's garage but I was not ready to take my car out yet as I had a few places to visit. The first was only a few blocks away where the Scandinavian Airline offices were located. I had not had the time to reschedule my flight, and was hoping it was not too late to do so. Fortunately, I was able to make the change without any problem. I paid a small surcharge and left.

It was almost two thirty when I checked my watch. I needed to get to my bank before they closed at three o'clock. I walked through the streets as fast as I could and arrived with ten minutes to spare. I entered the bank building and headed down a narrow staircase to a small gated area. A woman was sitting behind a desk under a sign that read, "SAFETY BOXES-SHOW YOUR KEY."

"Dr. Feelgood, how are you? We haven't seen you for some time"

I'm always taken aback when people use the royal "We". It's as if this clerk somehow managed to get the authority to speak for the whole corporation, which

I might add, included three hundred plus locations worldwide, and God knows the rest of the stuff you can't see.

"We're feeling fine," I answered sort of sarcastically.

I told her that every now and then I have to show up just to assure myself that I'm getting my money's worth.

"Well, then let me open the vault door and safety box for you. I'm sure you will find everything exactly as you left them."

"I'm certain of that," I replied. "After all, this department's specialty is to do nothing. Do they dust sometimes?"

"Not under my watch," she teased.

I spent just a minute emptying all the contents in the box into my attaché case, only glancing briefly at papers I didn't recognize or forgot were even there.

"That was fast Doc," she said as I returned to her desk.

"No sense in lingering," I replied. "Everything is in order just as I left it. Exactly as you promised."

I walked back up the staircase. The guard was waiting at the street door to let me out. It was one minute after three and the guy looked like he was ready to put his life on the line rather than to allow one more person into the bank. I reversed my direction and headed back to retrieve my car.

I arrived home somewhat later than expected. I had forgotten about rush hour traffic at this time of day, as for years I had never left the hospital before eight. Anna left a note for me that she had gone shopping, but had prepared some simple meals for me before she left. I pulled one out of the freezer and placed it in the micro. I went upstairs to change out of my dress clothes and noticed that my answering machine was blinking. There were two messages. The first was from a telemarketer informing me excitedly that I had won a free trip to Hawaii. All I needed to do was to call back a toll free number within twenty four hours.

"What the hell," I thought to myself. I dialed up the number and was connected to a prerecorded message congratulating me on my good fortune and directing me to mail in a two hundred dollar "no show deposit", in case I decided not to go. This money would cover the expenses that would be entailed in making my arrangements and would be refunded when I returned. This deposit was to be sent to a PO box on Wake Island, or somewhere like that. Not a bad idea, at all. I should have done the same thing to patients of mine who cancelled operations leaving me twiddling my thumbs. If I had done this I would not have the financial agony I am now experiencing.

I heard the ding ding from the micro and decided that the other message could wait a few minutes until I finished my supper. Having now been fortified with a dish of macaroni and cheese, I returned to the bedroom. I hit the button to listen to the other message. It was from Barry Hodges wanting to know if I could meet with him at his office on the upcoming Monday. He explained that his son was graduating from Sanford University next week and he and his wife were planning to extend their time on the West Coast for a little vacation. He thought that it would be a good idea to put some things into play before he left. I guessed the challenge to extract five million dollars from the insurance company was also a factor in squeezing me in. I returned his call and since the staff had already left for the day, I left my return message thanking him for thinking about me and pushing the appointment up to the front burner. This was a good opportunity to introduce him to the concept of cancellation fees, but Barry doesn't joke about money, so I just skipped it.

Later that evening Barry called me back to set the time for ten o'clock and told me to bring an original death certificate, and a copy of the life insurance policy. I asked him if I should also bring a copy of the will as well.

"Not yet," he declared with authority.

I knew what he meant and what he was thinking. It was all about getting a favorable closure on the policy, for without this he would have no reason to read the will.

CHAPTER 4

June 21st

I AROSE EARLY this day. The crematorium called and told me that I could pick up Sophia's ashes after ten o'clock this morning. I also needed to get her death certificate from them for my Monday morning meeting with Barry. I decided to visit my office first and make copies of the medical file covering my deceased patient while I had the opportunity to do so. Other then these two stops my day was relatively free until my early evening flight to Denmark.

The mail usually arrived early. Anna had brought it into the house and left it for me on a table at the entrance door. The overnight delivery from the insurance agent was also there. I tore open the envelope and pulled out the contents. I walked over to a garbage basket and tossed the quotes away without even looking at them. I only glanced at the cover sheet of the life policy with all that fancy old fashioned art work telling me in very bold letters, FIVE MILLION DOLLARS AND NO CENTS – BENEFICIARY, CHARLES FEELGOOD. The rest of the pages were full of bla, bla, bla.

I hoped to arrive at my office during the staff's morning break so as to avoid meeting many people. I entered through a back door which would maximize this effort. Only a few cleaning people were in the hallway. I unlocked my office door and closed it shut behind me. I went right to the file I needed and pressed the button on the copier to warm it up. As I was waiting I looked about and had a funny feeling that things were not exactly as I had left them. In fact some things were in places where I would never leave them. The ding ding from the machine told me to get going. I began to make copies of the file which took about ten minutes. I shut down the copier and returned the original file. I now noticed that my desk had a red sticker pasted on it. It read, CONTENTS OF THESE PREMISES EXAMINED BY SEARCH WARRANT ON 6-20-77 BY NYS SUPREME COURT ORDER 89052, NASSAU COUNTY, N.Y.

To say the least, I was very much surprised, but there was not much I could do about it but just tell Barry on Monday. I would however, enter this incident on my "B" list because there was nothing here that had anything to do with Sophia's death in any way. I checked my watch and it was almost twelve o'clock. I left the hospital as inconspicuously as I had entered. I could have walked over to the crematorium, but I wanted to get my car out of the hospital's parking lot. I drove the two blocks and figured out during this time that the reason the crematorium was located where it was is no accident. It just put them closer to their supply of product.

Sophia's ashes were waiting for me when I arrived. The manager greeted me holding a tin box. I noticed that the cover had a white ribbon taped to it in the form of a cross. I told him that we were Jewish. He apologized, and offered to give me a ribbon in the shape of a star. After checking around through boxes of bows, he announced that he could not find one and added, "You know, not too many Jewish people cremate." He picked out a ribbon in the shape of a rose and adhered it to the boxes cover. He looked at his work like an artist and boasted, "now there, isn't this nice!"

I carried the box of ashes to my car, opened the rear door and placed it on the seat. Sophia had rarely ridden in the back seat of any private car with the exception of limos. If I had thought of this earlier I would have gone there by limo. As I drove away it seemed like a stupid idea. I stopped at McDonalds for my first non-kosher meal. I pulled into the drive-in lane. I did not understand that one ordered into a microphone, used numbers to identify the full meal they wanted, and then waited for an inaudible confirmation by someone either inside the restaurant or at McDonald's headquarters somewhere in the Midwest. With horns honking behind me I finally made my way to the pay window. The guy there stuck his hand out of a little window, tapped on my glass and mouthed, "roll it down mister!" He must have thought that I had just arrived from Mars. I was even embarrassed having Sophia in the back seat as a passenger.

CHAPTER 5

June 22nd

T HE LARGE AIRPORT sign read, "WELCOME TO COPENHAGEN." The words were in English, meant for tourists. The Danes were already here. It was very early in the morning when the plane taxied along the runway towards the terminal building. There was a ground crew assembled to meet us, but very little other activity going on. I had not checked any luggage. There was no need to as I was just staying over-night.

With an attaché case in one hand and a carry-on-bag in the other, I headed directly for the customs area. I was the first of the passengers to arrive there. The agent asked me to unzip the bag. He peaked in and rezipped it closed. Pointing at the attaché case, he inquired as to its contents. I stated that there were only papers and some used jewelry I was bringing to a friend who had left them behind during a trip to the United States. If I had just stopped at papers, I think that he would have shoed me in. However, I knew the word jewelry would intrigue him. I didn't even wait to be asked, as I quickly flipped the case open. The agent perused the various pieces of jewelry as if he were at a craft show. I'm sure that he had no idea at what he was looking at. He shut the latch and stamped my passport as my fellow passengers began to line up behind me pushing carts full of luggage.

I walked a few feet to a large swinging door and pushed it open with my elbow. A small crowd of people were pressing against a guard rail. A few held cameras. I spotted Harriet, Hans, and Susan standing against a rear wall. They moved forward upon seeing me as I made my way around a series of barriers. We all embraced each other. The children were shy at first. I couldn't blame them as they had not seen me for several months. Harriet asked me about checked luggage when she noticed the minimum amount of bags that I carried. I explained that I had to cut this trip to a one night stay as there were a few details that needed immediate attention back home. I did not want to go into detail as the kids were with us and as kids they listen closely to talk. As we strolled out of the terminal we decided that we would plan to all have lunch together, but leave dinner only for the two of us so we could talk.

The lunch was uneventful chit chat. We selected an outdoor restaurant so the children could watch the world go by. It was one of those perfect summer days and so it gave us an opportunity to take a stroll in Copenhagen. The Danish capital is not handsome architecturally. Most of its streets are narrow and old fashioned. Yet this city has two very noticeable characteristics, cleanliness and cheerfulness. The faces of the passing Danes beam with calm contentment.

Although it was only the two of us at dinner I decided not to go into much detail about the events of the past week. I did not worry that Harriet would become very upset. I just did not know myself where the real problems were. However, I had to give her a smattering of what was developing. I must have used the word glitch a dozen times. Harriet's English was as good as anybody's in Denmark, but some American idioms often eluded her. While she shook her head knowingly, at one point she interrupted me and asked exactly what a glitch means. I told her it was like a bump in the road. She thought for a moment and put it together.

"Well Charles, it sounds to me like there are lots of glitches but if you tell me not to worry, then I will not worry, so there!"

It was getting late and I wanted to discuss the one important reason I made the trip even though my lawyer advised against it.

"Remember the attaché case I left at the house."

Harriet nodded.

"I'm leaving it in your care for safekeeping. It contains investment papers, bonds, stock certificates, and Sophia's better jewelry. It's not a great deal, but it's not chopped liver either. When I return home I'm going to draw up a new will leaving these funds to you. I also plan to include you now as co-owner of my rental properties."

Harriet shook her head that she had absorbed everything that I just threw at her, but I doubted she understood what chopped liver had to do with anything. The baby sitter could only stay until eleven o'clock, so we headed home.

The house was quiet, but we tip-toed in anyway. The baby sitter was in her usual position, bending down and peering into the refrigerator. She was a little startled to see us as she straightened up and moved to the side of the door. Harriet and I glanced at the index finger marks cris-crossed upon a chocolate cake.

"Take the cake home, honey. My wife and I just had enough dessert to last us for a month."

"Thanks, Mr. Leeds," she responded."

It was the first time I was called Mr. Leeds, but this was no time for explanations.

We checked in on our children who were sound asleep, said good night to the sitter and headed for our bedroom.

"Come on," Harriet beckoned. "Come over here. You can touch me wherever you like. I know you want to."

I did. I ran my hands slowly all over her body. Her eyes were closed, her head back, her feet stretched apart. Her hands were draped around my neck. After five minutes of private foreplay she gently lowered me onto the bed and climbed on top of me. I was grateful to see her take the lead because I had not slept for a long time.

She slid down my body, her tongue peering out of the darkness searching for my penis. She did her thing for about ten seconds, knowing that any longer would end our adventure. With her tongue still whipping around like a viper the search was on for my mouth. I placed my hands on her large breasts and rubbed and squeezed her outstretched nipples softly between my thumb and index finger with the detachment of a biologist noting the responses of a new specimen. Her hand was now on the hunt for my penis, which I might add, was getting easier and easier to find. She gently wrapped it in the palm of her hand and lowered herself onto me and positioned herself carefully. I wanted to prolong that first moment of entry. I wanted to move lightly so the result of the union would be pleasurable. To this end I began to move in easy circles letting her pace her own ride. As I involuntarily started to pick up speed going faster and faster back and forth she began to groan and gasp. We were both getting nearer to our goal. She arrived there first and I responded with a sudden gush of hot juice. I was sleepier now than I had been before and was grateful that I would doze off soon.

"That was wonderful Harriet," I murmured.

"What do you think I am, chopped liver?" she teased.

Sunday was just as beautiful as the day before. We had promised the kids that we would take them to Tivoli Gardens. There were lots of special events for children on this day of the week and so after a light breakfast we were on our way. The light breakfast incidentally was to make room for the junk food ahead. Why should we be different? After all, we were raising the baby sitters of the future.

For Harriet and me, the gardens were a place to find some peace of mind. It was an opportunity to spend some time, however limited, with body and spirit in God's out of doors haven. Nowhere in this city could we find a quieter or more untroubled retreat. I truly believed that the hardships I was bearing today was only a breath away from the pleasures I would have tomorrow and those pleasures would be all the richer because of the memories of what I'm enduring now.

As we walked through this beautiful landscape, I began to regret that time was getting short for us. I had a return flight at four o'clock and we would have to depart for the airport shortly. We both decided that I would leave alone as airport goodbyes are always depressing and a farewell in the midst of a sun drenched flower bed would be so much better.

CHAPTER 6

June 24th

I ARRIVED AT Barry's office promptly at ten o'clock. I brought the death certificate and life insurance policy. His office was rather sparse; more so then I had remembered as I had not visited here for some time. Only a phone, a yellow legal pad and two sharpened pencils messed up the desk that was otherwise clean as a whistle. Barry offered me a chair, which I might add was the only available seat. To me, this was proof that he only worked one on one. He picked up one of the pencils, tested it's sharpness with his index finger and said, "OK, let's get going." I had the feeling that he was about to make a quick determination of his interest in handling all my legal work. One thing I knew, for certain, was that his middle name was not pro-bono. I handed him the envelope containing the two documents that he had requested and sat back in my chair watching him peruse them.

"This death certificate was issued to a crematorium."

"Yes," I agreed.

"I was under the impression that cremation was not sanctioned in your religion."

"Well, that's what she wanted," I explained.

He did not reply back, but it always left me astounded that Goyim (non-Jews) always managed to know these rules.

"So, I gather that the DA doesn't think it was a suicide."

"It seems that way," I responded.

"Do you?"

"Of course," I asserted.

"So, what's the DA's problem?"

I explained the testing that was done on Demerol both by the medical examiner and the DA.

"Doc, this sounds far fetched to me."

"Me too," I assured him.

"That's not enough to build a case on. Did he ask you about anything else?"

"No," I replied. "In fact, he told me that this was the only detail which needed to be cleared up. When he suggested that I get a lawyer, I felt that the clearing up was my responsibility."

Barry leaned back in his chair, looked up at the ceiling, and just nodded his head.

"There is another thing that you should know even though the DA never got into this area."

"What area?"

"Fingerprints," I responded.

"Whose?"

"Mine."

"Yours?"

"Yes, mine."

"Where?"

"On the Demerol bottle."

I went on to explain how I picked the bottle up off the night table and how John, the cop, got upset because I placed my prints on it. I also told Barry that when leaving the bedroom he swung around, and waving the Demerol bottle, berated me again.

"He sounds like a Columbo impersonator to me."

"He seemed like a real Columbo character to me," I assured Barry.

"Look Doc, don't worry about this?"

"Don't worry! Why not?"

"Think about it. You handled the bottle in the morning, right?"

"Right!"

"So, placing your prints on the bottle again means nothing."

"Of course," I replied. "How stupid of me?"

"But what about her prints," I questioned.

"Well, she could have wrapped her thumb and index finger around the neck of the bottle in order to swallow the pills. Right?" Barry proposed.

"That's probably what happened," I asserted, thinking on my feet, as this was clearly an important point.

"Was the cap off the bottle when you left it on the table that morning?"

"I'm not sure," I said, still a step behind Barry.

"Think about it," he counseled. "If the cap was on, then in order to remove it there will have to be evidence of her prints."

"Now, I remember," I replied. "It was off, definitely off, because I usually take two tablets out, so the cap had to be off. I took the pills out but forgot to take the bottle away."

"That's the way to remember it," Barry instructed.

"Of course, of course," I assured him.

"Why didn't you trust just leaving the entire bottle there?"

"It was only a feeling. I just thought it is better to be safe then sorry."

"What made you think that she might take her life?"

"She never threatened suicide, but she would sometimes say that her back pains were so unbearable that she wondered how much longer a person could take it. She never said how long she could take it, but rather always used the word person"

"Perhaps then, it was an accident," Barry speculated, with the thought of double indemnity going through his mind.

"Perhaps," I answered.

"Anything else I should know?"

"I don't think there is Barry, except for Harriet and my children in Denmark."

"That's a non-issue. As far as I'm concerned, it's not important until the primary problem is solved favorably."

I knew exactly what he meant. He was talking about money and how available it would be. We would get to that shortly, but while he was asking me, 'what else?' and I'm sitting on such a comfortable bridge chair, I decided to continue and throw in the entire kitchen sink.

"What about the malpractice problem?"

This question made Barry stand up and pace behind his desk. He twisted his chair around enough to create four non-stop spins. One of his pencils dropped onto the floor.

"Do I look like a fucking legal machine. Wait and see what happens, for Christ sake. Most of these suits are settled out of court. Often the hospital's insurance covers the doctors as well."

Barry picked the pencil up off the floor. The point was broken, and this seemed to disturb him. I felt like telling him, "get over it, look, take a good look, see the other pencil on the desk, that's what a second pencil is all about."

I was now a glutton for punishment, so, as Barry kept staring at the broken pencil point, I blurted out.

"By the way, I spent this past week-end in Copenhagen."

He looked me straight in the eyes and winced. "Sorry, I didn't hear what you just said."

"And, one more thing," I threw in, "I went back to my office last Friday to make copies of the medical history of that patient. I figured that I should have these while I still had access to the files."

"Finally, I'm hearing about some solid thinking," he chided.

I went on to tell him of my discovery that my office was searched with a warrant probably secured by the DA.

"That's good news"

"Good news! How is it good news?"

"T-h-i-n-k," he spelled out slowly. "It shows that the Demerol testing is all they got, and damn weak at that, so, the DA dispatched a witch hunt."

I would never have come to such a positive scenario. Barry was absolutely right. He was always ahead of the curve. I appreciated his legal mind prompting me to figure out how I would get all the money needed to pay him for all my situations. I had not forgotten that he looked upon me as five clients.

Barry sat down and studied the death certificate more closely. He turned it around on the desk so it would face me, and placed his index finger on the section that read, "Cause of death."

"See this," he said as he pounded his finger repeatedly on this spot. "It states that the cause of death is 'drug poisoning'. Can you see it?"

I nodded that I saw it.

"Good!" he said. The coroner's office in Nassau County, and in fact, in most jurisdictions never commits to the intent or non-intent of the deceased. They don't fill in this box with wording like 'hit by car'. Maybe the person jumped in front of the car? Hit could mean accident, or homicide. Jump could mean suicide or fainting at the wrong bus stop. You get it? Who the fuck knows for sure? So, the cause of death is only stated in pure medical terms."

Barry was giving me an interesting interpretation of causes of death, but I knew it was only a foundation for him to build on in my case, and I was right.

"So Doc, as you can see, we can have a suicide here, or we could even have an accidental suicide, or even, God forbid, a murder!"

The top of my forehead started to bead upon hearing that word. I prayed that he did not notice. Barry leaned back in his chair as far as it would go.

"As far as I am concerned, this policy is in force until there is conclusive legal proof through the courts that it is not valid."

He went on to lay out what he thought must be done at this stage. It seems, that under Federal law, insurance companies are required to pay off this type of policy in full within thirty days after they receive a claim.

"They either pay the beneficiary or the estate," he explained in the tone of a school teacher. "That's you, the former."

I nodded, showing that I understood what former meant.

Barry directed me to return the claim form which came with the policy as soon as possible. "Like today," was how he put it. He also urged me to use registered mail and return receipt requested, adding, "you can never trust those bastards." However, I think he trusted me to follow his instructions, because he pulled out his notary public stamp from the desk drawer and notarized the claim form even before I signed it.

"Remember," he said to remind me, "use the same cause of death wording on the claim form as was used on the death certificate."

"What about the insurance agent? I told him that it was a suicide."

Barry leaped out of his chair again as he had done a few minutes earlier. I guess I was pushing the wrong buttons again. He paced around the room and raised his voice to a louder level.

"Fuck the agent! He's out of the damn picture for Christ sake. He's just another little runt representing twenty odd insurance companies, pitting one against the other. When he mailed the policy to you he completed his obligations and his commissions stopped. Believe me, he doesn't give a rat's ass whether you collect or not. It's us against the insurance company. Your company is located in the middle of Nebraska. You may ask, why Nebraska? I'll tell you why! It's because their state laws are friendly to their needs in all ways, that's why! This is the way Nebraska attracts this industry. Do you think that high salaried executives would live in a corn field voluntarily?"

"Do you expect a dispute here,?" I asked sheepishly.

"It's hard to say. Who knows? The word poison doesn't sound like pneumonia! You may receive a follow up letter requesting other specific details."

"Like what?"

"Like autopsy and police reports and God knows what else they dream up during hay rides. These follow-ups also serve to extend the legal time frame for payment."

"Then what?"

"Then if they reject the claim for what they deem as good cause, and we feel confident and rich enough, we can either try to negotiate, petition for impartial arbitration, or take the matter into court."

"I wish you would throw in some good news now and then, something I can hang my hat on."

"OK, I will," he responded, "how about hanging your hat on this. The policy has a stipulation that will pay double indemnity for accidental death. Have you ever cashed a check for ten million dollars tax free?"

Finishing the meeting on such a thought seemed like a good thing to do. Barry placed the documents back into the envelope, handed it to me and led me to the door where he patted me on the back. It reminded me of Dr. Frank's pat at the hospital assuring me that my patient will do fine. Perhaps Barry had a better touch.

CHAPTER 7

June 25-July 1

THE NEXT FEW days were somewhat uneventful, and a marked difference from the past stressful and busy week. However, this time was productive for me. The weather had turned from nice to hot and humid. I spent most of the time at my swimming pool. I decided to emulate my lawyer. I set up a patio table with a yellow legal pad and two sharpened pencils. All that was missing was the telephone. I replaced it with a large pitcher of lemonade and an eight ounce glass. It was better to answer to my thirst than to answer to the phone. This quiet environment offered me an opportunity to take stock of my situation by reviewing my A and B concern list. Barry had given me lots of food for thought. What may have been on my A list could be shifted to the B list or visa versa, or wiped out entirely by two virgin erasers poised for action on the top of my pencils.

What had really stuck in my mind from the meeting with Barry was his telling me to T-H-I-N-K and spelling it out! Now I decided that he was right, except I needed to start thinking out of the box and come up with a "Plan B." I turned to a clean page on the pad and titled it "OPTIONS." There was a trend in movies and books to use one word titles that would describe the entire story. I used the word option thinking it to be so perfect that I underlined it on top and bottom, threw in an explanation mark and placed quotes around it as well. I had taken myself with that one magnificent word out of the box and now all I needed to do was to think that way.

Efficiency called for a plan in chronological order, and did not necessarily have to be completed at one time. However, the big picture had to be known. The big picture was to flee! Now, every clandestine operation needs a code word. This is something that I learned from Watergate. My code word would be T-H-I-N-K F-L-E-E! I set "Plan B" in motion by listing things that must be done immediately. Thursday, the day after tomorrow seemed like a good start date. Depending upon my initial success, I would move the plan along the same way kids play hopscotch, take a small leap, stop, look around, see where you started from, check where you are, look ahead and take the next leap.

Thursday required visits to Scandinavian Airlines, The U.S. Passport Agency, and the law library at Hofstra University in that order. At the airlines office I purchased round trip tickets to Denmark two weeks out from today. There were no plans to use them, but I thought it would be good to have with me when I requested that the passport agency expedite a new passport to replace the one which I will claim that I lost. The tickets would show them that I was leaving in two weeks. The fact that I would be able to use the tickets within the year made it a no-brainer to buy them now.

The passport agency was very busy as the summer vacation season was in full swing. The lines were long, the room was hot, the noise level high and tempers short. I did not seem to mind what was happening around me. People, Democrats and Republicans were cursing out the government. Finally it was my turn. I stood in front of a caged window, while a harried clerk ignored me completely. She was ruffling through a mess of paperwork from the person who preceded me. At last, she raised her head and greeted me "warmly".

"Yes," she barked.

The best answer was to say nothing. I simply shoved my application to replace a lost passport towards her. I knew she would be able to figure it out.

"Was it lost or stolen?" she quizzed.

"Definitely lost," I replied.

"How are you so sure," she challenged.

"Well you see, I was reading the Sunday papers, actually the travel section, to see if I had enough time to purchase airline tickets cheaply as I needed to leave for Europe shortly. I took out my passport from my desk to check the expiration date and to my joy it was still current. I placed the passport on the pile of newspapers and forgot about it. My wife threw away the entire pile as Monday is garbage day. That's it! I called the sanitation . . ."

She stopped me cold in the middle of my sentence. I was either putting her to sleep or she was ready to throw up. I wasn't sure.

"Please don't go on," she said as she grabbed one of her rubber ink stamps and pounded my application with it. I could read it upside down. It read in bold letters, "LOST". I paid twenty five extra dollars for them to expedite the application. I did not even need the air tickets to prove that I was departing out of the country shortly. The twenty five bucks satisfied the agency.

"You'll receive your new passport in five to seven business days," she volunteered. I thanked her and headed out the door.

A young lady at the exit door carrying a magazine called "Rome Now," excitedly asked me how it went. "How what went?" I replied. People always asked me the same question as I left the operating room at the hospital. I decided to give her the same answer that I gave to them . . . "just wonderful, couldn't have been better!"

So now, if my passport were to be pulled, I would have a back-up. This idea came to me at my meeting with Barry who readied two pencils for himself, and low and behold, he needed the reserve. This was 1977 and computers were either not in use extensively or used primarily by the military. Having two different passport numbers today would be flagged down in fifteen minutes or less. In those days it would take fifteen months or more. The fact that the authorities would have my passport in hand would preclude them from thinking that I could be out of the country. Las Vegas would be a place of first choice for them to search. They always start in this town. Look, detectives are human too.

I felt very satisfied as to how the day went so far as I headed for the university. I hoped that the law library would help me locate those countries that did not have extradition treaties with the United States. I managed to come up with the names of some of them. Most were third world countries where I could not live anyway and others were Arab states, not exactly perfect for a Jewish boy. Central and South America had a few possibilities as well as some Caribbean Islands. My time here was well spent because I learned things in this area were not black or white. Many acceptable places had some treaties or understandings with the United States that included exception clauses which often changed as the political climates between the countries changed. I realized when and if the time came for me to flee, I would need expert legal guidance. As I drove back home, I thought that if the first steps I had taken to kick off "Plan B" were not outside the box, then I did not know what outside the box meant.

The telephone message light was blinking as usual. The indicator showed that there was only one message waiting. It was from a woman who identified herself as the secretary to Sophia's lawyer, Ron Black. She informed me that a reading of the will was scheduled on Tuesday, July 2nd, at eight o'clock, at their law offices. She added that my children and father-in-law had been notified and indicated that they would be there. We were the only four people involved. I thought that only an occasion such as this would entice my children to come to New York from Europe and the West Coast on such short notice. I was instructed to call her back if I could not attend nor send an authorized representative. I didn't call back, I'd be there. I guess the late hour was set to accommodate me thinking that I needed to be at the hospital before that time. Little did they know that I could be there at eight in the morning if necessary.

Tomorrow was Friday, and the forecast was for temperatures in the nineties. I decided that for the near future I would avoid planning any activities on Fridays. I gave myself three day weekends. Why not! I had piles of unread magazines and books and now was the time to catch up with my reading.

CHAPTER 8

July 2nd

I WAS SOMEWHAT apprehensive this day. Tonight was the reading of the will and I had not heard from my children or from my father-in-law, nor had I made any attempt to contact them either. I reread the copy of the will I had found in the house. I came to the same conclusion. Under state law I would be the recipient of a third of the estate, but an estate of little value.

I arrived at the lawyer's office promptly at eight o'clock. I, of course, knew Ron Black, who was Sophia's family lawyer as well. It appeared as if I was the first to arrive. However, Ron explained that the others decided to give him a proxy to act on their behalf at the reading of the will. His secretary had stayed to be the witness.

Without wasting any time he told me that the will was filled with legal jargon and while he was obliged to read every word he intended to move through it very quickly. I did not tell him that I'd found a copy of the will at home. As he moved along with the reading I became aware that my copy must have been updated. Basically the estate was bare. It was worse than I thought. I stopped the reading, and asked him when the will was dated. Ron flipped to the last page and read off a date which was about four months ago. Undoubtedly, this new will was recently drawn up by Ron Black. He checked the date as if he was searching for a date somewhere in the sixties.

I refused to watch this actor fuck with my head, and decided to take the high road.

"Lets stop here," I kind of ordered. "I'm willing to say that I heard the will read. Whatever it is, it is!"

"I hear you," he replied. "However, I must advise you of one key thing."

I told him to go ahead. What the hell, I'm here anyway, and I've made my point already.

"All personal possessions have been willed to your children."

"Does that include the jewelry that I bought for her during all these years?"

"Yes!"

So, I could add another concern to my "A" list as all the good stuff was now in Denmark. As of now, I retained the house which I shared with Sophia under a tenancy by the entirety. I also had a few rental properties which I owned by myself and some money in a savings account. All this was not nearly enough to cover potential malpractice liabilities plus supporting my growing family in Copenhagen.

I lifted myself up from my chair and was about to leave when Ron handed me a paper to sign.

"What's this?" I said.

"Just a formality," he replied.

With those three words I thought it best to sit down again and read it carefully. I would declare that I had been present for the reading of the will, and that I had no intention to contest it.

"I can't sign anything like this," I declared.

"Why not?" questioned the dope.

"Don't be ridiculous Ron. I can't sign this until my lawyer has a chance to advise me."

He did not reply. Instead he pulled out a similar paper all typed up and ready for signature that simply stated that I was present for the reading of the will. Since the paper was void of fine print I agreed to sign it. The secretary signed as well as a witness, and Ron showed his "officer of the court" authority by stamping the document hard and with a flourish I haven't seen since the Rabbi signed my wedding contract.

I thanked Ron for his time, even though I knew that my father-in-law had kept him in Brooks Brother's suits for years. As I was walking towards my car it occurred to me that while Ron Black knew everything about these private matters, he did not know about the five or ten million dollar life insurance policy that slipped below his radar screen. Hopefully, it will become a reality for me.

CHAPTER 9

July 18th

I T WAS NOW the middle of July and I had not heard from the DA, or from the hospital, or the life insurance company. I received my new passport a few days ago and had been speaking to Harriet several times a week. Most of the conversations dealt with speculation because everything was hanging in limbo.

It had been almost a month since the hospital suspended me. I was getting anxious to return to the operating room. I had always questioned their decision and since so much time had gone by, I decided to call the administrator to find out what, if anything, was developing. This must have been a psychic moment for me. When I reached his office his secretary informed me that Gary was away on vacation, just like me, but the hospital had just received a bunch of legal papers. An action had been placed in motion. All she could tell me was that it was directed at the hospital, and I was named along with the two nurses and the head nurse who had read me the riot act. It appeared as if a giant net had been cast. Perhaps, Barry was right about nurses not carrying insurance because the hospitals assume responsibility for them. Hopefully, they may handle me in the same way.

I had not talked with Barry for several weeks. Now was a good time to update him about the malpractice law suit.

He spoke first without a hello.

"Hey Doc, did you hear from the insurance company yet?"

"No," I answered.

"I see," he replied.

He sounded disappointed. I felt instinctively that in order for the two of us to move forward as a team I would have to tell him something I had not done, but would do now.

"Barry, I placed a check for five thousand dollars in the mail to you yesterday."

"Thanks," he replied. "So what's up?"

I informed him of the information I received from the hospital about the suit, and explained the background of what happened with my patient that day as well as the care procedures that have been in effect for the past two years.

Barry related how malpractice is often difficult to prove. He said that the measurement of proper care is usually based upon federal, state, or local standards. The major issue in my case, as he saw it, was that the suit is predicated upon the hospital's self-imposed requirements.

"It seems," he went on, "that mandating written care instructions from one caregiver to the next one is a very good idea, and probably, put in effect to avoid a malpractice law suit. Ironically it has worked in an opposite way here. However, here is the rub . . . the litigants can argue that even if all this is so, patient care was set up this way and hospital staff members could become confused when they don't receive expected written instructions. More important, is that one never knows what a jury will do. That's why I always shoot for a settlement out of court, no matter how strong I feel my case might be. My guess is that 90% of the staff at one time or another neglected this rule at least once."

"Or at least a hundred times," I added.

"Doc, I must ask you before I forget if the hospital is aware that you do not have malpractice insurance."

"They are not aware, and would be surprised to find this out."

"Let them be surprised. Tell them at the first opportunity. After considering this, they will realize that it is in their best interest to protect you financially. If they don't, they may run the risk of having you expand the situation to other incidents, giving the litigants the chance to widen the picture of incompetence by the hospital."

"How will this happen?"

Barry explained that if I were left to defend myself, my defense would center on the fact that this was a very common occurrence and the hospital failed to monitor their own patient procedures. Staff members would be called to testify, and under oath, be forced to admit to their own failings at times as well. This could also induce new law suits when some sharp lawyers, with their eyes and ears open to court cases, contact the families of former patients who have died in the hospital, and possibly were subjected to the same neglect.

Barry's scenarios were making me dizzy. I thanked him for his time and advice. I knew, however, that at this point in time everything was only conjecture and not reality. Barry always seems to have the answers, usually on the positive side. That's his job after all. He was not only a good lawyer, but a good salesman in order to keep his clients happy and his income rolling in. All I can do now was to hope and wait for events to develop. Of course, I still had my ace in the hole . . . "Plan B" . . . T-H-I-N-K F-L-E-E.

CHAPTER 10

July 22nd

I RECEIVED A call early this morning from Gary, the hospital administrator. He wondered if it were possible for me to visit with him today so we can discuss some matters. I offered to be there after lunch at about two o'clock. He agreed.

I had been checking my mail delivery each day expecting some notice about the law suit. This morning an envelope arrived from the life insurance company. I was anticipating either a check or a follow up to my claim form. The envelope was very thin. So, I thought, if there wasn't a check inside, their new inquiry form would be short. As I walked back to the kitchen I speculated upon which of these two probabilities it might be. In any event, I would have to call Barry. I decided to place this call after my meeting with Gary. Waiting would give me the advantage of covering two areas with him, the suit and the insurance. Any conversations I have with him has its price. Getting your money's worth with Barry will always be a challenge.

I decided not to open the envelope until I returned from the hospital. I did not have it in me now to deal with bad news on top of bad news until I was alone at the end of the day. As I left my house I thought that this day would not be the same as the lazy days I'd been living recently.

On my way to my meeting I had a yen for a McDonald's lunch. This time I knew the ropes. The same guy was at the window to hand me my meal and to take my money. He sort of smiled at me and said, "See, it's a piece of cake!"

An elevator near the main entrance of the hospital took you straight up to the administration floor. I was a bit early, and the staff had not returned from lunch yet, but my nemesis was there to greet me. He got right down to business. First, he told me that he had good news. The executive board voted to reinstate me. I could return the next day or wait until after the weekend and come back on Monday. I chose the latter as I was getting paid anyway.

"I understand that a malpractice law suit has been filed," I stated.

"Yes, that's true," he replied, "but we are confident that it has no merits for success."

"How is that?" I questioned.

"Well, the suit contends that the hospital and others named, including you and three nurses, failed to monitor our requirements for leaving written care instructions to the chain of the patient's caregivers. However, our legal team maintains that this is our own internal procedures. It is not normal care practiced in other hospital, nor does it violate any codes anywhere.

This conversation sounded remarkably very familiar to me. It placed Barry at the top of his profession as far as I was concerned. At that moment I was happy that he was my lawyer.

"So, how will this action be handled?"

"Well, as I just said, we contend that the suit's premise is based on a weak foundation. Yet, they may move forward and get the case in front of a jury. Juries are generally not friendly to the profession. So, it's prudent to settle out of court if the price is reasonable enough. Our insurance will cover us and in any settlement I'm sure that your insurance would cover you as well."

"I don't have malpractice insurance, I never did. You see my wife was well off personally, and so was her family, and they still are, I might add. As such, we decided, even before I began my career, to self-insure. This worked well until now."

"So, I assume her estate has the same funds in reserve if needed in this case."

"I wish I could say, yes, but the answer is no."

"I don't understand?"

I went on to explain that my wife and I did not have a good relationship for many years. When she passed away her fortune was still intact, but taken out of the estate and given directly to the control of the children.

"While I am the executor, there is nothing to execute. It's a cruel joke, wouldn't you say?"

He gave no opinion to my question. Instead he persisted on.

"What about life insurance?"

"Nothing!" I answered.

Since I had not opened the envelope from the insurance company, I continued to tell the truth, at least at this moment in time. I watched him searching mentally for other areas that might shake cash out of me, but he came up empty.

"If we can obtain a reasonable settlement perhaps our policy can cover you."

"I hope so," I replied. "However, I would like to know this in advance with a written statement to this effect. It would make me sleep better at night."

Barry was not with me, but I knew that this would be the direction he would have taken.

"I'll get back to the board on this," he responded. "Hopefully knowing of your situation they might agree. After all, you have been at the hospital for almost twenty years."

I felt that I was moving and continued pushing buttons.

"By Monday," I responded.

"I'll try," he replied. "I'll send in a memo of our talk to the board before the day is up. How's that?"

I thanked him for his help and expressed the hope that things would shortly return to normal. I wished that Barry could have been a fly on the wall during the meeting. He would be proud of himself to have hit the nail on the head.

As I was walking out of the office, and as I had experienced with John, the cop, Gary pulled a Columbo on me.

"Oh by the way, Doc, some police investigators were here recently. They had a court order to search your office. They wouldn't say why."

I responded with my first lie.

"I'm aware of that. In fact they notified me that morning to tell me, and even invited me to observe."

"Really," replied Gary. "That seems highly unusual."

"It was about an old real estate deal that went sour. This nut has pursued me in court claiming that I was hiding records he needed to sue. To sue who, I'm still not sure of."

I left the hospital thinking that my concern lists needed an update. The malpractice problem can be transferred from the "A" to the "B" list, at least for the time being. I needed to add Gary's comments about the search to the "A" list because I'm not certain he believed me. However, my attention now turned to the mail from the insurance company.

Back home I searched for a letter opener to make certain I did not damage whatever was in the envelope. I then carefully slipped the opener under the flap. I couldn't believe my eyes as I looked at a check drawn for five million dollars and no cents, made out to Charles Feelgood. There was no explanation included, no nothing. It had not even been sent by special mail. Barry would have said, "Those cheap bastards." The back side of the check had a printed statement that read, "AGREED TO BE CASHED AS COMPLETE AND FINAL PAYMENT FOR LIFE INSURANCE POLICY 12B1674W5."

I was so exited that the first time I tried to call Barry I dialed the wrong number. When I reached his office he picked up the phone himself and barked, "Hello!" I blurted out loud, "the check came, the check came!"

Using his rare sense of humor, and while he obviously recognized my voice, he asked, "whose calling?" We both were ecstatic and for the same reason. At that moment, in his eyes, I became whole again, as the five clients became one entity.

Barry surmised that the cause of death may not have raised any flags. On the other hand, he theorized that if they pursued, and found out that an accidental suicide might have been involved, they would have had to shell out ten million bucks. That's why they needed me to sign a waiver on the check accepting the money as full payment.

"Those guys don't like to shoot craps," he added.

I began pushing buttons again. I suggested that perhaps we should send the check back and redo the claim for double indemnity.

"What are you, a fucking idiot or what?" he bounced back excitedly.

"I was just kidding, just kidding."

"I hope so," he responded.

I should have known better then to play games with him when it came to money. I had to calm him down some more, so I asked him if they decided to pay the claim during a hayride."

"No, at a barn raising!" he said almost proudly as he knew that he upped me.

I now turned the conversation to my meeting with Gary at the hospital. I told him exactly what had transpired between us, and that things ended on a positive note. I also complemented him upon being so accurate in appraising the situation that the hospital will find itself in. He suggested that I not give him that much credit, because they thought of everything first.

"Yeah," I said, "but you didn't know that!"

"I guess that you are right," he answered, "maybe I am a good lawyer after all."

There was one point he cautioned me about. While the promise to cover me financially is all well and good, it only applies if there is a settlement. If the case goes to court, the deal is out the window.

"Oh, my," I thought, "now this matter is back on my "A" list.

I asked Barry what would happen if the hospital elects to take the case to trial. He laid out a strategy that follows:

"I'll take over myself at that point. I'll urge them to negotiate harder towards a settlement by upping the ante, so to speak. I'll point out the downside, spelling out the defense we would be forced to take, as we had discussed. However, from the results of your meeting today, they are aware of the awkward position they could find themselves in without you in the loop. However, my personal involvement and my presence will indicate to them, in no uncertain terms, that I can execute what I say. Anyway, all this is for another day that may not come to pass. My advice now is to do nothing, let things work themselves out wherever the chips may fall. So, just report back to work Monday."

We had covered everything for now. I was very pleased how things were developing. Yet, there were many hurdles to jump, the biggest being the DA, who has remained quiet. I told Barry that I would send him a check for ten thousand dollars on account. This seemed like chicken feed to both of us now. He thanked me anyhow, for Barry was a patient man.

CHAPTER 11

July 23rd

I STILL HAD those round trip airline tickets to Copenhagen which were purchased in anticipation of having to prove to the passport office that I needed my new passport expedited. There were a few days left between now and Monday when I was expected to return to work at the hospital. With not much to do at home, I called Harriet and told her that I decided to take a quick trip over to see her and the kids.

I booked a flight leaving this evening and returning on Sunday. I packed a small bag which included a few more pieces of jewelry.

"Estate bullshit," I thought, "I bought her all this stuff. I did the operating to pay for this. My children couldn't even remove a splinter from an elephant's ass."

I looked forward to a stress free weekend, so I ordered car service to drive me to the airport to avoid the agony of driving myself in the early evening rush hours and parking when I got there. The international terminal at JFK was always busy in the evening as most flights destined for Europe took off at this time for early morning arrival at destination cities.

Having skipped lunch, I stopped at a cafeteria for a bite. I managed to find a seat at a table for four. Three other people sitting there were finishing up their snacks and shortly left the table. It occurred to me after sitting alone for almost five minutes that while the restaurant was jammed with customers nobody took the empty seats at my table. As I wondered about this, two men sat down. I noticed that they did not bring with them any food or drinks. This seemed strange. One man cupped something in the palm of his hand.

"Dr. Feelgood?" he asked as a question.

"Yes," I answered, astonished.

He opened his hand exposing a police badge.

"Police," he announced.

A third man appeared and stood directly behind me. I noticed that all the surrounding tables had been emptied of patrons.

"You are under arrest, sir. I am going to read to you your rights under the law." A fourth man handed him a 3x5 index card and he proceeded to read my rights in a whisper.

"Could you please stand up now and place your hands behind your back," he ordered.

I stood up as directed. The man behind me closed the handcuffs and threw a small towel over them. They apparently wanted to whisk me away without having the people there peering at the cuffs.

As we exited the terminal two autos were waiting for us at the curb. We left like a mini caravan. The route took us through Queens and into Nassau County.

We pulled up at a police station which I had passed for many years but never had the reason to see the inside until now. The reception area featured an oversized desk on a platform perhaps a half foot off the ground. This gave the desk sergeant an authoritative appearance to the poor soul standing in front of him. The police officer who had handcuffed me escorted me to a room where I was to be booked and fingerprinted. His presence was necessary, for he had the key to the handcuffs in his pocket.

The desk sergeant informed me that because of the late hour I would be held overnight for a court appearance the next morning. He advised me that I would have to have an attorney with me. If not, then there would be a postponement.

"Can I call my lawyer now?" I asked.

This was no problem. In fact, they let me use a small cubicle to place the call. A policeman was stationed nearby, but not in listening distance. I hoped to reach Barry at home, and I did.

I told Barry of my arrest. The first thing that he wanted to know was what I was doing at the airport? Of course, he didn't like my answer. He kind of read me the riot act. I was half listening. All I remember now is that he must have used the word shmuck at least a half dozen times. When he calmed down he asked me to put the sergeant on the phone to introduce himself as my attorney, and assure him that he would be present in court in the morning. He was told that arraignments start at ten o'clock.

I was grateful that I just had to get through one night in jail. Now I had the time, without the commotion, to try and figure out how they knew that I would be at the airport tonight. I came to the conclusion that they must have been tracking my telephone records and noticed a number of calls to Denmark. I guessed this prompted them to monitor any airline ticket purchases and flights I may have booked. Thus, when I became a passenger on a flight tonight a red flag went up. The DA needed to act quickly whether he was ready to indict or not. At the worst, he could depend upon pulling my passport. This would at least put him ahead of the game.

CHAPTER 12

July 24th

T HE PROCEEDINGS BEGAN at 10 o'clock sharp, to my surprise I might add. The DA's staff presented the indictment to the judge. They argued that a three million dollar bail be posted, and that my passport be surrendered. The judge agreed to the latter only. As I had the passport with me it was confiscated then and there. Barry rebutted the request for bail by referring to the trappings of the indictment claiming that it was based solely upon conjecture and circumstantial evidence.

"Where is the motive? Where are the witnesses?"

At the time there was a television commercial which asked the question, "Where's the beef." Barry threw this in as well as he waved a copy of the indictment high in the air. He had a talent for getting his point across in a way that everybody could understand.

Barry then continued to lay out a laundry list to support the reason that bail should not be considered.

1) My passport had already been surrendered.
2) There is no past police record
3) I am a respected surgeon practicing at the same hospital for twenty years.
4) I own an expensive home and other properties in the community.
5) My family roots are local.

Then, with the five million bucks on his mind, he added, "there is no doubt that Dr. Feelgood's wife's death was a pure and simple accident that . . .

The judge interrupted Barry in mid-sentence.

"There is no need to go on counselor. I am dismissing the indictment on the grounds of insufficient evidence,"

The judge then addressed the members present from the DA's office.

"More than once you have clashed with this court in the same way that you have done this morning. The results should be predictable by now. I have to warn you again to avoid taking premature, reckless and irresponsible paths towards justice. Be advised that I am sealing the arrest record here. Both parties can consider the arrest as a non-happening, at least for now. I will give the State thirty days from today, if they wish, to present a new and solid indictment and to renew a plea for bail. I will allow the DA's office to continue to hold Dr. Feelgood's passport for this period of time. These are my rulings."

The judge briskly walked off the bench ignoring one of the prosecutors shouting, "But your Honor, but your Honor, wait."

As we left the courthouse I thanked Barry for his efforts. I had gained a month of freedom and continued to have complete control over my assets. Now was the time for Barry to move in for more money.

"Doc, we are now in the thick of things and I will need an additional payment. I'll send you a schedule of future fees in the mail."

"How much do you need now?" I questioned.

"Twenty five thousand," he answered firmly.

"OK," I replied meekly.

I had nowhere else to go at that moment. Opening an oyster without a knife is as easy as opening Barry's mouth on my behalf without a fee. For the promise of twenty five thousand dollars he began to feed me additional legal information.

"Do you know Doc, that the judge in sealing the arrest record saved you the embarrassment, at least temporarily, from any media exposure. For this alone, consider this your lucky day."

Barry went on to give me an oral list of do's and don'ts. I might add, mostly don'ts.

"The court will deal with me directly from now on. I will only contact you if there are any developments prior to the thirty day period. So, I suggest that you go about your normal business. Don't use you home phone. Use phone booths and change locations often. On incoming calls at your home tell the caller that you will get back to them unless the call has nothing whatever to do with these legal issues. The phone at your office should only be used for hospital related business. Now, for God's sake, don't buy anymore airline tickets!"

"I can't, I don't have a passport."

"I mean not even to Dallas or Peoria."

"Why would I want to go to those places?"

Barry shook his head, "Who knows? Who knows?

Let me tell you something else to think about. The indictment was drawn up quickly within the last twenty four hours and was flawed through and through. This was not the first time, as the judge said, that this DA arrested a person and then built his case afterward. I guess the judge was tired of this tactic. However, let me caution you that at the next bail hearing the judge could reverse himself or there could be a new judge presiding, and so we may not be so lucky."

"What will happen if things work against us as you just described?"

"In order to stay out of jail during a trial you would have to put up your home and add another million or two in cash to make bail. Let's hope the three million doesn't turn into five million."

I did not reply, but only nodded to show that I understood. All I could think of was "Plan B."

I returned home to begin some serious thinking. My best thinking is done in solitude, the worst in turmoil. I have learned in life to keep silent and draw my own conclusions. The hardest things to decide are which bridges to cross and which to burn. I knew that it was time to stop going over old ground, and prepare instead for what is to come. Do I want to experience peace of mind or do I want to experience conflict, or even worse, incarceration? The latter was now looming as a real possibility. It was a no-brainer for me. "Plan B" was definitely the future. Concern and impatience always drove me into action. I know myself best. Once I prayed to God asking him to give me patience, and I added, "I want it now!"

"Plan B" demands that I must now act deliberately and be aware of the consequences. Plans that do not result in an action are nothing much, and an action which has no plan behind it is even worse. However there is a cautious element here as well, for there's a mighty big difference between good sound reasons and reasons that sound good.

I will have to resign myself to abdicating my medical license to practice surgery. This sort of relieved me in an odd way, as I always had an inner conflict between my religious beliefs and having been thrust into the role of playing God. The practice of medicine is a thinker's art, but the practice of surgery, like mine, is a plumber's. Every surgeon carries about a little cemetery in which from time to time he goes to pray. It's a cemetery of regret, where he seeks the reasons for his failures. Before I entered medical school I toyed with the idea of becoming an architect rather than a surgeon. In retrospect, I now recognize that the former is a kinder and more honest profession. A surgeon must bury his mistakes, but an architect can simply advise his clients to plant vines.

The next stage of "Plan B" called for a change of lawyers. I no longer needed a lawyer to tell me what I can or cannot do. I now needed a lawyer to tell me how to do what I want to do. There would be no trouble finding such a lawyer to execute my wishes as long as I paid his fees in a timely manner. I drew up a list of assignments. There were only three.

1) Replace Sophia's name on the house and other properties we shared, with Harriet's name.

2) Research up-to-date information covering the absence of extradition treaties between the United States and other countries.
3) Open a Swiss bank account.

In a decision about burning bridges, I decided to pay Barry the twenty five thousand dollars I promised him under a "you'll never know" heading.

CHAPTER 13

July 27th

I N A WAY it felt strange returning to the hospital. I'm sure that everyone from the janitor up was aware of my suspension. I decided that I would answer all well wishers in the same way. I would smile and hold out the palms of my hands and say, "see not guilty."

I arrived at my office earlier than normal. There was a memo left on top of a huge pile of files. It was from Gary welcoming me back and explaining that I would not be assigned to operate on patients, but rather, I would spend my time supervising the surgery department full time. This would be effective until the malpractice law suit was "put to bed."

I was angry that he did not tell me this when he announced my reinstatement. I would have protested in no uncertain terms. Upon reading this directive I felt like the cop whose tool, his gun, was taken away. As with me, they are always assigned to desk duty until matters were satisfied. After I calmed down, I began to understand the hospital's position and so it was useless to fret over their action as I was winding down my career anyway. However, I did toss the memo away in the waste paper basket. Being human, I must admit that I was provoked to anger.

I began to examine the contents of the files in front of me. I needed to prioritize the most serious cases. My responsibilities to serve the hospital and its patients had not been diminished by past events. I also wanted to leave the profession on a high note.

Between two files I found a directive to all personnel. Basically, it explained that the policy covering written care procedures would be discontinued immediately. The memo went on to emphasize that these rules had only been instituted as a two year test, and now will be further evaluated. To me, being on the inside of what prompted this action, I viewed it as a lawyers' move downplaying what the memo referred to as an "experiment."

My first instinct was to grab the phone and tell Barry about this. "Why?" I said to myself. I'm into "Plan B" and looking for a new attorney. It's hard to get use to, but Barry is history!. At that moment I was happy to know that I was master of my own destiny.

It took several hours to sort out the hospital's paperwork. I did not plan to eat lunch in the cafeteria which would have subjected me to showing my outstretched palms, an idea that did not appeal to me anymore. I walked over to a candy machine and selected a bag of potato chips, two Mars bars and a Coke. Clutching my purchases against my chest, I returned to my office.

Four more weeks to another bail hearing seemed like a long time away, but, in fact for me and for "Plan B" it was pressure. I placed a call to the New York Bar Association and spoke with a Mrs. Spencer. I explained to her that I was looking for a good lawyer or law firm, expert in international law, and in establishing a Swiss bank account. I also needed some light work on property transfers. She gave me three recommendations. I told this very bright woman who was trying to help me that the work had to be done rather quickly and that I did not have the time to interview all three.

"Well," she replied, "if you want me to pick one, I'd go with SHERWOOD and SHERWOOD."

"Which Sherwood?"

"Gus," she answered.

"Gus it is then."

I thanked her for her knowledge and recommendations. I wasted no time and called the law firm as soon as I hung up with Mrs. Spencer. I introduced myself to their secretary and explained that the ABA had recommended Gus Sherwood as an attorney who could handle all my legal needs. I also need my work completed quickly, I added.

"We work quickly," she replied, "but did they mention quality?"

"That's why we are talking," I answered.

"When would you like to come in?"

"As soon as possible, hopefully this week."

She placed me on hold while she checked his calendar. Returning to the phone she told me that he could see me Friday afternoon at three o'clock or if I could make it he had an open hour the next morning at eight.

"Which would you prefer?"

I didn't even think twice. I agreed to be there the next day.

She asked me for some specifics in order to prepare Gus. I told her briefly of my needs as she took notes. I thanked her and hung up the phone. "Plan B" got out of the gate quickly in what I considered to be its phase two. I was very pleased with myself. I returned to my work. I never had a problem going in two directions at the same time and now was no exception.

CHAPTER 14

July 28th

G US SHERWOOD WAS not the type of person that I had imagined. I was thinking "Sherwood", a lanky WASP with straight blond hair and blue eyes to match. Gus on the other hand had a dark complexion and sported a short stocky frame. He spoke with a slight European accent which I could not quite pinpoint. However, during our conversation he told me that he had been born in Turkey and came to the United States as a teenager with a twin brother, the other Sherwood on the billing. Obviously, neither the name Sherwood or Gus appeared on his birth certificate. We hit it off well right away, as he too was a Harvard graduate. A better student than I was, I thought. He was a Harvard grad in his second language.

"So, let's see if we can help you," he offered.

I explained the three specific areas where I needed assistance as best as I could. He listened, took a few notes and did not interrupt.

"That's it in a nutshell," I concluded.

"I can tell you that you have not presented any challenges that we could not handle."

"At a fast pace?" I added.

"Yes, at a fast pace," he confirmed.

Those words made me feel very comfortable.

"The simplest task are the property transfers. You call them transfers, but they are only simple name changes to replace your deceased wife's name with that of Harriet Leeds of Denmark. Is that correct?"

"Yes," I confirmed.

All Gus needed was Sophia's death certificate, the deeds, and copies of the original filings. Once I would secure these for him the proper forms would be sent to Harriet for her signature. She then would have to return them notarized for the new recordings.

"Is notarization from Denmark OK?" I inquired.

"Of course," he assured me. "One can even notarize in Pago Pago and it would be valid here."

I now tried to pin down the important time frame. Gus promised a done deal a few days after Harriet returned the paperwork.

I then asked about obtaining a Swiss bank account.

"This office has opened more than twenty five hundred Swiss bank accounts, and not one is mine," he joked.

All he required was specific information about the accounts I wanted transferred, which was all of them! I promised to gather the details he needed including transfer codes from each institution.

"If you can get me all this information within a few days, then I can answer your next question. The account at that point takes two days to open."

"That's great," I said.

"Now to the part I thought about all night," he chuckled. "What's with the extradition treaties?"

I told him that I needed a detailed report of modern countries that do not have an extradition treaty with the United States or a limited treaty. I also want to know the up to date exclusions or exceptions as well.

"Is this a rush job as well? he questioned.

"Within three weeks," I responded.

Gus then explained that this research would have to be turned over to a law student and then a lawyer from his staff will check it out for accuracy.

"Is this OK with you? I work with several law students. This work helps them pay for their tuition."

"Fine," I answered.

"Look, I did not ask you who Harriet Leeds is, and we never ask clients why they want a Swiss account, but this is the first time we have been hired to research extradition treaties. I am very curious, can you tell me why you need this information. You know that there is such a thing as a lawyer-client confidentiality code."

"Of course, I am aware of this. Even though we just met I trust you, but sometimes the government or the authorities and often the courts throw this rule out the window and try and break this trust. I don't want to place us in this position in the name of curiosity. I hope you understand."

"Completely," he responded.

I was quite satisfied with our meeting and asked the final question.

"Can you give me a ball-park figure of the fees all this will entail," I explored.

"I cannot see more than thirty hours work in total," he responded "I would estimate about seventy five hundred dollars the most plus costs for filings and so on. We require half down and the balance settled upon receiving our final invoice.

Without hesitation I took out my checkbook and wrote out a check for four thousand dollars to the firm. Gus reminded me of my role to help expedite the necessary paperwork and information needed to meet the time frame that I required.

"Don't worry Gus, as far as I'm concerned, this is all I have to do," I assured.

He did not know it, but I was prepared to pay a fee of twice as much or even more.

CHAPTER 15

August 21st

D URING THE PAST few weeks leading up to T-H-I-N-K F-L-E-E day I followed Barry's advice and led my normal life except for daily phone booth calls to Harriet plotting our future. Before settling permanently in a new land we decided to visit the exotic places of the world first. The kids would be placed in boarding school and Harriet would ferry back and forth as necessary.

I was just two days away from leaving for Hong Kong and today was also five days before the scheduled court date. This morning Barry left a message for me to call him back. This meant that I had to drive to a strip mall near my home to use their telephone. As far as I was concerned, I had lost all interest in Barry. However, with only a few days to go it was best to keep our communications going.

He told me that he had received advance information from the DA's office covering the general nature of the new indictment, which included the names of possible witnesses.

"I was surprised to receive this witness list," Barry said. "They don't have to reveal this yet, but my guess is that because of the debacle the first time around, they want to show the judge a tighter indictment now. I placed a copy of all this in the mail to you the other day. Please review the list of names so we can discuss it. Frankly, I never heard of half of them."

"I'll check the mail when I get home," I replied.

Barry also told me that the DA requested a two week extension until September the ninth, and the court granted it.

"It seems as if those guys are getting their act together," he added. "So Doc, be prepared to possibly post bail. As good as the judge was before, that's how tough he could be this time. You just can't trust those bastards!"

All this was easy for Barry to say. I was listening to him as if he was relating this whole sad tale about somebody else. In a way he was, because unknown to him, the State and I had been going through divorce proceedings for irreconcilable differences and the decree will take effect the day after tomorrow. Barry can call them bastards all he wants, but I can make them disappear.

It occurred to me that the two week extension would be helpful for me. While my plans were already in cement, the extra time would give me an undetected two week head start. So, I told Barry that since I'm terribly stressed out, that I will take advantage of the delay and go away to some secluded beach resort by myself. He agreed that this was a good idea.

I had never received the letter that Gary sought promising me that the hospital would cover me financially if there would be a settlement on the pending malpractice law suit. I had now lost interest in the whole affair anyway. Yesterday he called me to his office and told me that the legal department will honor an oral agreement only and would not consider putting it in writing. As he was explaining all this to me I had the same feeling of disengagement that I had just experienced with Barry. Now, I'd use that decision as an excuse to tell Gary that that I needed to take two weeks off blaming the stress that the hospital board created in me.

Staring at the phone perched on a post outside of a drugstore, I had the opportunity to make two calls for the price of one car trip, so I dialed the office of the hospital administrator. Gary listened to my plans without comment, so I threw in the clincher by offering to wave my pay during this time. That should help to calm down those bastards.

I returned home to find that the mail had arrived from Barry. I walked with the envelope to the pool area, curious its contents. There were eight names on a witness list, numbered from one to eight. The first was detective John LaGotta from the Nassau County Homicide Division. Just as I had suspected, this must be John the cop, for sure! A real Columbo dressed in a policeman's uniform.

Anna Wyoski, my maid, followed. I guess that she had been too scared to tell me that she had been interviewed by the police.

Ron Black, esquire, was number three. He must be their motive witness having drawn up a new will for Sophia which isolated me financially.

Rene M. Bellwood, Chase Bank. Ron must have led the DA to the safety box with a court order to open our box and found it empty. Rene M. was probably just as dismayed as the authorities because it was emptied "under her watch!"

Howard Kanter was listed next. He is the pharmacist at the hospital. I can't remember for certain but he could have been the person who filled my order for Demerol capsules. For the moment I could not figure out what bearing that would have on anything.

"Nassau County Laboratory." This must be the coroner's in-house lab.

"One Stop Medical Laboratory." This one must be the lab the DA used.

My thoughts went back to Howard Kanter, because I had the need to understand why his name showed up on this list. It suddenly struck me that the records would show that I only ordered Demerol one time while I was claiming that Sophia had been using the drug for a long history of back pain.

"Yes, that's it, of course," I said out loud.

Dr. Sam Klein was the final name on the list. He was Sophia's private physician. I completely forgot to consider him in the whole picture. It was a serious blunder on my part. My perfect murder was not only tainted here, but also made me realize that I left a trail of other mishaps as well. With all these mistakes, Barry would have had a difficult time and probably gone down in flames. However, he would become richer nevertheless.

"I was not aware that Mrs. Feelgood had back problems," Dr. Klein would testify.

I now shuddered as I could hear those words followed by a gasp in the courtroom, as the judge pounded his table calling for order. The jurors would then look at one another and then stare at me. These thoughts made me hear in my head the thunderous sound of a jail cell door smacking shut while I grabbed onto the bars for dear life. What a nightmare!

It became obvious to me that the DA had begun to tighten a noose around my neck. With all these people recently contacted, the media publicity could crack open at any time even if the fact of my arrest was sealed. However, there was one potential witness that they missed. Barry called him "that runt." The insurance agent could cause havoc by revealing the existence of the insurance policy. The five million dollars would be recovered immediately and I would lose the option of using the money for my legal defense or as a necessary ingredient of "Plan B."

I was not sure if I was upset or not with Anna. Since I had to let her go anyway, it would make me feel better if I found out that she was disloyal. I left the pool area and headed for the house. I found Anna in the kitchen where I asked her straight out if the police had spoken with her.

"Yes," she admitted.

"When?" I asked.

"About a week ago or maybe it was ten days."

"Why didn't you tell me?"

She did not respond right away so I decided to say nothing until she replied.

"I don't know," she finally blurted out.

"What do you mean you don't know?" I challenged.

At this point she had to tell me something, so I just waited for an answer.

"Well, they asked me questions about the time that I found Mrs. Feelgood in bed."

"Like what?"

"Like if I noticed a medicine bottle on the night table."

"What did you tell them?"

"I told them the truth."

"What's the truth?"

"That I did not see a bottle."

"Is that all?"

"They asked me over and over again if I was very sure that there was no bottle on the table."

"So!"

"So, I told them I was positive."

"And I guess they asked you what made you so positive?"

"Yes, they did."

"What made you so positive?"

"I told them that I had knocked the phone off the table, and if there were a bottle there it would have fallen off with it."

"Did you agree to testify to this in court?"

Anna looked down at the floor and did not answer. I had heard enough. This conversation was like pulling teeth, and I'm not even a dentist.

"Look Anna," I said, "I'm going away for a few weeks and then when I come back I will be moving into an apartment near the hospital, so I have to dismiss you."

Anna remained quiet. In a way I felt sorry for her. She was caught in the crossfire. I sat down at the kitchen table and wrote her a check giving her two weeks pay.

"You can gather together all your personal things. It's OK to leave today."

I had contracted with a management company to take care of the house, several other properties, and manage some personal work. Now was the time to place a message on my answering machine explaining that I had left for vacation and would be back on September the eighth, which was the day before the new court date. Essentially, I shut myself down until then.

I walked back to the pool area. I poured myself a glass of scotch whiskey even though I had never taken a hard drink in the middle of the day before, and proposed a toast into the air.

"Thank you, 'Plan B'. You saved my life. I have my passport, I have my new family, I have five million dollars, and more, socked away in a Swiss bank, and I have my health. To all the DA's, cops, detectives, coroners, testing labs, litigants, nurses, pharmacists, doctors, runts, maids, safety box attendants, children, father-in-laws, Rons, Garys, and Barrys of the world, God bless you all. I'll see you on the other side one day."

CHAPTER 16

August 23rd

T-H-I-N-K F-L-E-E DAY FINALLY arrived. As I had expected, I was energized. It felt like the first day in a new life, and in a sense, it was. However, there was a tinge of sadness in me as I glanced around the house for what was probably the last time, aware that I might never lay eyes on it again. As I walked from room to room I was reminded of past events, both good and bad. More than anything else, I realized that I associated this place with my failed marriage.

I sold my car to my automobile mechanic. I told him that I would be on vacation and he could pick up the auto in the driveway anytime after today. My flight was scheduled to leave in the early evening to Los Angeles. I would layover for the night which was doable because of the earlier time difference there and continue on to Hong Kong the next day.

Packing was my number one priority this morning. I did not want to burden myself with too much luggage. I selected just one large suitcase which I loaded with basic summer clothing. I didn't imaging Hong Kong would be very formal. By the time I'd packed everything I wanted, I had to sit on the suitcase to get it closed. I then filled a briefcase with some personal papers, toiletries, and clean underwear. I was about to leave the bedroom when I eyed my doctor's black bag. I hesitated a moment and turned away.

The airport service limo arrived at three o'clock. I was sitting on my front steps with my luggage at my side when the car pulled up to my door. In all the years that I had lived here this was the first time that I had sat on these steps.

I was dropped off at Northwest Airlines and headed towards the ticketing counters. It was a long walk through the terminal building. This gave me the time to reflect on the past a bit and think how my new life was starting out in the unique fashion of defying the court. I did not know much about the finer points of the law, but I knew that I was turning myself into a true fugitive.

My new and very valuable passport was tucked safely into the inside pocket of my sports jacket. As Hong Kong was my final ticketed destination I was obliged to show my passport to the agent. I was naturally apprehensive as I approached her. However, this was 1977, and the whole security scene would not be upon us for a decade or more in the future.

The agent flipped open the passport and thumbed back the pages until she found my picture. Then she glanced at me, looked again at the picture and handed the passport back with a smile.

"Yep, sure looks exactly like you," she quipped with a pride of meeting her responsibilities.

My one piece of luggage was checked and off I went to my gate. As soon as the flight was called I pressed to get on the plane. I couldn't wait to take my seat. With my briefcase secured in the overhead compartment I leaned back and closed my eyes. The moment for a reality check was upon me. The seriousness and irreversibility of what I was about to do began to sink in. There was no turning back and I felt no regrets.

The cabin attendants were busy slamming all the overhead bins. A gate agent came onto the plane and handed a final manifest over to the pilot. The door to the cockpit was closed with a resounding click, followed by the heavy sound of the plane's door closing. The engines were turned on at a noise level almost as low as that of an automobiles as the pilot backed away from the terminal gate. The engine noise increased dramatically as the plane picked up ground speed towards its take off position. We were cleared to leave immediately and lifted into that wild blue yonder. As we gained altitude the aircraft shifted around slowly towards the setting sun. All that came to mind at that moment was, "go west young man, go west!"

CHAPTER 17

Hong Kong/Macau
August 25th-September 16th

D ESCENDING INTO HONG Kong's
Kai Tak airport, the doorway to Asia's
number one tourist destination, is like coming down a hotel's glass elevator. While
gliding by the high rise buildings one can almost touch the faces visible in the office
and apartment windows.

I arrived at the Peninsula Hotel, considered the best among other large great
luxury hotels here. Two Chinese porters grabbed my luggage out of the taxi. They
were garbed in stark white outfits, with matching white berets and white cotton gloves.
They almost faded away into the huge white front entrance doors as they approached
them. Inside the spacious and ornate lobby I was greeted by a host dressed as if he
were part of a wedding party. However, I knew better because it was only eight o'clock
in the morning. He escorted me to the registration desk, stood at my side, and then
handed me over to another member of the wedding party whose job it was to walk
me over to the elevators and push the correct floor button.

I checked the suite assigned to me with the guidance of a concierge. Each floor
had its own concierge desk. He made a point of letting me know that it was almost
required that I leave my shoes outside the door before retiring. They would be
returned all shined up by five the next morning. In return, I made it a point to notify
him that my wife was joining me shortly and so I didn't want him to think that I was
sneaking in some chick. Undoubtedly, this was one reason these floor desks were
manned around the clock.

"I'll leave a note for the others on duty," he promised, smiling.

I could have sworn that I saw him give me a slight wink.

I joined the hustle and bustle of early morning pedestrians on Nathan Road, the main drag near my hotel. I stopped at a currency exchange window. As the clerk was processing the five one hundred dollar bills that I gave him, he threw me a question.

"How long will you be in Hong Kong?"

Since I don't give that kind of information out even to my mother, I replied, "three days."

"You're not changing enough money for three days," he declared.

"What do you suggest?" I replied.

"How about another five hundred?"

So, I handed him another five bills. We were, in fact, planning to stay about a month. I hoped these Hong Kong dollars I just received would at least give me pocket change for the month. As for Harriet the story will be different, for all she talks about are the tremendous bargains available here.

As I strolled through narrow winding streets I counted enough tailor shops to clothe half the world. A man sitting on a piece of cardboard with a threaded needle in his hand and a sewing machine in front of him could also be considered a shop as well. There was a good reason not to be part of the custom tailoring experience except that I didn't think I'd ever wear a suit again for the rest of my life. There was one way out of this predicament, and that was to go the sports jacket and matching pants route.

The tailor told me that purchasing a full suit was a better deal.

"How much better?" I inquired.

He replied that suits ranged in price from thirty-two to forty-eight dollars. The cost for a sports jacket and matching pants ranges from thirty-nine to fifty-five dollars.

I stared up at the dirty ceiling and tried to appear as if I was contemplating a decision seriously.

"What the hell," I proclaimed, "let's shoot for the sports jacket and matching pants, you only live once!"

I selected my fabrics from what appeared to be over one hundred rolls of cloth. I did not ask about price. I knew instinctively that whichever choice I made the price would be fifty five dollars. This was confirmed when the tailor told me that I had good taste.

"You picked out the best fabrics in the store!" he announced.

An old gent suddenly appeared from behind a curtain and began to take my measurements. The tailor told me that the order would be ready to be picked up after six o'clock the following evening.

"It takes that long to make," I joked.

"Three o'clock then, OK," he responded. "Just for you! Tell all your friends that we work fast, OK."

"Sure," I answered, even though I didn't have a friend in the world at this point.

I decided not to test his promise. The following day I returned to the shop after dinner, perhaps it was about nine o'clock. The tailor and the fellow who took my measurements met me at the entrance to the shop. He was holding up my order in his hand. It was all wrapped up in plastic.

"You said three o'clock," he admonished.

I apologized, paid him fifty five US dollars and did not have the guts to ask them if I could try the clothing on. I just did not want to hear the tailor say:

"You want try on! You want try on! What for? What do you think we are, chopped liver?"

I took my goodies back to the hotel and tried on the clothing in the privacy of my room. Everything was just perfect. There was even a label sewn inside the jacket that read, "CUSTOM MADE EXCLUSIVELY FOR CHARLES FEELGOOD." It was now time to meet Harriet at the airport and so I hopped a taxi and we sped off.

Harriet and I spent much of our time taking in the sights and sounds of the city to appreciate why this place is called "The Pearl of the Orient." On her first day here we took the famous Star Ferry from Kowloon Island, where our hotel was located, to Hong Kong proper. This ten minute ride gave us a waves' eye view of the very busy deep water harbor filled with large container ships to small one man Sanpans.

Victoria Peak hangs high above Hong Kong. To reach the top, pedestrians must board a tram which travels at a snail's pace at what appears to be a forty five degree angle. There are several stops along the way as the mountain is spotted with expensive homes, some of mansion proportions. The ticket taker rides with the tram and moves from car to car punching tickets. He has mastered the art of walking up and down a staircase without the stairs. There is a reward once the peak is reached, an unforgettable breathtaking view of the harbor, outlying islands, and the city below.

In between Harriet's shopping excursions we managed to squeeze in a dinner one evening at a town named Aberdeen. The entire area itself is a fishing village where thousands of boat people live on the water. Some of the boats also serve as floating shops for food, clothing, fishing supplies and the like. Young children earn their keep diving off their family boats to locate and secure coins tossed into the water by passing tour ships. Colorful Chinese junks ferry diners to large floating restaurants specializing in seafood, of course. We had dinner at the Palace Restaurant. I ordered turtle soup and a three pound lobster stuffed with crab meat. I asked the waiter if all this was kosher. He looked at me somewhat puzzled. This confirmed that, indeed, I was as far from New York as I planned to be.

I was not certain what the date was in Hong Kong, as I could never understand the intrusion of the International Date Line. I knew for sure that it was September ninth in New York, the day of the new court appearance. I had arranged for my management company to have my phone disconnected this morning. I figured that having the phone operational until now with my message that I was away, would prevent callers from thinking anything out of the ordinary was happening. I was to learn in the future that during this time all hell broke loose. For example, Gary, the hospital administrator, left a message wanting to discuss why the police interviewed Howard Kanter from their pharmacy department about a prescription I had filled for Demerol in late June.

"Sorry to bother you while you are on vacation. If you get this call please contact me."

He then went on about damn Howard Kanter and how upset he was.

Of all people my father-in-law called and left a classic message. I'm certain the call was prompted by his attorney, Ron Black, who led the DA to the safety deposit box. I don't want to paraphrase his memorable message as it is more meaningful to capture his words verbatim. This is what the shmuck said:

"Charles, whom do you agree you are already! What's with Sophia's jewels from the vaults? They should be possessed by the kids. Wills are legal tender, you know. Do the right thing. Don't be a shnorrer (cheap skate) for God's sake!"

Note, that he did not open the call with a hello, or identify himself, or say goodbye.

There were a few more enlightening messages. One was from the "company" who had informed me that I had won a trip to Hawaii. They were inquiring if I had sent them the two hundred dollars "no show" deposit.

Then there was a message from Barry. It was simple, to the point, but cautious.

"I see that you're not home as yet. The court date tomorrow is set for two in the afternoon. Meet me at the courthouse steps at noon. We can grab some lunch and talk about whatever we have to talk about."

I figured out what the code word "grab" meant. Grab meant a cheap lunch and he would grab the cheap check. At that appointed time I could imagine Barry frantically pacing up and down those steps and then frantically calling me at twelve fifteen or so, only to hear the phone companies apologetic disconnect message. They used the same words that have incensed creditors since Alexander Bell received his patent.

I felt comfortable with my conscience because I did send Barry a check for twenty five thousand dollars as I had promised. In my mind I labeled the check a "no show" deposit.

It was now past midnight in Hong Kong. I cracked open a bottle of champagne. Harriet and I proceeded to drink it all.

"Now for the real celebration," she said, and dropped to the floor to give me a blow job.

"Better than a kiss!" she then bragged.

After three weeks here we realized that while Hong Kong was certainly an exciting place, it was small. As with most island paradises, it became confining. We needed to expand our own territory.

The Portuguese territory of Macau is an island which lies off the coast of Red China. This place is a hot bed for legal casino gambling and other not so legal activities as well. Harriet and I were eager to test our luck there as we were living on the edge anyway. Luxury hydrofoil boats riding above the ocean water ferried passengers from Hong Kong to Macau in about an hour. We both enjoyed sightseeing in Hong Kong and planned to check out Macau which was considerably smaller in size. As such, it would take less than a day to capture the flavor of the island. Then we could attack the casino in the evening. However, as it turned out, not until Harriet could make one more stop. She insisted on going to the barrier gate between Macau and China to get a glimpse of Communist soldiers peering back at us.

As we approached the area, a policeman coming out of nowhere, stopped us a block away. He explained that since the riots in 1966 foreigners are requested not to go nearer the border than where we were standing now. By the way he pronounced "requested" I knew he meant "not permitted." As far as I was concerned, there was no sense in arguing with him. Harriet's plea for "just a little peak" was ignored. As the guard walked away to wherever he came from, Harriet said:

"Maybe we can bribe him?"

"Not a good idea," I responded.

However, in my heart I knew that's what we would wind up doing.

"You bribe him, if you wish," I said to her after I saw her pouting.

"Sure," she shot back. "Give me a saw buck. That's a week's pay, you know."

I waited until Harriet found the guy. She then returned very excited.

"Hurry, let's go to the gate. He suddenly had to go to the bathroom. He says that he can pee for up to five minutes. I promised not to show the soldiers the finger, as one riot was enough. I closed the deal on this quid pro quo!"

It couldn't have been more than five minutes when the policeman showed himself in the distance. Our time was up and we headed for the casino.

I recalled that the few times in the past when I had visited Las Vegas I would budget myself three hundred dollars to lose in the casino. The prophesy always came true. Now I wondered with great excitement what it would feel like to play for thousands of dollars. Harriet found a seat at the higher paying slot machines. She chose one at the end of a long row of them near the entrance of the casino. Her theory was that this location attracts new people coming in who pause and watch the action.

"Casinos always rig these machines to pay out quicker where visitors can observe how easy it is," she explained.

"We'll see," I thought.

I left her sitting there wrapped up in her confidence and began wandering around the casino floor. I checked out the crap tables and all kinds of card games, and finally felt more comfortable finding a seat at the roulette wheel. Like the slots, roulette required the minimum of thinking and the maximum of luck. Both these games enabled Harriet and I to shut down our brains and drink exotic South Pacific liquors that the casino so generously plied into their guests. This strategy in approaching gambling may sound good on paper, but did not work in reality. In less than an hour I was in the hole for five thousand dollars. Harriet was not looking very happy either for she only broke even at this point. It seems as if the crowds of people entering the place and stopping briefly to peer over Harriet's shoulder came in good spirits. However, this state of mind would be taken away from them in short order.

It was time for us to take a break. We made our way through the crowded casino floor to a lounge where we found a corner table and ordered drinks. A young Australian man who sat across from me at the roulette table approached us. I had earlier determined that he was Australian because he called everyone "mate."

"Well, I guess it wasn't our time. I lost a bundle as well, and I consider myself a good roulette player, so don't feel bad," he said.

The waiter arrived with our drinks. I thought that if he fathoms himself a roulette maven, I should talk to him. I invited him to join us. He accepted, ordered a drink for himself and handed the waiter a card and told him to put the entire tab on his account. I argued, he insisted, so I let him have his way.

"How long are you guys staying in Macau?" he inquired.

I told him that we just came for the day and that we have been in Hong Kong almost a month. I then challenged his boast about his roulette savvy.

"So, I imagine that you must win more than you lose!"

"I'm going to tell you a little secret, mates. When I lose, I never lose, and when I win, I win double."

"Is this a riddle that we have to unscramble," asserted Harriet with a tinge of sarcasm in her voice.

"You'll never figure it out, but it's worth a fortune," he boasted.

"A fortune!" exclaimed Harriet.

"Well, if you are both interested, then I'll reveal it to you."

"Shoot!" I said.

He leaned across the table and looked around the room to see if we would be alone. Stupidly, Harriet and I looked around the place as well. When the three of us were satisfied of complete security, he began to talk slightly above a whisper. This made us drop our heads closer to the top of the table. At that moment a roving camera girl came by.

"Picture today, no charge if you don't like it!"

Our friend lifted his head up, glanced at her, nodded no, and said:

"Couldn't that shit head see that we were leaning down!"

That comment nearly cracked Harriet up, but she managed to contain herself with a cough. He was none the wiser.

"Listen to me carefully," he whispered. "I can only repeat this one more time."

We all laughed at his little joke.

"Just tell it one time mate, we're no dopes, you know!" Harriet added.

"As I was about to say when that jerko interrupted, China, as you may or may not know, is a major source of high quality opium. This has been the case for three thousand years and maybe more. The stuff is easily brought to Macau by dingies floated down the Pearl River. The problem for sellers is that the supply here is far greater then the demand. This is because Macau has a small population and a high poverty level. Hong Kong, on the other hand, with millions of people living or visiting there in a flourishing economy, is the real market. The price is more than double on the street then it is here. The dealer's problem is to get it to Hong Kong safely. This is often difficult for the Chinese or other Asians, but not for Westerners who pass through customs between these two islands unscathed. All others are subject to spot checks, particularly if they are noted coming and going too often.

"All this is very interesting," interrupted Harriet, "but what's it got to do with your riddle, mate?"

With her voice dropping off a full octave, she whispered as she looked around the room, "you know the one worth a fortune!'

"Hold your horses," he replied "I just gave ya some background, now I'll tell ya!"

"Shoot," I interjected.

"You see, I've got a compulsive gambling problem and the first to admit it. Now I've found a way to gamble risk free by carrying bags of the stuff from here to Hong Kong."

"What's this mean to us, mate?" Harriet said.

"OK, let me lay it out further. For every person I recruit I earn a bonus of one thousand US dollars. Right now I'm looking at two thousand bucks."

"The riddle mate, get to the damn riddle already," insisted an impatient Harriet.

"If both of you are of the mind to be carriers as I am, here is how it works. You both play roulette for as long as you want. When you quit the game ask the pit boss for a receipt reflecting your winnings or losses. You can get this if you tell them before you start playing that you need this for tax purposes. When you arrive in Hong Kong and deliver the stuff the guy on that end will reimburse you with double your winnings or return your loses, if that's the case. That's it in a nutshell."

"Boy, that was some nutshell to crack," commented Harriet. "I see now, so we earn double our winnings, or if we should lose, our losses will be returned. That's what you mean by risk free I gather."

"Exactly," he replied "and that's the answer to the riddle as well. So, are you guys interested?"

"One minor point. What if by chance one is caught? Is that a fair question?" I asked suspiciously.

"That's a fair question," he responded. "Being caught is rare for Westerners, but that does not mean it can't happen. Only a fool would think otherwise, and you've already told me that you're both not stupid, or did you say dopes. I can only judge from the past. I personally have made over one hundred trips. My bosses use more then a dozen carriers every day without an incident yet. I say yet, because as we say, nothing is for sure except death and taxes. I'm giving you an honest answer."

He went on to explain that some Asians are searched randomly on Macau. If a customs agent finds anything he is more likely to confiscate it rather then to arrest that individual.

"You see," he added, "these inspectors, making about one hundred dollars a month, have nothing personal to gain from an arrest. Do you get the picture, mates?"

I felt that he needed a response to show him that we understood exactly what was going on, so I blurted out, "gotcha!"

"Are we paid in US dollars," Harriet asked, beginning to uncover final details.

"They pay in Macau's casino chips. You must cash them in here. The exchange rate is only three or four percent less than US, so it's no big deal."

I glanced at Harriet.

"Let's go for it!" she said.

"Great!" he responded, "I can always use some bonus money for my bar expenses. By the way, what are your names, mates?"

"I'm Charles and this is Harriet," I replied.

"What, no last name?"

"Of course, Wilson," I asserted.

"And my name is Willy Armstrong, the all Australian boy," he quipped.

I told him that we were fairly certain that we would give it a try, but first we needed to observe for ourselves the custom officers when we leave Macau today and then when we arrive in Hong Kong as well.

"If it's a go, then we can meet again in a few days," I offered.

"How about this Saturday, at ten o'clock, in the morning? We only work on the weekends because the crowds are real thick then. Custom agents are busy keeping the flow of humanity moving. The three of us can meet here at this same table. Don't forget to bring two backpacks with you."

"That sounds good," I replied.

"Sounds good," repeated Harriet.

"One more thing," Willy proclaimed.

"What's that?" I responded, thinking that there is always one more thing with these kinds of guys.

"Set yourselves up with a twenty five thousand dollar credit line each. This will also give you all sorts of comps from free rooms to free meals, as well as access to the pool area and other junk. Can you manage this, mates?"

Harriet replied for the both of us:

"What do you think we are? Chopped liver?"

We had satisfied ourselves that passing through customs on both ends was as easy as a walk in the park. There was no problem establishing casino credit either. All we had to do now was to purchase backpacks and show up Saturday morning and meet Willy. All of this excited us, as this was the kind of adventure we had planned.

The three of us met in the lounge. The bar itself had not opened as yet for business. As such, there was no need to lean over the table and converse in low tones. In a way it did take the clandestineness out of the equation.

"Glad to see that you remembered your backpacks and I hope you're all set with credit lines," Willy commented.

"Don't you remember what I told you the other day?" jokingly scolded Harriet.

"I remember," he said, "but honestly, it's something I've been thinking about since then."

"Like what?" I added.

"Like, what does chopped liver have to do with anything?"

"That's our riddle to you, mate!" Harriet teased.

Who could ever explain it to the all Australian "GOY." I realized that there must be much fewer Jews in Sydney than I had imagined. It was time to get to the guts of why we were here.

"OK Willy, take us through the day," I began.

"It's very easy for Americans, so don't worry" he replied with a smirk on his face. At this point he laid out some suggestions to follow.

"Remember, winnings are doubled. Play as if it's your own money. You're not stupid and you're not dopes. Do not go back into the well even if your losses are covered. Take it from me, a professional gambler, the well is dark and deep."

"Not to change the subject," said Harriet, "but what about getting the opium?"

"Let's call it 'the stuff', that's the correct terminology," Willy insisted. "When you are ready to return to Hong Kong go to room 711 in the hotel. There is someone there at all times who will have the packages ready for you."

"711, is there any significance to that number," Harriet questioned.

"Yes," replied Willy, "only if you're playing craps!"

Willy went on to explain that this person notifies Hong Kong that we are on our way. At the pier when we arrive we had to look for a uniformed chauffeur holding a sign reading, "WINNERS' CIRCLE." We then would be driven to a luggage shop where we will hand over our packages and be reimbursed in casino chips for the winning or losing amount on the tax receipt.

Just to make sure Harriet repeated the agreement.

"Double winnings, all losses returned. Is that correct?"

"Who could forget?" he wisecracked.

"Sounds easy for Americans," she chided back, "but what about Danes?"

"Much easier," he assured, smiling widely.

As we all began to leave the lounge area he stopped and said, "just one more thing."

"There goes that one more thing again," I thought.

"From this moment on we don't talk or acknowledge each other in public, OK."

I must admit that after Willy left us we became a little nervous being on our own. We had not come half way around the world to make money. We had come to spend money! At this point we still had the option to bow out and gamble like the rest of the suckers. On the other hand, we would then be just like everyone else and that's not much of an adventure, so we decided to take the plunge. What the hell!

We spent the time now hanging around the swimming pool of the casino's hotel. Dinner was taken at five o'clock when it would be quieter and the food prepared better with attentive service. We each finished our own bottle of wine.

"There's no thinking at roulette," we toasted ourselves, as the last glass of wine was gulped down.

We were seated at the roulette wheel around seven o'clock. I called over the pit boss and told him that I would need a tax receipt for either winnings or losses.

"No problem," he replied, "after you put your chips down they have to be counted and you can't remove any until you leave. If you add any while you are playing, you have to let us know, OK."

"OK," I replied.

I know what the expression beginner's luck means, but I was rarely the recipient of it. However, this night I was, and to a lesser degree, so was Harriet. Within an hour we had won fifty-five hundred dollars together. Harriet tapped me on the knee.

"Let's go," she urged, "Willy says we should never go to the well, whatever wells have to do with it!"

"One more play," I begged.

I placed five hundred down on red trying to increase our winnings to six thousand dollars for a total of twelve thousand when we got to Hong Kong. That little ball skipped around and settled on black. My five hundred dollars worth of chips was whisked away by a disinterested croupier.

"I think I know what a well is now. Come on Charles, we are out of here," she directed, as she lifted herself off her stool.

I motioned to the pit boss to check the value of our chips and requested my receipt or whatever they called it.

"Here ya go sir, sorry ya leaving us so early."

"Oh, we'll be back tomorrow," I assured him, hoping not to place our lines of credit and comp possibilities in jeopardy. However, I really believed that this stoic individual didn't personally give a shit whose asses occupied the stools tomorrow.

We cashed in our chips and walked over to a bank of elevators. The seventh floor's hallways were decorated with expensive art and antique furniture. We approached room seven-eleven and knocked on the door.

"Just a minute," cried out a voice inside.

The door was opened and to our surprise there stood Willy.

"What are you doing here?" I exclaimed.

"Minding the store," he answered, "the regular guy needed the weekend off, so they enlisted me for duty. So, how did you mates do?"

"Five gees!" Harriet announced proudly.

"Now don't forget to collect five more in Hong Kong," he reminded.

"Don't worry, she won't," I assured him.

Willy took our backpacks and placed a paper wrapped package the size of a small cereal box in each one.

"I'll notify Hong Kong that you will be on the next ferry."

Willy led us out the door and wished us luck.

"We'll see you tomorrow if we don't find ourselves in the slammer tonight!" I joked.

Willy did not laugh.

Harriet and I left for the pier which was only two blocks away. Crowds of people were moving along with us to catch the next hydrofoil boat. Now we witnessed why Saturday evening was a key time for this sort of thing. All the customs agents were busy just moving the hoards of people as quickly as possible. When we arrived in Hong Kong we did notice that a guard had pulled a Chinese man out of the rushing crowd and began to check his briefcase. That was one in a thousand, good odds, we thought.

The streets were full of the cries of vendors and the sounds of honking car horns. The chauffeur holding a "WINNERS' CIRCLE" sign spotted us before we saw him.

"Are you the Wilsons," he asked.

"Who the hell are the Wilsons," I said to myself.

"Yep, that's us," Harriet quickly replied.

"Follow me," he instructed, "my limo is parked around the corner."

After twenty minutes or so, we arrived at Good Luck Luggage and Handbags. The chauffeur jumped out of the car and scurried around to open the rear door for us. This was comical in a way because the "limo" was only a black Lincoln Town Car. Then again, if it's bigger than a rickshaw. I guess that one can call anything with wheels a limo here.

The three of us walked towards the shop's entrance. An extra large man sitting on an orange crate box in front of the store greeted us and we followed him into a back room. The driver took the man's place on the crate. We removed the stuff from our backpacks and placed them into his outstretched hands.

"Do you have your casino vouchers?" he asked.

"So that's what they are called!" I blurted out.

The guy looked at me kind of funny. I gave him the slip of paper and he handed me a sealed envelope.

"How did you know how much it was?" I questioned.

"Willy told me," he replied, "it's all there in casino chips."

He offered to have us driven back to our hotel. I thanked him, but told him that we preferred to stroll back. If they knew us as the "Wilsons" then why should they know the name of our hotel? We walked for a few blocks, spotted a taxi stand and drove to the ferry slip and crossed over to the Kowloon side.

After arriving at our hotel we decided to visit the bar for a nightcap to unwind. I scribbled some figures on a paper napkin and said to Harriet, "The score so far after tonight puts us ahead ten thousand dollars. Subtract the five thousand lost on the first night and we wind up with a net of five thousand bucks. Now, that's great!"

"I don't think so at all," she responded. "We are here for high excitement. I don't see why we each shouldn't have the kick of playing for the full amount of money. If we lose, we lose nothing. If we win, then that just tops the experience."

"I agree Harriet," I replied back. "I don't know why we are futzing around for, and don't ask me what that means. From now on we're going all the way every weekend starting tomorrow until we decide to leave Hong Kong. Willy said to treat our betting as if it was our own money and this is the way we treat our own money. Fuck 'em, win or lose, that's the deal we made!"

We slept late Sunday morning, had lunch and headed for the pier. Today was the casino's busiest day. The hydrofoils increased their crossings from on the hour to every half hour.

We were greeted at the roulette table like old friends. The pit boss asked if I needed a receipt again.

"Yes," I replied, "I'll need a voucher."

I think he was pleased that I had learned the correct terminology. We spent about four hours watching that little devil of a ball bounce around the numbers. Harriet hit a rare double green just as we were thinking of leaving the table.

"Oh shit," she reacted, "now we gotta play some more!"

We must have seen more than fifty faces come and go that evening, most walking away with less chips then when they first sat down to play. Finally, after another hour, it was all over for us. We had lost fifty thousand dollars and high fived each other. The pit boss upon watching us turned white from yellow. The security guys hiding in the ceilings must have gone ballistic to see our joy. Surely, nobody working there had witnessed anything like this before.

We followed the carpeted path to the elevator, arrived at room 711 and knocked on the door. Willy unlatched the locks.

"Hi mates, how's it going?"

"Great," we replied in unison.

"Let me guess. I think you guys won a couple of thousand bucks today. Am I right?"

"Wrong, very wrong." answered Harriet.

"How wrong am I?" he wondered.

"We lost fifty gees," she replied.

"You are joking around, right?"

"Cross my heart and hope to die. Here Willy, see for yourself, look at this voucher."

"Were you ever ahead?"

"Oh sure," I answered, "We were ahead often. At one point, by almost eighteen thousand dollars. Now that's damn good because some people we met today told us that the wheel is fixed."

"So, why didn't you quit then? What happened to the rules?"

"Rules, what rules?" answered Harriet, "we only took them as suggestions. We don't give a hoot about the money we lost because we get it back anyway. Remember what you told us. When we lose we never lose. So we decided today to go to the well."

Willy turned paler than the pit boss did. He grabbed our backpacks out of our hands and shoved in two packs of the stuff in each one.

"I've doubled up to defray the cost of the money you lost."

He instructed us to wait two more hours for the next boat when the crowds thicken. As we walked back towards the elevator Harriet muttered, "What's he so upset about? What does he care, he's not the boss!"

"Maybe he's afraid of the boss," I pondered. "After all, I'm certain nobody has fallen into that well as we did."

We moved through customs with ease again. On the ride back we agreed that if we couldn't play for the kick of it anymore then we would quit this "job."

The same chauffeur met us at the dock. This time he took our backpacks right away. He drove to the luggage shop and as talkative as he was yesterday, that's how quiet he was now. The crate man was sitting outside the shop waiting for us to arrive. He led us into the back room.

"Here is our voucher," I said as I handed it to him.

He glanced at it and at that moment the curtain behind us pulled away. Willy stepped out holding a revolver in his hand. The crate man gave him the voucher, calling him boss.

"Tear it up," Willy ordered.

I now felt the gun against my temple. Willy began his tirade. "If you clowns haven't figured it out yet, I own this fucking operation. Losing, you say is exciting and better than winning. If you really think so then I'll make you very happy. I hope that you will be glad to know that you lost fifty gees for real today. I'm not only in the opium business, but I'm also a hired killer. Today I might work for myself. Relax, we provide proper burials at sea. That's what those extra large trunks at the front of the store are for. Can I drop the Wilson and call you Feelgood instead? If you both want to continue feeling good as your name suggests, then make sure that you are out of Hong Kong by five o'clock tomorrow. Now both of you march out of here and consider yourselves lucky to leave alive."

"I have one question," perked up Harriet.

I could have kicked her in the ass at that moment.

"If we had won fifty thousand instead, you would have paid us fifty thousand more, right?"

"Don't be a fucking imbecile," he responded. "If people told you that the wheel was fixed, do you think they would allow you to win that kind of money? I was surprised they let you get up to eighteen grand, unless you're bullshitting me. Now get the fuck out of my face and be gone by five tomorrow. As you leave, take a good look at those large trunks out there. That should make you decide that it's more exciting to leave then to stay here.

We left the place shaken up to say the least. When we arrived at our hotel I spotted a note sticking out from under the door. It simply read "five o'clock." They not only knew our correct last name but the name of our hotel as well.

We booked a noon flight for the next day then and there. Perhaps in our quest for high adventure we would take it down a notch or two at our next stop.

CHAPTER 18

Taiwan
September 17th-October 4th

O UR PLANE TAXIED along the runway at our new destination. The Island of Formosa had established itself as the Republic of China after World War II. It had been ruled by Japan for fifty years and then renamed Taiwan. This did not bode well with China which considered the territory an integral part of the Mainland. To add fuel to the fire, millions of people fled to Taiwan to escape Communism.

We checked into the Grand Hotel located on a mountain top overlooking the capital city of Taipei. It was common knowledge that the place was owned by Chang Kai-shek and his wife. Since Chang was dead it was now solely her possession. We tried to verify this with the room service waiter who confirmed it and added:

"Anything worth anything is owned by the Madame, including the museum!"

We gathered that he must be pissed off being a room service waiter. The museum he was referring to was considered one of the world's best for Chinese art. Most of the paintings and objects were probably stolen or smuggled in from the Mainland. No wonder Mao Zedong was foaming from the mouth.

It was some sort of a holiday and we were promised a festive atmosphere by the concierge, who hired a private car for us to tour for the day. Our driver and guide was named Charlie. As soon as we were seated comfortably, he raced away from the hotel and penetrated the bedlam of traffic along one of the main thoroughfares. Exhaust fumes clouded the air. Cars, buses, and taxis clogged the four lane boulevard. Obviously Taipei was suffering from the pangs of progress.

Our car continued to a suburb of Taipei where we viewed a festival at a temple. Lanterns on bamboo poles swayed high above the town to guide the spirits, according to Charlie. We stopped to watch opera troupes and puppeteers performing ancient plays of Chinese mythology with high pitched voices and whining music. In the main street huge pigs lay split and spread over bamboo frames in front of shops and homes. There were tables laden with cooked chickens and ducks plus fruits and rice cakes. All these foods were offerings to the Gods.

"You mean, Charlie, that people can't eat any of this food?" Harriet questioned.

"Not unless you can prove that you're a God!" he responded.

We stopped at a small restaurant for a late lunch. They served a variety of soupy stews over rolled rice. After the meal Harriet asked Charlie what we had eaten.

"You may be sorry you asked." he grinned. "The one with the yellowish lumps is pig's bowel and ginger. The milky one with brown squares, well, that's coagulated chicken blood with turnips. And that . . .

"I've heard enough!" she interrupted with a smile.

The following day we decided to visit the museum.

"What the heck," Harriet remarked. "We might as well see it since it's owned by the same landlord who owns our hotel."

In all the high ceiling rooms there stood guards dressed as soldiers or visa versa, we couldn't say for certain. We stopped to admire a cloth woven portrait of a Chinese farm scene dated two centuries before Christ. A well dressed Chinese man, perhaps in his early forties, although one should never guess the age of a Chinese person for money, came up to us.

"This is either an original or a damn clever forgery," he proclaimed.

"You must be kidding," I replied in a shocking voice.

"Not really, I'm serious," he answered.

"How would we know?" Harriet questioned.

"We don't, but do you how many fakes they have pulled out of the museum?"

"I have no idea." I admitted.

"Over one hundred since the museum opened. Those are the ones they have discovered, so there must be a few more, and others keep coming in."

"That's simply incredible," Harriet responded. "You mean we could be admiring a piece of shit here? Pardon my French!"

"Anything is possible in the world of art. Take it from the horse's mouth."

"Are you that horse?" questioned Harriet.

"You might say that. I'm here on a busman's holiday today. I own an art gallery at the Royal Hotel in downtown Taipei."

"I bet a person could make a bundle of money selling copies of expensive original art?" Harriet speculated.

"That's for sure! The best thing about it is that the seller and the buyer are happy. We have a Chinese proverb which translated says, 'happiness doesn't depend upon what I have, it depends solely upon what I think I have!"

"I never heard a Chinese proverb that I couldn't relate to," Harriet asserted.

"If you are both interested in the art business, either real or fake, then why don't you visit with me at my gallery. We could have some tea together. It's best to come mid-morning before the tourists arrive."

I told him that this would be something we would look forward to doing. He handed me his business card.

"Where are you staying and how long do you plan to be in Taiwan?" he inquired.

I told him that we were at the Madame's hotel and planned to stay for two or three weeks. He smiled and advised:

"Don't steal the ashtrays. They are tempting, but they're fakes, you know!"

The art dealer bid us goodbye.

When we returned to our hotel Harriet was chomping at the bit to contact our new friend, Thomas Wong. She did, and made a date to meet the next morning.

It was close to ten o'clock when we arrived at his store, located with other upscale shops in the hotel's shopping mall. He asked us to call him Tommy. We introduced ourselves as Harriet and Charles. Tommy decided it would be more relaxing if he called me Chuck. I didn't object out of politeness. I'd never been called Chuck in all my life.

Harriet opened the conversation. "You have a wonderful art gallery here Tommy. Don't you think so, Chuckie?"

I did not acknowledge the wisecrack.

"Can you point out the fakes?" she continued.

"This one here is a fake and so are those two on the end," he replied without hesitation.

We followed him into a back office for tea. The walls were decked with art work, including the ceiling. Harriet made some comment about never having to paint the room. Adjacent to the office was a large showroom chock full of Oriental statuary, vases and other antiquities. Harriet was still on a fake kick.

"Any fakes in that room?" she inquired.

"Some," replied Tommy. "I get burned often even though I pride myself as an expert. Most of the collection is originals from the Ming Dynasty. When I discover a fake, I classify it as a Shming. I try to unload it to someone who only has price on his mind. As I told you, Ming, Shming, everybody is happy. When I run out of Shmings, I buy a half dozen more at a Shming price, of course, to satisfy the bargain hunters."

"Of course," volunteered Harriet, who was beginning to sound like an art dealer.

Tommy poured more tea for us out of a beautifully hand painted tea pot. He stopped Harriet from asking her next obvious question by pointing out that the tea pot is a fake.

"It's from the Madame's hotel!"

"You are kidding," responded Harriet.

"Yes," he replied, "but it's fake anyway. The tea is fake as well, – It's Liptons!"

Tommy went on to explain why the art business was so tricky. It seems that after the Second World War the Taiwanese developed a publishing and music industry which totally disregarded world copyrights, patent laws, and agreements in these fields. The country became the leading supplier of "knock off" best sellers and other desirable books and music recordings by the top performers in all languages, undercutting the world's markets by as much as 90%.

The art dealers at the time took note of the success here and realized that they too could operate in a similar manner. A flood of tourists and business people began visiting Taiwan. Many would stroll into the numerous art stalls and galleries around Taipei seeking out original oils from well known painters. Those that ran these shops found it difficult to tell them the truth. The original art could only be found in the West.

The Chinese people hate to lose a sale and developed a way to avoid it. Their best artists and painters were among the millions who fled Red China. These people figured that if they remained they would be relegated to painting houses and factories for the rest of their lives. In Taiwan they became adept at copying the styles of the Masters, producing bogus art work to satisfy new demands.

Tommy remarked that Rembrandt painted about five hundred pieces of art during his lifetime and of these three thousand were still in existence.

"All in Taiwan!" exclaimed Harriet.

"Not all, Harriet, a few in Denmark," he chuckled.

She realized how foolish her question was. We all just laughed it off.

"What are forgeries worth anyway?" I asked Tommy.

"Chuckie," he replied, having heard Harriet call me that and concluding that I preferred it to Chuck, "everything is worth what the purchaser is willing to pay for a one of a kind forgery, believing that it's the real thing. Of course one has to consider the price that the seller is willing to let it go for. Usually the seller always manages to make the sale. It's just a matter of time until the guy tells the customer that he's stealing it and says, 'cash only.' If the client doesn't have that kind of funds on him, he will wind up paying any way he likes. However, to answer your question, prices range from five hundred to fifty thousand dollars, although I never personally sold one that high. Not yet, anyway."

"Of course," agreed Harriet.

"Think about it this way," said Tommy, "originality from the Masters is nothing more than undetected plagiarism. You have a saying in the West that states, 'there is nothing new under the sun.'"

Out of curiosity, Harriet asked Tommy which type of art was his favorite.

"When I am selling in my gallery, just like an auctioneer, I'm impartial to all schools of art. I advise businessmen to buy old Masters as they fetch a better price on the market than old mistresses."

Tommy must have liked that line as he laughed out loud, while Harriet looked at him silently. I took my clue from her.

"Art for art's sake," she blurted out.

I'm sure that she didn't know what that meant, but it got a yes nod from Tommy.

I thought about our recent experience dodging customs and so I asked him about this aspect of the business. Tommy informed us that no declarations are required for books, music or art. He then added proudly:

"You must admit that we Chinese pick our spots. After all, we have been trading for over five thousand years. We have learned how to avoid annoying problems by concentrating on free goods. We also give the middle classes the opportunity to enjoy the pleasures of the very rich. In a way we are the Robin Hoods of the cultural world!"

"Let me think about that," I said.

"What's to think about!" shot back Harriet.

Tommy appeared quite pleased with her.

At that moment we all glanced at our watches. It was nearing eleven o'clock and the gallery was due to be opened shortly.

"Let me get to my offer now," Tommy urged.

This surprised us because we didn't think we came here to hear an "offer". Anyway, we were always open to this kind of talk.

He went on to explain that the art business is very competitive. Visitors are leery about doing business with the Chinese when it comes to large purchases. They need reassurances from other Westerners as to who can be trusted and where to shop for original art. "It's like shopping in Hong Kong. If one wants a custom suit at a fair price they will only go to the place that somebody recommends."

"So, Tommy, what's the offer?" questioned Harriet.

Tommy looked at his watch again and probably thought that he better get going.

"You guys are living in the best and largest hotel for Western visitors in Taipei. Since you plan to stay there for several weeks, you will meet lots of people at bars, on tours, while shopping and so on. Turn the conversation to art. Tell them about my gallery and that I have the best prices for original art from well known artists. I will give you a supply of my business cards. Offer the people you are talking with an extra card that you just happen to have with you, and write Harriet or Chuckie on it. Tell them that we are friends and this card will get them an even better deal."

"And then?" asked Harriet, awaiting a payoff.

"Then, if I collect say twenty of your cards, for example, I will offer you free a legitimate piece of art with a market value of twenty thousand dollars. If I collect five cards then the value of the art will be five thousand dollars, and so on, up or down. Also, it doesn't matter how many sales I make. I'm only looking for opportunity."

I glanced at Harriet. She had a familiar look in her eyes.

"Where are the business cards, Tommy?" she questioned.

We were happy with the decision to agree to Tommy's proposal. It gave us an opportunity to meet new people and to satisfy our thirst for adventure without having a gun pointed at our heads. Then, of course, there was a valuable painting at the end of the road. Who in their right mind could turn down a deal such as this. Not us!

We spent the first few days handing out the business cards to such an extent that we needed to return to the gallery and pick up a new supply. At this visit Tommy showed us that eight of our cards had already shown up and four translated into sales.

As expected, we began to tire of this "adventure" at the end of the second week. At this time we purchased our flight tickets for our next stop, which was Singapore.

"Let's relax now, and throw in the towel," urged Harriet.

We returned to Tommy's place and told him of our plans. He was sorry to hear about them, but understood. He went to his office and returned with twenty business cards bearing our names on them. Some signed Harriet and others proudly signed Chuckie. He offered us a choice of five oils. He opened an art value catalogue to show us that each had a market price of twenty thousand dollars.

"You choose," I said to Harriet.

She selected a beautiful 9x12 Chinese village street scene.

"That's the one I would have selected as well," Tommy volunteered.

"Bullshit!" she shot back in a joking way.

We told Tommy that we would return before we left Taiwan to say goodbye.

We spent the balance of our days hanging around the pool area of our hotel. It was good to know that we no longer had to talk to strangers hawking Tommy's gallery. As we had promised, the day before our departure, we went back to thank Tommy for providing us with a memorable stay.

When we arrived, the gallery was closed. There was a large notice plastered on the front door explaining in Chinese and in English that: THESE PREMISES HAVE BEEN CLOSED BY ORDER OF THE TAIPEI POLICE DEPARTMENT UNDER CITY ENFORCEMENT CODES 1674 and 3418.

Harriet and I glared at each other in disbelief. There was a hairdresser's shop next door. We went in and inquired about what had happened.

"Do you know Tommy?"

"Yes," we said in unison.

She put down her scissors and comb and handed us the morning edition of an English newspaper.

"Here," she said, "You can sit down and read all about it."

The headline of the story read, "HOTEL ART GALLERY SHUT DOWN FOR ALLEGATIONS OF FRAUD." The article reported that a Thomas Wong, owner of this gallery, was arrested for art fraud. It seemed that we were not the only ones handing out his business cards and touting his place to strangers. Unfortunately, for Tommy, one of the cards was given to an undercover art fraud investigator. It could have been us! It seems that the investigator purchased a Ming, but got a Shming instead.

The story went on to explain that art fraud was not similar to the knock off publishing industry. The government closed its eyes to illicit sales of copies of books and music. Art forgeries, on the other hand, were sold as the real thing. Naturally we felt quite nervous as we could be considered accessories to the scam. We were happy to be leaving Taiwan the next day.

We arrived at the airport hours before we were scheduled to depart because we were anxious to get away. I noticed several art dealers in the shopping area. Since we had the time Harriet suggested that we try and get an appraisal for the oil painting given to us by Tommy.

We walked into a shop where there were no customers. The woman inside introduced herself as the owner, and offered to appraise our painting at no charge. Harriet unwrapped the oil and laid it down on the counter.

"This is very beautiful, and I am familiar with the artist's work. Let me find a catalog and determine the value. You know, I'll give you the market's retail price. If I were to purchase it the price would be about half."

"Thank you, but we have no interest in selling it," Harriet said.

Well, we were relieved that she recognized the artist. The woman returned with a huge book and laid it on the counter next to our painting. She studied the painting closely again and then flipped to a page in her book filled with columns of signatures of artists. She matched the name in the book against the signature on the painting. After a few seconds, she asked us to come behind the counter.

"I still maintain that your oil is beautiful and an original, but it is not painted by the well known artist."

"What artist then?" questioned Harriet.

"A talented forgery artist," she replied.

"How do you know that?" I asked.

"I wouldn't have except for one little thing," she responded.

"What's that?" Harriet said anxiously.

The woman pointed to the artist's signature in her book. It was in Chinese as it was on the painting.

"See this letter. See how it is repeated as you might repeat an "R" twice in English."

"So," Harriet questioned.

"So, now look at the signature on your painting. One of the double letters is missing. The person who painted this picture is a genius, but couldn't spell the real artists name correctly enough to save his paint brush. Where did you get this painting from?"

"It was a gift," I answered.

"Then you are very lucky," she replied. "To tell you the truth, you should never have brought it in here for an appraisal. There's an old Chinese proverb that says, "Happiness doesn't depend upon what I have, it depends solely upon what I think I have."

CHAPTER 19

Singapore
October 5th-17th

N OT KNOWING MUCH about
Singapore, we purchased a guidebook
before departing Taiwan. During the flight we perused it together. Singapore is a City
State Republic where the government is dominated by a single party and takes strong
actions to suppress dissent. The laws are enforced with fervor. Spitting in public can
land one in the slammer. Sales of chewing gum are prohibited. Try and bring a Playboy
magazine through customs and you'll be one unhappy camper.

Somehow these types of restrictions excited us and we were not sure as to why.
Perhaps another challenge or another adventure? Our guidebook also informed us that
the international free zone designation of the city opens up opportunities in widespread
illegal money exchanging, money laundering, and even counterfeiting.

"Pick your poison," I proposed to Harriet jokingly.

"We won't know until we experience them all," she retorted.

We selected the best hotel rated in our book and made reservations there when
we landed. On our way from the airport we passed through the financial district
where I spotted a branch of my Swiss bank. I developed a good feeling being closer
to my money. We were not disappointed when we arrived at our hotel appropriately
named "The Shangri-La." The place was truly five stars in every way.

Today must have been a holiday, as we witnessed a festive mood in the streets. It
was only steps away from our hotel door where we had the need to crouch behind an
alter of a temple, and watch in fascination as a Chinese spirit medium hurled coins and
small rice bags over his shoulder to a scrambling crowd. The whole atmosphere was

deafened by crashing gongs as he leaped convulsively around the temple lashing the air with a murderous snake-head whip. He'd seemed a fearsome figure and it was best that we stayed well out of his way, so we moved toward the back of the crowd.

"What's he so angry about?" Harriet whispered.

"I think he just got up on the wrong side of the bed this morning," I responded.

"The guy needs a good dose of Valium," she calculated.

Since we had to leave Hong Kong abruptly on short notice, Harriet missed the opportunity to purchase a sapphire pendant she had her eye on. Singapore had an upscale jewelry district and so the following day we headed there. After visiting several jewelry outlets we came across a place with a large selection of the type of stone Harriet had in mind.

The owner was a British gent who told us that until 1959 Singapore was a British colony and that his family had been here for over a hundred years in this business. Harriet selected a pendant that cost twenty thousand dollars. As was the custom in the Orient he gave us a "special discount" of 10%. To show off my shopping skills I told him others were offering 20%. The man played around with all sorts of numbers on his pad for a few minutes, studied the pendant as if he was about to lose a dear friend and said:

"Well, if that's what I have to do to satisfy you, then OK, I'll go for 20%."

"No tax!" I added.

"OK, no tax," he agreed, "but it must be for cash."

I peeled off sixteen one hundred dollar bills and recounted.

"Are they real?" he asked.

"Are you joking?" I responded, "Why would you think they may not be real?"

"Where did you get them from?" he went on.

"I withdrew them from the Swiss bank in town where I have an account," I replied.

"Fine, I accept your word. I just needed to hear your answer."

"Why?" I questioned.

"Well, there is a great deal of counterfeiting going on in Singapore."

"See honey, remember what the guidebook said," piped up Harriet.

"Let me ask you guys a question."

"Shoot," Harriet interrupted.

"Would you be interested in doubling your money risk free while staying in Singapore?"

"That depends on what risk free means?" questioned Harriet, leery of hearing a 'doubling your money bit'. This was something we had just gone through which ended with a gun held at our heads.

The man looked at me, for we were in Asia where men make all the decisions, and he addressed me to the distain of Harriet.

"What about you, do you want to know what risk free means?"

"Sure!" I answered.

"First of all my name is Edward and I've picked up on your names. This whole thing is quite simple. You determine how much money you want to double. You give me that amount in one hundred dollar bills from your bank in Singapore. In return, I give you six one hundred counterfeit bills for every one of yours. Let me show you what a bogus one looks like and then tell me if you can tell the difference."

Harriet and I inspected the money closely, and as we had expected, they were the same in all ways.

"How do we know that your hundred is not counterfeit?" questioned Harriet.

"That's a smart question, Harriet. Not many people would even consider something like that."

Edward left both bills with us and went to a back office to retrieve a small black box and proceeded to plug its wire into an electric outlet which lit up the top glass surface. First he slid my hundred into a slot below the glass.

"Look here," he directed us, "see these watermarks. There are two on the front. Now I'll reverse it and you will find one on this side."

"OK, slide your bill in," directed Harriet.

He placed his hundred under the glass and challenged us to find any watermarks, front or back. There were none.

"So Edward, where do we shine in?" questioned Harriet, and my husband wants to know as well," she added sarcastically.

Edward did not answer her, for he got the point.

He went on to explain that he works with money exchangers and money lenders who earn their living selling counterfeits. Their legitimate business is regulated by the government which only allows them to charge very low rates for their services. Edward supplies the bogus money to them through runners. That title would be ours. When, for example, we would deliver six hundreds, the dealer would then deposit two hundred dollars into the Swiss account, thus doubling our money. The deposit could be in Francs, Liras, Pounds, or whatever they have equaling the two hundred US dollar value.

"The dealers unload the counterfeits at a good profit and I keep a small amount of the money that you give to me to purchase the fakes."

"If you have a counterfeit detection gizzmo, don't others have one as well?" asserted Harriet.

"That's also a good question Harriet. Anyone can obtain one of them if they find it necessary. However, tourists and businessmen don't check money and the locals don't care. The people here simply pass them along into the chain of commerce. A fake could circulate for years. Only financial institutions such as banks check all large bills they handle. This is a guarantee to you that the funds that are deposited into your account by the dealers are real, as those people are not going to mess around with the banks."

"So, where is the risk?" I asked.

"You tell me, I don't know," he responded. "Believe me you are not going to be pioneers in this business!"

"I bet!" added Harriet.

"Now, I gave you an example for just a one hundred dollar bill," Edward continued. "However, I must buy the counterfeits at a price I need and the money brokers don't want to deal with a transaction less than five thousand dollars. That translates to a minimum of a ten thousand deposit into your account."

"How often can this be done?" I asked, knowing full well that if I didn't ask, Harriet soon would have.

"Transfers to your account should only be done once a day," he responded.

"Are there many suppliers?"

"Plenty," responded Edward. "However, one has to be a runner before they can be a supplier. Unfortunately, Harriet, you have to begin at the bottom."

We all laughed. At this point she gave me that familiar look again.

"OK, we'll give it a whirl," I said to Edward.

"That's great," he responded. "This will be the easiest and safest money you guys will ever make."

I didn't tell him that he was wrong. I had done it before. That's why I wore a mask in the operating room.

Edward told us that when prepared to just return back here with a minimum of five thousand dollars and he would trade it for thirty thousand counterfeit bills and instruct us about how and where to get to the dealer.

I assured him that we would return in a few days. As we were leaving the shop Harriet turned around and yelled back to him.

"Hey Edward, are you sure the sapphire is real?"

He laughed and responded. "Of course, have it appraised. I'll even pay for it! If it's not I'll give you triple your money back. Wait a minute, I'll put it in writing."

"Not necessary," assured Harriet, "I believe you."

As we headed for a taxi stand Harriet remarked, "I guess this is what the guidebook warned us about . . . money laundering, and counterfeiting. We found these all rolled into one . . . how exciting, so exciting!"

We set a twenty five thousand dollar budget for our little escapade, expecting to double it. I had a sinking feeling in the pit of my stomach that we were counting our chickens before they hatched, surely an idiom Harriet must have come across. Before we decided to return to the jewelry shop, I suggested that we first test the transaction at the five thousand dollar minimum level and then, if successful, continue four more times at the same rate. The less conservative Harriet had other ideas.

"We should learn from our experiences," she argued. Willy Armstrong taught us never to go back into the well too often. Every time we go back into that dark, dark well there is a chance something can go wrong. Why stretch it out five times? I know that we set a twenty five thousand dollar budget, but it's not large enough. Our profit from all this work and possible risk will amount to less than one month's interest on the Swiss account. We should double it to fifty thousand, ten for the test, and forty for the final shot."

Somewhat apprehensive, I gave into this logic forgetting that it was my money. We needed a day to assemble the cash and to buy an oversized attaché case to carry the money for this transaction and the next one.

"Gee," said Harriet. "Willy's Good Luck Luggage Shop had great attaché cases!"

"Let's not re-visit that scene. It sends chills down my side." I gulped.

The following day we returned to deliver the goods.

"Are you guys all ready?" he questioned.

This must have meant did you bring money. To answer his question I removed the ten thousand dollars in hundreds from the case.

"Ten thousand, is fine," he said.

"How do you know how much it is?" I questioned.

"I can just look at rolls of hundreds and come up with the total amount within two bills on either side. That's an acquired talent, you know. It comes with the territory!"

"What territory?" Harriet asked.

She knew damn well what that meant. However from time to time she puts on that "me no speak too good English bit."

Edward ignored her question, and went back to his office and returned with sixty thousand counterfeit dollars and proceeded to write out the name and address of the person we needed to make the delivery.

Harriet always thought of one more question and now was no exception.

"What if the guy fails to deposit money into the account?"

"That's not possible," Edward responded. "That could only happen if they planned closing up business today after thirty years. Secondly, and I don't want to scare you, double crossers, as you might describe them, tell no tales in Singapore!"

Before leaving I told Edward that if all went well we would up the ante the next time to forty thousand dollars. Harriet asked if there would be a problem accumulating the almost quarter of a million counterfeit bills. He told us to return the day after tomorrow and so we set our appointment at the noon hour. We then grabbed a taxi and set off to our contact's place. The whole transaction took as much time as he needed to count the money. The next morning I checked my account. There had been an overnight deposit of English Pounds amounting to the value of twenty thousand US dollars.

We were now a threesome. Harriet, I and Mr. Attache arrived at noon on the day of our appointment with Edward. I flipped the case open and challenged him,

"OK, my friend, how much is this, within two bills on either side?"

He looked into the case, stared at the money, said nothing, and then we all laughed out loud. He told us that his source for this much money insisted on payment at the same time the fakes would be handed over. This sounded reasonable to us. We agreed to return at four o'clock, giving Edward the time he needed to complete the deal.

We returned to our hotel for lunch and planned to take a leisurely stroll back to the shop later in the day. When we arrived there were a few customers being waited on by a middle aged woman who we assumed was a clerk. After the shoppers left we approached this woman and inquired where Edward was.

"Edward!" she almost barked.

"Yes, Edward, the owner," I asked firmly.

"Owner, ha, I'm the owner!"

"Oh, we just assumed he was the owner, that English gent."

"He's English alright, but I'm not so sure about the gent part."

She told us that she was away on vacation for a month and just got back today.

"Look," she explained further, "Edward, who knows the jewelry business inside out, was minding the place for me as he had done many times in the past. He's the black sheep in his family, but I like to help him out now and then with some employment. God knows he can't work for his family."

"What's a black sheep?" Harriet asked her. Evidently, this one she really never heard of. The woman did not reply, but went on to tell us that she had to fire him today from ever working in the shop again for sales irregularities she had spotted.

"Did all this just happen? We saw him here only a few hours ago," I asserted.

"Yes," she replied, "he walked out about a half hour ago."

"Where is he now?" Harriet asked nervously.

"God only knows," she answered, "sometimes he disappears for weeks at a time, maybe longer."

"Do you have his phone number?" I gasped

"Phone number!" she laughed. "He never had a phone because he moves around so much. His phone number is any public phone he's near."

"What about the money we left with him," Harriet exclaimed.

"What's your name, dear," the woman asked her.

"It's Harriet!"

"Well, Harriet, I have no idea what you are talking about!"

"Did he mention us at all?" she continued. "We had a four o'clock appointment with him here."

"I'm afraid not my dear," she responded.

Harriet cupped her hand to her ear and whispered to me, "I think I hear the fat lady singing!"

"Where did you get that pendant?" the real owner asked Harriet.

"We bought it from Edward, why?"

The woman asked to be excused to check recent sales. While she was away it gave us the opportunity to discuss our course of action. I suggested that we go right to the police.

"And tell them what? Tell them that we were laundering money and counterfeits, to boot, and today our laundry got dirty, so please help us!"

The owner returned carrying a piece of paper in her hand.

"I found your transaction, and it's an example of why I had to get rid of Edward for good. I see that he sold you the pendant for sixteen hundred dollars which was too much for glass, no matter how well cut it is."

"Sixteen hundred!" Harriet blurted out. "It was sixteen thousand!"

"Oh my God," bellowed the shocked woman.

After we all calmed down she offered to make some amends. She explained that the retail price was one thousand dollars and they always gave the traditional 10% discount.

"My cost is four hundred and fifty dollars and I received sixteen hundred, so I'll write you a check for eleven hundred and fifty dollars"

"That's very kind of you," I responded. "Now we are only out fourteen thousand, eight hundred and fifty dollars!"

"That's the best I can do sir," she stated. "It's OK with me if you wish to file a complaint against Edward with the police. However, let me tell you that they are not hot to trot on petty crimes. The police spend their efforts on the big stuff like money laundering and counterfeiting. This gives them the opportunity to throw someone in the slammer for twenty or thirty years. Anyway, I hope you enjoy wearing your pendant. In a way I'm sorry that you know it is not real. There is an old Chinese proverb that says . . .".

Harriet interrupted. "Don't tell me, I've heard it before."

We waited for our check and left the shop. During the taxi ride back to the hotel we had little to say to each other. In the lobby of the hotel high tea was being served, a remnant from the "British Invasion." We found a small bistro table and joined the crowd.

"You know, Charles," Harriet said, "it's time to leave this place and think of settling down somewhere to a more normal life. We discussed India as a possibility but decided to visit Bangkok first.

With some small gains and large financial losses our adventure so far cost eighty nine thousand and eight hundred and fifty dollars. Then there was also a twenty thousand dollar painting worth perhaps two hundred dollars. Harriet was very dejected by all of this. I tried to comfort her by reminding her that this was only a drop in the bucket for us. I held my tea cup high and told her to raise hers as well, for I had a toast to make.

"Fuck the Chinese proverbs. It's what you know you have, not what you think you have! That's an American proverb."

Those words put a smile on her face and we finished our tea and crumpets feeling much better. We spent one more week in Singapore just hanging around the pool of the hotel and seeking out interesting restaurants for dinners.

Over breakfast, the day before our departure for Bangkok, I was perusing the newspapers and a story caught my eye. It told of a man named Edward Barron and his wife Hedy, who were arrested for passing counterfeit money and for money laundering as well. The article said that they owned a fine jewelry shop in downtown

Singapore. They had been arraigned and then jailed without bail pending a formal court appearance. I shoved the paper towards Harriet almost knocking over her coffee pot.

"Read this!" I urged, pointing to the article.

After reading the story quickly, she put down the paper and exclaimed out loud, "holy shit!"

This caused the couple sitting at a nearby table to turn their heads around.

"I bet Edward was back in his office all the time listening to us as his wife related a bullshit story and then so generously wrote out a check returning eleven hundred and fifty dollars of the sixty thousand they stole from us. I'm not as upset about the money as I am about how those fucking crooks hoodwinked us!"

This time the couple next to us picked up their coffee cups and moved to a table on the other side of the room.

"As they say in French," Harriet continued, "it's time to vamoose from Singapore, and luckily for us, it's tomorrow."

The next day we boarded our flight to Bangkok.

CHAPTER 20

Bangkok
October 18th-26th

W E CRAWLED ALONG the streets in heavy traffic on our way from the airport to our hotel. A man holding a fistful of flyers shoved one through the cab's window. It was an invitation to attend a real cock fight.

"Let's go tonight," pleaded Harriet.

After dinner we waited in line outside our hotel for a taxi. I handed the driver the flyer which included directions to the site of the cock fight. He glanced at it and acknowledged that he knew where it was. He asked us if we were sure that we wanted to go there.

"Sure," Harriet responded.

"Why are you asking?" I said.

"Have you been there before?" he questioned as he made his way from the hotel's driveway onto the busy street.

"First time for us," I answered.

The driver didn't reply nor did he explain why he questioned our going. The drive took about an hour. The place was located down a dusty dirt road about a mile off a secondary highway on the outskirts of the city. From the outside the building looked like a huge barn. Fifties vintage automobiles were scattered about upon an adjacent field. Men were lingering around the cars drinking beer and jabbering away with each other. It was not quite dark yet, but the outside flood lights already began illuminating the building. The taxi driver collected his fare and handed me his company's business card and told us to hold onto it in case of an emergency.

"What sort of emergency do you have in mind," inquired Harriet.

"I'm not sure," he replied, looking around nervously.

He told us not to accept any offer of a ride back to Bangkok, especially if we won any money, and suggested that he would return for us after the fights, around eleven o'clock. We agreed and filed into the building with the people leaving the parking lot area. The inside was one big room which housed a miniature arena in the round. There was seating on tiered benches circling a small dirt patch, and enclosed with chicken wire fencing. The top rows filled up first, so we guessed the higher up one sat, the better. However, we chose to sit on the bottom row to be closer to the action. When most of the crowd was seated we estimated that about two hundred people were here. Harriet counted four women including her. Uncovered light bulbs, some lit, some burned out, hung off exposed electric wires hanging from the ceiling. A free standing spotlight focused on the fighting area. Programs of the events were scattered about for the taking.

Just before the first fight was scheduled to begin, men with white armbands walked around the arena taking money from the spectators. They hand back red or green tickets, which was a receipt for bets placed on one or the other fighting cock. Neither Harriet nor I had any clue of what was about to happen. However, this did not matter to her. She waved down a runner and placed a five hundred dollar bet on one of the cocks. When she asked him about odds, he told her that at cock fights the odds were always even. I thought her selection looked scared shitless thinking about being thrown into the ring. I was proven right as his life span lasted as long as Harriet's five hundred bucks – about three minutes!

I questioned her why she bet only five hundred dollars when the maximum bet was five thousand. I asked this sort of sarcastically based on her knowledge of picking winners.

"Because I don't think they have ten thousand bucks in the till to pay me off if I should win, and I don't want to be paid off in fighting cocks!" she explained, adding, "one cock back at the hotel is more than enough for me!"

For some reason this remark caused me to have an erection.

Harriet placed another five hundred on the next fight, this time studying the combatants more carefully. As in the first fight the screams of the crowd became deafening. When the contest ended the groaners competed with the cheerers to express themselves. This time Harriet was a winner. The runner returned and counted out ten one hundred dollar bills in front of her. The owner of the winning cock noticed her getting a payoff and came over to where we were seated to congratulate us, and to thank us for having confidence in his bird.

"I don't know your bird from Big Bird on Sesame Street but I liked the way he strutted about"

"Who is Big Bird from Sesame Street?" he questioned.

"All I can tell you is never put your cock in the ring with Big Bird!"

Again, listening to her comments caused me to have another erection after I'd just settled down.

The next fight was set to start in twenty minutes. Most of the spectators took off to a liquor bar set up in the far end of the arena. Our new cock owner friend squeezed in next to us and helped Harriet select the cock to bet on at the upcoming fight.

"If I bet twenty five hundred dollars now, do they have enough money to pay off five thousand in US bills?" she questioned the man.

"These people can buy and sell you ten times over," he responded.

We knew this boast wouldn't apply to us, but it gave Harriet the confidence to up the ante. She called "Mr. Armband" over and placed her bet on the cock the man had recommended. My body language must have shown my reluctance for the heavy bet, and it deserved an answer from her.

"Chuck," she said, "do you think that guy is chopped liver?"

It was time for the next contest to start. The whole scenario repeated itself. The bright floodlight hit the arena floor. The crowd began to scream, some calling out the nickname they had christened their cock, and then came those familiar groans. When this fight was over, to my relief, Harriet won again. The runner handed her five thousand dollars in one hundred dollar US bills. However, this time an armed guard stood by.

"Are they real?" she asked.

This made me recall the question our friend from Singapore, Edward Barron, asked me when we first met.

"Real what?" responded the runner somewhat perplexed.

Despite the fact that Harriet was on a roll, we decided to quit betting because we wanted to avoid having more cash with us then we now had. We hung around until before eleven o'clock and then waited outside the building for our taxi to return for us. We stood close to a guy seated at the door with a rifle laying on his lap for all to see. Our new friend, the cock fighting entrepreneur had followed us outside. He asked us if we were interested in making more money but in a much better atmosphere.

"Why not?" Harriet answered.

He handed her a business card reading "GEORGIO LEWIS, BEST OF THE COCKSMITHS INC." A telephone number followed. It was his personal joke.

"Give me a call at your convenience. I'll meet you at your hotel for lunch and it's on me, as long as you don't order chicken!"

We laughed together at the thought, said goodnight, and spotted our driver making his way towards us. In the cab Harriet studied the business card again and thought that it was a funny name for his business. I didn't want to explain the obvious with the driver in front of us, so I just nodded in agreement. We returned to our hotel after mid-night and slept late the next morning. After breakfast we took a stroll through this interesting city to see some of their well known sites.

If Bangkok had any problems at all, it was prompted by prosperity. Not unlike Taipei, the most striking of these was the excessive motor traffic. We did manage to traverse the streets like pros, after all, we were gaining experience. After visiting the "Grand Palace", the "Marble Temple", the "Temple of Dawn" and the "Temple of The Emerald Budda, Harriet announced that she was "all templed out . . . please save me."

With a few more hours left for sightseeing, we joined a boat excursion leaving on a trip through the city's famous canals. The barge passed between wooden houses on stilts, surrounded by big leafy greenery. In slim wooden boats women vendors were delivering the daily shopping needs of the inhabitants – vegetables, fruits, ice, charcoal, and other necessities. These women were gossiping and spitting red streaks of Betel Juice into the water. Our boat churned up the water with its motor, and once the wake jostled a woman and her floating notions shop, almost dumping her supplies overboard. I could almost guess what she was thinking. We glided into a narrower canal past a general store on stilts. Our boat poked around another corner so congested with water vehicles that a policeman had to direct traffic from the shoreline while standing on a docked barge.

We tied up at an enormous shopping bazaar offering, under one roof, a wide variety of merchandise made in Thailand. We were also given time to grab a snack. However we could not identify anything familiar so we skipped this "opportunity." Our fellow passengers marveled over how cheaply all hand woven Thai silk was.

"No wonder," one commented in an angry tone, "I understand, they make about ten cents an hour!"

I whispered to Harriet that I thought that she might be a union shop steward in the United States. The hustle and bustle on the canals was no longer evident as we made our way back close to dusk in the late afternoon. The silence was now almost total.

"Earlier I was templed out, now I'm canaled out," proclaimed Harriet. "Let's head back to the hotel for a drink."

All Harriet had on her mind now was to contact Georgio Lewis and set up a lunch date as he had suggested. He was available to meet us at our hotel the following day at noon.

At lunch we were anticipating some sort of proposals from him based on our recent experiences with Willy Armstrong, Tommy Wong, and Edward Barron. However, Georgio just spoke about the opportunity to make money at cock fights if one knew the best strategies. He told us that he entered his birds at exclusive high betting private clubs, attended only by invitation. Only champion cocks that had never lost a match are pitted against each other. This type of match up makes the results less certain. One of these events was scheduled a few days away with only fifty people accepting invitations. Georgio planned to enter his three best cocks and was very confident that they could win all their contests.

"I will be betting on my cocks, and you are invited to come and bet along with me, for more or less money, whatever makes you more comfortable. The surroundings are very nice. We all sit on velvet sofas with drink service and small sandwiches available."

We accepted the invitation. He went on to tell us incredible tales about his cock fighting experiences. Before he departed he handed us two tickets to the event.

"Those were some stories," I remarked to Harriet.

"They were all cock and bull stories Chuckie," she shot back. "The guy is a real cocksmith alright, just like his business card touts, but we'll go anyway!"

Harriet never ceased to amaze me!

The fight was scheduled for nine o'clock that evening at a private club not far from our hotel. We arrived a little early to get the lay of the land. We spotted Georgio fussing around his cages. He saw us and called across the room.

"Sit over there," pointing to a large red couch, one of many circling the ring, "I've reserved it for us."

There were a dozen or so men already seated. A small desk in a corner of the room had a sign on its front panel which read, "PLACE BETS HERE." The only other woman in the place sat there with an adding machine and paper slips on the top of the desk.

Georgio came over to our couch and sat down between us and began to explain the betting process. He told us that because of the high stakes, some of the people coming tonight had established a line of credit for this and other cock fights.

"So, hopefully you guys brought cash?"

"How high are the stakes?" Harriet asked him hoping we brought along enough money, because (thank God) we certainly didn't have a line of credit for the event.

"The minimum bet is twenty five hundred dollars and the maximum is twenty five thousand," he replied, as a matter of fact. "Are you covered?"

"What do you think we are – "

I stopped Harriet mid-stream and chimed in.

"Of course, we have twenty five g's with us, and we only intend to bet when your cocks fight."

He thanked us for the confidence and returned to manage his cages as the time neared for the matches to begin. The lighting in the room dimmed and a spotlight was thrown onto the ring. An armed man took a seat on the side of the desk where bets were being placed.

"How can you guard a line of credit?" Harriet quipped.

I had no answer to that one.

Georgio's cocks were not scheduled in the opening event. This gave us the opportunity to observe procedures before actively betting. Basically things went the same way as we experienced at out first cock fight. After a short break the next fight was set to begin and Georgio's cock was a participant.

"How much are you betting?" Harriet asked him.

"Twenty five thousand," he replied. "I always bet the maximum when my champion undefeated cocks fight. Why fool around?"

Georgio excused himself to tend to necessary last minute preparations.

"Let's put down the whole twenty five g's now," urged Harriet. "If Georgio is betting this kind of money, he's got a sure winner. As he told us, why fool around?"

I assured her that if there was such a thing as a sure winner everybody in the world would bet everything they owned or could borrow on the winning horse. She thought about the truth in what I told her and agreed to begin betting at the five thousand dollar level. We walked over to the betting desk and handed the woman the money.

"Cash!" she exclaimed. "You know that we pay off bets this high by certified check only. It's something you can easily cash at any bank,"

"That's fine," I replied.

Georgio's cock won in what he described to us as, "in record breaking time!" We went back to the woman and stood in line for the payoff.

"We issue the checks at the end of the night," she said, "unless this is going to be your only bet. If so, I can give you your check now."

"Hold on to it," Harriet instructed, "we're not finished yet."

We waited through a few more contests before Georgio's cock was scheduled to battle next. He returned to us with a broad smile on his face.

"I wish that I was allowed to bet more then the maximum. It's a sure bet."

We put down five thousand dollars again and sure enough his cock was victorious. So after two picks we were ahead by ten thousand dollars. There was one fight left for Georgio and it was set as the final event of the evening. He approached us with his bird under his arm.

"This one is my very favorite. His name is Rocky. He bought me a new car last month. This is going to be a fight you'll both never forget, believe me."

Georgio patted Rocky's mouth, and the cock almost took his finger off.

"He saved the best for last," Harriet exclaimed after Georgio returned to the arena to get ready. "Let's bet Rocky. Let's shoot the works on this one. Georgio's made fifty g's already to our ten betting the same way."

"OK," I agreed, "but I hope that cock won't take us down a Rocky road."

We now had thirty five thousand dollars in our possession, and had to split our betting to observe the maximum twenty five thousand rule per person. In my guts I thanked God that we had no line of credit as well.

This fight was considered the main event of the evening. The opponents entered the ring to the roar of the excited crowd. Believe me, it didn't take more than ten seconds and Georgio's favorite bird, a never defeated champion, was laying belly up in the middle of the ring. Rocky was dead as a doornail.

One guy jumped on his couch screaming, "get up you son-of-a-bitch, get up you fucking cocksucker!". Rocky paid the gentleman no heed. He wasn't moving for anyone.

Georgio didn't lie. After all, he had told us that this was going to be a fight we'd never forget! A few people approached Georgio and offered him sympathy as if his mother had suddenly died. He turned to us, and of course we had no kind words for him.

"I hope you guys bet the same as before," he muttered.

"We bet the maximum and more," complained Harriet. "We thought it was a sure thing as you promised."

"I guess nothing is sure but death and taxes!" he responded.

Harriet could have belted him in the mouth then and there for saying that. The woman at the betting desk called him over.

"Please excuse me," he said. "I've got to sign some checks now, but listen; it was nice to have met both of you. I hope one day our paths will cross again."

To say that he fluffed us off would be an understatement. A furious Harriet told him to be fruitful and multiply, but not in those exact words.

The club had a bar in an adjoining room. Harriet and I wandered over there in semi shock, sat down at a table and ordered two stiff drinks. One of the men who attended the fight sat down at a table next to us.

"I lost a few bucks, how'd you guys do?"

"Not too good," I admitted.

"When fights are fixed you need pure luck," he volunteered.

"Fixed!" Harriet gulped. "So why are we betting on them?"

"It doesn't matter," he asserted.

He went on to explain that since the odds are always even the chances of winning are no different than picking heads or tails on a coin toss, or black or red at the roulette table. A fix does not affect us. We depend 100% on a lucky pick.

"If you are interested I can tell you how cockfighting works."

"It's a little late, but we sure would like to know," I replied.

"First of all, owners of the participating cocks cannot bet, period. They are paid by the house a flat amount for bringing their birds to the event."

"You're kidding!" exclaimed Harriet.

"I did say period, didn't I? It's illegal!"

"The fix needs the cooperation of the owners. Before each contest the house signals the winner to the two owners."

"Please explain, I don't understand that at all," urged Harriet.

"Here's how it works," he went on. "The first thing the house does is to tally up the betting. For example, if 60% bet one way, you better believe the opposing bird is going to win. It goes without saying that the house has to come out ahead on each fight, just like the casinos must on every roll of the dice or pull of the slots."

"Now wait a minute," I interrupted, "how in the world can you fix a cock fight at that last moment?"

"Easy," he replied, "you could substitute cocks. That's why the owners bring a dozen birds along when only two or three are scheduled to fight. For example, tonight that man they call Georgio must have substituted a lemon in that last fight. No doubt, but there had to be heavy betting on his original entry."

"We were the cause of our own demise," I disclosed to Harriet, if she had not figured it out already.

"Since we are dealing with animals," the man went on, "there are times when the fix backfires, but not very often. This is the way it's been for hundreds of years. Anyway that guy Georgio and his wife have a nice business going."

"His wife!" gasped Harriet.

"Yes, the woman at the betting desk. They run cock fights throughout Bangkok. He is a very clever person. I've heard that he makes most of his money touting people to one of his fights and then manipulates their betting patterns.

"So Georgio never bet at all," Harriet said to me.

The man answered her by restating that owners could not bet but in this case Georgio was also the house!

"Who would he bet with? Himself?"

"Let me tell you it's easy to lose a bundle with the minimum and maximum rules enforce tonight," I said to the man.

"Rules?" What rules are you talking about?"

"Twenty five hundred minimum, and twenty five thousand maximum."

"Nonsense," the man answered, "most bet a few hundred bucks. Some who have had too much to drink might go for a grand or two."

"Does everybody use their line of credit?" Harriet asked digging deeper.

"What line of credit are you talking about?" he responded. "We are at a cock fighting arena, not a bank!"

"So, I guess there are no certified bank checks issued either?"

"Checks for what purpose. They run a cash business. I bet in cash, and when I win I damn well expect cash back."

I think at that point we heard the whole sorrowful tale. I thanked the guy for setting us straight about the world of cock fighting. However, for us, it was too late. Obviously, he sought us out because he noticed that we had spent the evening with Georgio and knew that we had been fleeced and wanted to be sure that we became aware of what had happened.

Harriet looked into my eyes in disbelief, but we had been down this road before.

"He put in that lemon when his wife must have signaled him that we had placed big bucks on Rocky. The fix was directed exclusively at us," Harriet said, summing it all up.

The whole experience was a rude awakening and Harriet found the words to describe her feelings.

"That fucking cocksmith," she blurted out in a raised voice. "What the fuck are you looking at?" she yelled at an innocent guy who happened to pass our table too closely.

"Why don't we just get our kicks from sex from now on?" I suggested. "It's better and certainly cheaper, dear!"

"I can live with that Chuckie. I can even begin tonight and I won't charge you a dime! That's how cheap it will be."

"I'd pay a dime," I assured her, "That's why they call this place 'bang cock!'"

"You're going to be sorry for that comment," she retorted jokingly.

We finished our drinks and headed back to our hotel.

As we entered our room Harriet closed the lights that I had just snapped on except for the track lighting running along a twelve foot clothing closet. She stood in front of the mirrored closet door and began to massage her breasts through her clothing. She closed her eyes as feelings overtook the viewing. I watched her for several minutes before approaching her from behind. I pressed my body against her back, slipped both my hands over her neck, slid my fingers inside her bra and moved them around her nipples very slowly. She moaned quietly as tiny capillaries dilating rushed blood into her nipples. I settled my fingers here where I felt pop outs of at least a half inch. The moaning picked up a notch into loud groans. She whispered that I had fantastic fingers and asked if I had considered being a surgeon. As she slumped involuntarily down to her knees, who would doubt that she was right.

As she lay on the shag carpeting she took over the massaging as I quickly peeled off my clothes allowing everything to fall to the floor around me. Harriet slipped out of her skirt and undies, now naked from the waste down. I spread her legs apart and sat between them. I leaned over to find my target using my tongue first and then my mouth. I kept this going for almost an hour, stopping now and then to allow her to slow down from unrelenting wiggling. My fingers reached her face and began to probe her ears and move around her lips and settling inside her mouth and over her tongue. Harriet latched onto my thumb and worked it with her tongue and cheeks simulating a blow job. She then searched for my penis and finding it began to caress it slowly. It expanded to a length I had never achieved before. She pulled away at the right moment to keep the evening going.

"Harriet, what can I do for you tonight? What would make you happy?"

"You've done enough already," she replied. "Now I'm in charge!"

She threw off her blouse and tossed away her bra hanging off her shoulders.

"Now you'll be me and I'll be you," she said as she directed me to lie down as she had.

She slowly knelt on top of me and began to caress her genitals with my penis as I remained passive and relaxed.

"I'm ready now!" she announced, as she slowly squatted her strong leg muscles around me and inserted my penis inside of her using it to explore her vagina as she thrust back and forth supporting herself on her elbows and keeping her buttock as high in the air as possible. It took no longer than a minute when she sprung a gusher and as I'd been ready since she stood in front of the mirror, I exploded inside her, joining the celebration.

The following day was Harriet's birthday. Sex does crazy things to the mind, for as we lay in bed I told her that I planned to put her name on the Swiss bank account. In the morning I contacted the bank to wire Gus Sherwood one thousand dollars to handle the details. Several days later we received and sent back to the bank Harriet's signature card. It was a done deal!

CHAPTER 21

India
November 1st-May 7th 1978

W E REMAINED IN Bangkok through the end of the month and left for India on the first of November. Ultimately this country was our serious destination as Gus Sherwood suggested that this choice would be one of the better places to consider. We settled down at the Park Hotel in New Delhi, renting a suite on the top floor. We planned to remain there through a trial period of six months. The hotel was very comfortable and met our needs. There were indoor and outdoor swimming pools, saunas, exercise gym, 24 hour maid service, and live music in the lounge every evening. Several good restaurants were backed up with timely room service.

Now all this may sound like a five star hotel. They called it five star and even the guide books listed it as such. However, against our own standards, five star was a stretch. After awhile Harriet and I stopped comparing things to our native countries and began to accept and appreciate the fact that we could afford to live at this high level in India.

There was a nervous vitality in New Delhi, particularly a few minutes before nine on weekday mornings and again a few minutes after five, when thousands upon thousands of office worker cyclists flow in unending streams along its streets. The busy thoroughfares reflect the very essence of the city. At the crack of dawn, a quieter time, vendors setting up shops on the pavement, prepare to hawk an incredible variety of wares. Many operate on a shoestring like a dealer in coconuts, offering one nut broken into several pieces. As if in a kaleidoscope, the pattern changes constantly.

Women in Saris and men in pajama like suits stroll here and stop there, oblivious to the traffic darting about them in all directions.

Harriet and I took a walk the day after we arrived along the main drag in Old Delhi. This extraordinary street begins at a centuries old fort. I believe the name is "Red Fort." At this end stands a strange little hospital, filled with the soft flutter of wings. This building is a haven for sick and injured birds, operated by a religious sect. Beyond this place lies a microcosm of all India. Here the street-side barbers squat on the sidewalk lathering up their customers for a shave. At a corner is a member of one of the city's strangest professions, an ear cleaner, who for a small fee will swag your ear with a sliver of bamboo dipped in sweet oil.

"Look Charles, this guy is almost like a doctor. You might want to try this work part time."

I thought about what she said and replied, "Only if I could get a good corner."

As we passed fruit and vegetable stands, we observed products we had never seen before. We were not certain if you would include them in a salad or in a fruit cup or none of the above. At our next stop we listened to a man proclaiming the virtues of bitter tasting twigs that serve as toothbrushes.

"Not a bad idea," I commented. "This could easily replace flossing in the near future."

"What near future," Harriet asserted. "Buy a half dozen, let's start now!"

A few yards further a bored snake charmer wheezes into a bamboo flute while two as bored Cobras slowly lift their heads up. Along the curbside, a sweeper labors bent over pushing a twelve inch brush of twigs bound together with twine.

"For God's sake," exclaimed Harriet, "hasn't anybody here invented the broom handle yet!"

A cow, not just any cow, but a sacred one, milky white, and dignified, but undernourished, browsed at discarded vegetable tops in the street deciding whether to eat some or not before the sweeper gets to them. After about an hour we both needed to reel away, sensing the onset of dizziness by the impact of so much going on in so small a space.

I had toyed with the idea of growing a beard and moustache since arriving in Hong Kong, but realized that I needed to look like my passport photo. Now that there were some long range plans to remain in India, I stopped shaving. The fact that this was "beard country" would allow me to mesh in with the crowd. The sunglasses and hats I now wore completed the disguise. My father in law might even say, "Whom are you?"

I didn't think that a disguise was absolutely necessary because I believed the authorities at home holding my passport would not cast their net beyond the borders of the United States. Harriet agreed, and joked that detectives must be scouring around Las Vegas and Miami reporting back to their bosses in New York that the trail was beginning to warm up, and all they needed was just a few weeks more.

Our plan was to take short side trips to visit other cities and confirm that New Delhi would be the best place to settle down permanently. When we approached the travel agent at the hotel and inquired about round trip airline tickets to Calcutta, the pleasant young woman looked at us and asked:

"Why?"

We were aware, to some degree, that no other city could have evoked such a negative response. There were many discouraging words associated with Calcutta, such as, dreadful, gruesome, frightening and worse. Labeled "the worlds largest slum" by experienced travelers who knew one when they saw one, I myself imagined it to be fifty Hobokens back-to-back, five hundred enclaves in search of a city, and a festering mud hole off the ocean where the tide goes out and is afraid to come back.

So, why are we going to such a place most people, along with the travel agent, might ask? I guess the answer is the standard one that most travelers offer . . . because it's there! However, Calcutta was more than the rude awakening we expected. The shock being, that when you get there, it's actually there!!

I told the travel agent that all we needed were quick in and out airline tickets and reservations for a two night stay just to get a taste of the place.

"What sort of a taste are you looking for?" she persisted, but with a wide smile.

Upon our arrival the living conditions we observed not only impressed, but depressed us. The driver on the sightseeing bus apologized for the tedious stretches on pot holed roads and for all the inching along in monumental traffic jams. However, without these delays we would not have seen as much along the way. Things such as a man urinating at the curbside in target range of others asleep on stone steps. Then there was an old man picking through garbage which miraculously kept him alive until this age. All of this took place in a twenty foot area. Soon we came upon a crush of women washing their hair at sidewalk water taps. A few of them were squatting to nurse their babies as nearby children wearing nothing but underpants were playing in the gutter.

I asked the guide why most of the manhole covers in the street were covered with wooden planks. Sort of ashamed, he explained that people steal the iron covers so as to have something to sell of value. He added that there are similar problems with people snipping off overhead commuter train copper wires and causing transportation delays. As if wall to wall people weren't enough, throw in the sacred cows wandering into traffic as well. If one took a snapshot of this scene, they could paste it in the dictionary next to the word chaotic to picture Webster's first definition, "in a completely confused or disordered condition."

"The cow dung never lies around too long," boasted the guide, "And that's a good thing!"

He pointed to hoards of men and women dressed in rags scouring around to collect it.

"They mix it with straw and sell it as kindling to start fires for cooking," he went on to explain.

"I can see why that's a good thing," Harriet commented to him sarcastically repeating the guides own words.

There was no getting around it. Calcutta was a dirty, hot, smoggy, but yet a friendly place. Back at our hotel in New Delhi we walked over to the travel agent's desk to show her that we made it back alive.

"So," she said, "what kind of taste did you get from Calcutta?"

"The taste of drek," I replied.

She smiled broadly not knowing of course that "drek" was Yiddish for "SHIT."

Harriet had flown to Copenhagen to bring our children back here for the Christmas holidays. Since Hanukkah fell at the same time we agreed to just refer to this time as the "holidays." After New Year's Day she returned to Denmark to drop the kids off at boarding school, where I might add, they were doing quite well. Harriet remained home for a week or so in order to tidy up her own affairs which had been neglected for some time now.

We had been in India now for two months. Harriet's absence gave me the time to evaluate for myself what this land called India is all about, and how we fit in. India showed us two faces, the disturbing poverty of life it offered on one hand, and the energy and imagination of the people on the other. There was no doubt in my mind that people are both India's pride and problem. I thought of the stark contrasts-automobile factories and wooden plow producers, jet aircraft travel and pedi-cabs, atomic physicists and naked mountain tribesmen, ruby-decked Maharajas walking alongside ragged serfs, and so on went the incongruities of the land.

We loved India despite all its problems and felt very comfortable living here. There was a strong possibility that we could settle here permanently. I went back to my old habit of putting pencil to paper to draw up a pro and con list.

The plus side developed quite strongly. First of all this, was an English speaking country, unless one lived in the boondocks. The people were very friendly, always trying to be helpful. The streets were safe. I rarely encountered a policeman on foot patrol. Yes, the beggars were plentiful and often bothersome. The young children in this group broke your heart. We ignored the sacred cows roaming about as did the natives, although we paid attention to what they left behind on the streets.

Of greater importance to me was the fact that India's extradition treaty with the United States was written in precarious language. After living for decades under British rule this government did not want any "Western" country telling them what to do. There was a clause in the treaty covering my case, but it was very difficult to enforce. During the legal process I would have total freedom to move about and possibly leave the country, without much trouble. So, while the treaty called for the Indian government to act as a watchdog "with due diligence," they usually chose to ignore this role placed upon them.

Another very important reason for remaining here permanently was so our children could join us and continue their studies at one of the very good American schools.

On the other side of the ledger, Harriet was not accustomed to the hot climate which persisted for a good part of the year. Also, India was in many ways, a second rate country, not a third world nation, but definitely a second. Then I added a thought: "So what? A world class power would kick my ass back to America with the first extradition request from the United States.

Finally, after visiting Calcutta I came away with one troubling thought. This government is proud of being a free Democratic society. Yet, if it cannot help the teeming millions who are dirt poor, it may not, based on history, in the future be able to save the few who are rich. However, I had enough on my plate not to worry about the future. Yet, this thought deserved a place on the con side of my paper.

When I finished, I perused my lists and to me the pros far outweighed the cons. It was important that Harriet agreed as well. When she returned from Denmark I showed her my pro and con listings. She studied them diligently.

"It's not so hot here!" she announced.

Thus, essentially, she put the con list to rest with five words.

As the weeks went on we settled into a daily routine of sorts. Harriet got involved with several local charities. Outside of my hobby for people watching, I had little to do. I realized that I missed practicing medicine. This prompted me to begin investigating opportunities that appeared available here in my field. Between the high demand for hospital and clinic doctors and low wages, I figured correctly that India in 1978, with an out of control population growth, should be an applicants' market. This shortage was also brought about by an exodus of India's best doctors to America, England, Canada, and even Australia. This trend began about ten years before and was not about to end.

I decided to try my luck and seek a position at a small hospital within walking distance from the hotel. For references, I listed the names of several hospitals I had worked in for short periods under an exchange of doctors' programs, which my hospital had participated in. I was, however, betting that these people, desperate for quality doctors, would not wait an eternity for my references to be acknowledged. This was confirmed to me by a gentleman from Italy who was applying for a physician's position that day as well.

"I have been practicing medicine in India off and on for many years because I am married to an Indian woman," he volunteered. "They never follow up on references anymore because they hardly ever received a response in the past. They do contact the medical schools and universities. You can't get hired without their confirmation of your records. Anyway these institutions usually reply promptly."

I handed my application to a woman sitting behind a glass cage. I was not certain if she was a clerk or a doctor because she wore the same white smock worn by doctors passing by. She checked my entries line by line with a pencil in her teeth. I did not indicate the name of my hotel but rather I gave them the PO Box number

I had opened. The woman did not question this, but did ask me about my telephone number. I'd written in that box "pending". I told her that I would give it to her at a later date as I was changing my number. She thought for a moment and then just shrugged. My plan was to use a telephone answering service, if pressed in the future. My application was filed and she told me that it usually took several weeks to have my references checked out.

Now was a good time to take another side trip away from New Delhi. We were told that we would never capture the true essence of India unless we visited Banaras, today called Varanasi. This teeming city on the Ganges River is a pleasantly old fashioned university town and also the holiest of Hindu cities where people throughout India flock to bathe in the waters of the Ganges. The young guide that we picked up at the railroad station when we arrived explained the religious importance of this place very concisely.

"The people look upon death as an impersonal and unimportant bit of punctuation along life's progression of birth, death, re-birth and death again. If they can die here and have their ashes cast into the waters, they believe that they immediately become one with God, free ever more of the cycle of re-birth."

"You mean," questioned Harriet, "that they are trying to escape re-birth?"

"Exactly!" he confirmed.

I asked the young guide if he personally believed this, so we would know how respectable we should act in this area as he guided us about.

"Of course not!" he replied, "I'm Jewish. My family has been here since the Spanish Inquisition."

"Why in Banaras?" I questioned.

"When you see the city, just look around. We have more learning centers then New Delhi. Jews and education go together, as you would say, like love and marriage and a horse and carriage."

Our first stop was at the riverbank where heaped bonfires crackle under shrouded figures lying at the water's edge awaiting their turns on the pyre. The Ganges looked like a stream choked with filth. Small boys shattered the illusion of sanctity with their joyful splashing.

As we walked along observing the whole scene a Hindu emerging from the dark river, whose hair still streamed water, nodded at us.

"You really should bathe in the Ganges. You will find it very refreshing as well as spiritually uplifting."

I thanked him for his suggestion and we all continued our stroll. All I could think about was the filth dumped into the river by the millions of people living and visiting at this place.

"Let's try it!" begged Harriet.

"Try what?"

"Taking a dip."

"You must be kidding?" I quivered.

"You know I'm not," she argued.

"Are you sure?" I replied, biding for time to think how I could change her mind.

"We'll just wade up to our knees. What harm would that do?"

I turned to our guide whose name was Josh and asked him what he thought.

"It's your funeral!" he responded.

When Harriet and I walked out of the river an orange colored clad priest motioned to us to come over to him. He dipped his index finger into a gray paste and pressed it onto our foreheads leaving a dime sized mark signifying our purification in the holy river.

"I forgot to tell you folks this." Josh said with a slight grin. "Very poor people are not cremated because their families cannot afford the cost of the wood. Instead their corpses are just dumped into the river."

"Oh, my!" gasped Harriet.

"One more thing," Josh went on.

"It's OK, you don't have to tell us one more thing," I protested.

"Let him tell it, Charles," Harriet insisted.

"Oh well, then go on," I urged Josh.

"It's not so terrible. I just wanted you to know that devout Hindus are reluctant to believe that a river as holy as the Ganges is polluted. So, the government has begun using a softer language by suggesting that "Mother Ganges is suffering."

We all smiled at each other. What was there to say?

It was now time for lunch. We stopped at an outdoor cafe along the bank of the river. Harriet I believe had lost her appetite, but not Josh. Whatever it was that I ordered had too much curry in it. Josh had the same dish and called the waiter back for extra curry. After lunch we walked around this very interesting city and learned much about this place and its history from Josh, an obviously well educated and bright young man, who probably would become this town's mayor one day.

Josh escorted us back to the train station in the early evening. As our train was pulling in I bid him, "shalom."

He replied back "shalom" and added, "YOU DON'T LOOK JEWISH!"

Some time had gone by since I put in my application at the hospital. Life was good, but I hoped I would get the position. I had never expected to receive mail at my PO Box, except from the hospital. Now, that I anticipated hearing from them, I began to check daily for their reply. That day arrived when I stuck my hand into the box expecting to feel air again, but touched an envelope instead. It had to be from them, and it was. I opened it up then and there. I found a one page form letter. There were two large boxes at the top of the page. One read "ACCEPTED FOR

EMPLOYMENT," the other, "REJECTED FOR EMPLOYMENT." The accepted box was checked off. I read on.

"IF YOU ARE ACCEPTED, PLEASE FOLLOW THE INSTRUCTIONS BELOW." The instructions directed me to make an appointment for a physical examination and to apply for a work permit. Apparently, wages were not negotiable. At the bottom of the form there were two options. You had to choose either three eight hour days or six ten hour days. The part time wage was listed at two dollars and seventy five cents an hour. The full time wage was three dollars and fifty cents, and included two weeks vacation after one year and free medical care for the family after six months.

I showed the form letter to Harriet and asked her if she thought they would be deducting for taxes.

"What do you expect, a free ride?" she retorted.

Of course, the money did not matter. What mattered was I could return to my profession and there would be no Blue Cross forms to fill out.

I reported to the hospital on February 20th. I had, of course, opted for the part time position. I was waiting around for my schedule and a tour of the hospital facilities when the woman in charge of personnel called me into her office. She asked me if I would consider working full time if they increased the pay. It occurred to me that the wages on the form were only starting points. I had been warned that almost everything in India was negotiable and apparently this job was no exception. Even though I had no intention whatsoever in a sixty hour work week commitment, I played along.

"How much?" I responded.

"Three seventy five US," she proposed, "That's a very big increase."

I did not reply until she spoke again.

"OK, three ninety five. It's the most we pay."

I told her that I was sorry but I only wanted to work part time.

"Four dollars, full time! That's final!"

I saw that I was getting sucked into a negotiating game that I had started, but no longer wanted to play, and which I had to stop.

"Look, please, don't go on. The money is not important"

"So, you'll work for nothing?"

Now she was beginning to steam me up. I jumped aboard her little game.

"I will only work part time for three dollars an hour, that's it!"

She must have thought better of it as this conversation could wind up raising the ante in my favor. I also believed that she didn't want to be responsible for personally loosing an American doctor from Harvard over pennies. She quickly ended it.

"OK, three dollars is fine, but you must promise not to tell anyone here. We pay two seventy five part time, you know."

I spent the first day getting acquainted with the hospital and the staff. One of them was the Italian doctor who had started working here only a few days before I arrived.

After two difficult months working at the hospital, I came to the conclusion that I had bitten off more than I could chew. My success in the States was due to an experienced support team, modern medical equipment, the newest in drugs, and great strides in rehabilitation. There was no team here, and little of the rest. I now understood first hand why the life expectancy in India was at forty seven years of age. One person, such as me with all my experience, could at best, have minimal impact, and so I decided to leave.

I returned to the personnel department and handed my written resignation to the same woman I had dueled with on my first day. She read my brief letter quickly.

"OK, three twenty five, we can't go higher then that. You're part time, you know."

I could have rung her neck. I just turned around and walked away expecting her to run after me screaming, "three thirty, three thirty five, three forty, but don't tell anyone." I had planned to give two weeks notice, but decided that since I was heading towards my hotel I'd just keep walking. I have to admit that the lady intrigued me somehow. I considered returning and try to reach the four dollar per hour level part time, and then bail out of the negotiations by saying that I can't promise not to tell anyone. On second thought I decided I didn't want to fuck with her head.

With time on my hands again, I suggested to Harriet that we visit the town of Agra. This was a must do one day excursion south of New Delhi where the famous Taj Mahal stood. While traveling by automobile is more direct and faster, we decided to experience an Indian train which we had read so much about. We could have taken a fully first class luxury train, but we opted for the "Peoples Express" instead. Here, lots of people are crammed into a little space and offered no-frills second class service. The fare amounted to about a half a penny a mile, but wound up costing us a few coins more. As the train pulled into the station in New Delhi a group of teenagers jumped on to take the seats of passengers getting off. Then they began to auction off these seats to the new passengers getting on. Failure to get a seat on a train where a deep breath helps one survive means standing for the full trip. Thus, the story of the extra coins.

Since the "Peoples Express" stops everywhere, it is probably the slowest express in the world. As we were not going very far the trip was bearable. However, there is one aspect of second class travel that must not be overlooked. This is the unexplained stop in the middle of nowhere, and the equally unexplained delay. At this time a dog is heard barking in the distance and a child emerges from the tall grass to sell the passengers tea in disposable clay cups. Then, a whistle suddenly sounds for some unknown reason, and a few seconds later, the train jerks back and forth, catches it's breath and slowly moves forward, picking up some steam as it rolls ahead.

It was a perfect day weather wise when we finally arrived at Agra. It was the kind of a day when National Geographic would have taken its pictures. The town of Agra consists of open air bazaars catering mostly to the tourist trade. The place is nothing to write home about, although I would not have been writing home to anyone at that time anyway. However, the Taj Mahal is something else. It is truly an architectural marvel, holding a distinction unique even in this land of overpowering spectacles.

"Do you know," our unauthorized Indian tour guide, walking behind us, volunteered, "that the minarets lean forward so if the vibrations from an earthquake would throw them down, the center would not be harmed" He then held out his hand and it cost us six cents for this tidbit of information.

Few buildings could possibly live up to its advance publicity, but the Taj does. It's more than a tomb. It's alive within its walls as proven by postcard vendors and grimy urchins who shriek to the tourists, "Very fine echo, listen, almost ten seconds!"

When they are out of sight, all tourists test it. Three seconds are more like it!

The story goes that once upon a time a Shah had this tomb created as a memorial to his beloved wife. That's all we knew when we arrived here. Since we would spend the day it was best that we purchase a guide book. We sat down on the one lone bench located opposite the tomb and Harriet began to thumb through the book's pages.

"He killed her," she shrieked.

"Who killed who?" I responded.

"That son-of-a-bitch killed the empress Mahal," she agonized.

Harriet urged me to read the text as her fingers followed the print.

"Shah Jahah stood bereft at the loss of his most prized possession. In 1631 she died bearing their fourteenth child."

"See what I mean," she shouted out loud, "he fucked her to death!"

A group of Indian monks passed us by at that moment and turned their heads around in our direction to see the source of this commentary.

"Keep it down, Harriet," I whispered, "they all speak the Kings' English, you know!"

As we were leaving to return home, I commented to Harriet that in just looking at the Taj Mahal one is certain to never forget it.

"It's hard to forget a place that one has walked around and gawked at for five hours," she retorted.

There was no need to think twice about it. We returned on a luxury train. There were comfortable recliner seats. No kids came on board to auction off "their" seats. In addition, there was a pantry car where food was cooked to your order and served by waiters dressed in traditional stark white uniforms. The train was fully air conditioned, and ran fast. The whole package made the Long Island Railroad, which I was so familiar with, look more like the train we had taken here earlier in the day. I could swear that I spotted a kid standing in the high grass with a tea bucket in one hand as our train whizzed through the countryside.

About two weeks had past since I resigned from the hospital. I was so upset that day I forgot to pick up my personal instruments. I had purchased them because the hospital did not have the proper tools for me. I felt bad about leaving without saying goodbye to a group of dedicated people who were just handicapped by the system. I decided that this day would be a good time to drop by there for a visit, say goodbye, and retrieve my instruments. I had not given up as yet on the idea of practicing medicine in some form at sometime in the future.

While visiting at the hospital my Italian doctor friend asked me to take a walk with him in a small garden behind the building. There he recounted that several days ago three men had shown up trying to locate me.

"The personnel department had no record of your address or telephone number. They suggested that they talk to me because we were the only foreign doctors on the staff. They found me here in the garden where I was eating my lunch."

"What did they want?" I questioned.

"They referred to you by name, and told me that they wanted to meet with you to discuss publishing a book about some new medical developments."

"What did they look like?"

I almost choked on my words because I was afraid to hear the answer.

"Well, they were all Americans, for sure. One was much shorter than the other two. I'd say that he was no taller than five feet six. They called him John and he did all the talking."

"Did he wear a mustache and have a mostly bald head?" I asked, hoping against hope that the answer would be no.

"Yes! Yes! Exactly as you described," he answered, sort of surprised.

I knew that it was John, the cop, for certain or more accurately, John, the homicide detective, AKA Columbo.

"And the other two, what did they look like?"

"Miles apart from the little guy. They were both over six feet tall, very muscular, and I might add, tough looking. If I didn't know better I'd have guessed that they were bounty hunters, not publishers."

"Did they ask what I looked like?"

"No, maybe they knew that already. You know, beard, mustache, dark skin, just like every one else here," he chuckled.

"So, what did you tell them?"

"Almost nothing. I just said that you were a nice guy but that I had no idea where they could locate you."

"Was that it? I pushed on, hoping for some more information.

"All I can add is that they were rude. They simply walked away from me without even thanking me for my time. Is anything wrong?"

"No, nothing at all," I responded. "I'm always being hounded to publish a new medical book because they are money makers in the United States."

"I wish I can say that," he responded. "If that were true in Italy I wouldn't have to work here, even part time for four dollars an hour."

I was flabbergasted, to say the least.

"You make four dollars an hour?"

"Yeah," he answered as a matter of fact. "I'm tired of negotiating with that woman! I also had to swear that I would not tell anyone working here. Did you ever, hear of such a thing in your life?"

I did not answer his question because all of this was not important now as I had just developed larger unexpected problems. Perhaps John would come back to ask my doctor friend some more questions, so I told him that I was leaving for the United States the following day. We shook hands and he wished me luck. I knew I needed it more than he did, after all, he was at the four dollar level here.

I raced home which was not an easy thing to do in the streets of New Delhi. I almost smacked into one of those cows refusing to move faster then a snail. When I reached the hotel I called Harriet at one of her charities and asked her to return back as quickly as possible. She did not ask me why, she just said she was on the way.

Harriet arrived at our suite in less then twenty minutes.

"Look, don't tell me anything yet. Let's first order up some lunch and then whatever the problem is can be discussed in a calm atmosphere."

She was good at quieting down situations such as this one, so I agreed. She called room service while I took a shower, my second of the day, given my perspiring experience. I returned to our sitting room all freshened up.

"Ah, that's much better," she remarked, "so, now tell me what's this all about, Charles?"

Before I had a chance to answer there was a knock on the door. I jumped out of my chair.

"What's the matter?" She cried out, "it's only room service. Come in," she shouted.

The waiter rolled in his cart and began to fuss around making certain everything was five star perfect. I can't complain but it was not quite there. The only thing five star was the price, about a days pay at my former job. The waiter backed out towards the door. This always made me nervous to think that I might have to treat this guy for a back injury on my living room floor one day.

"So, let's hear all about it now," Harriet urged.

"Well, for openers John, the cop, is in town with two bounty hunters!"

She bounced out of her chair just the way I had a few minutes ago.

"What?" she exclaimed. "Why? When? Where? How do you know?"

I urged her to sit down so I could relate the whole story. When I finished she asked the sixty four thousand dollar question.

"How did they learn that you were here in New Delhi?"

"I don't know the answer," I responded. "That's a total mystery to me."

"How long do you think that they have been here?" Harriet questioned.

"I think only a few days or so."

"Maybe they are checking all the hotels now, the good ones," she added.

"Most likely," I answered, "but you were smart enough to register and do other things here in your name."

"But they had a record of your phone calls to Copenhagen and might know my name that way," she speculated.

"They probably haven't thought of that. If they had, they would be sitting in the lobby of this hotel now waiting for me."

All Harriet could say now was "Oh, dear." She remained quiet, but the wheels were turning.

"What if they see you in the street by chance?"

"This is where I have half a chance, with my facial hairs, sunglasses, and pull over the eyes hat. Of course, I can't wear my Yankee cap anymore." Sometimes joking calms me down, but now it did not work at all.

"If extradition is such a difficult thing to execute in India, why worry about them finding you here?" she went on exploring.

"Bounty hunters don't wait for extradition proceedings. That's not the way they operate. They want to eat every day. Somehow they manage to find creative ways of spiriting people away through force or bribery. You can't beat them once they lock onto you. They don't play the legal game, but work outside the law in very grey areas. Yet, they manage to complete their work with impunity. I never understood how, and I don't want to learn now."

"Who pays them?

"Good question, Harriet. I think that it's always reward money."

"From whom?"

"Private parties."

"Like who?"

"I don't know!"

"I think I know!"

"You do!"

"Just a guess, but a good one."

"Who?"

"You're father-in-law."

"Damn it, you may be right!"

"So, what is John doing here with those two guys?"

"Beat's me Harriet. Either it's alright for him to arrest me in a foreign country or John quit his job and is chasing reward money. The fact that those goons are with him makes me believe that the latter is true."

We were both back to speculating again, but she insisted that we had to leave India.

"The quicker, the better," she urged. "No later then the day after tomorrow."

I told her that I mentioned to the Italian doctor that I was returning to the States tomorrow and perhaps, if John would return to the hospital to ask him some more questions, he might be thrown off the trail. Harriet cut me off.

"No more speculation, Charles. We are out of here!"

Of course, the unanswered question remained how they knew that I was here in New Delhi. So, let me relate now how events unfolded as I learned of them in the future.

First of all Harriet guessed right about my father-in-law putting up the reward money. It was one million dollars for, and I quote exactly from the terms, "TO WHOMEVER TURNS IN THIS FUGITIVE, DR. CHARLES FEELGOOD, MY SON-IN-LAW SO TO SPEAK, AND WHOM THEN IS BROUGHT TO JUSTICE AND CONVICTED OF A CRIME NO LESS THAN MURDER IN ANY DEGREE!" I'm positive that the last dozen words were added by his lawyer Ron Black trying to save him a million bucks, if at the end of the road, I'm convicted of a lesser crime, say like jaywalking!

I was grateful to learn that the reward statement never considered the words, "dead, or alive". As it turned out the reward money was enticing enough for John to take an unpaid leave of absence from the police department and team up with these bounty hunters who, I also learned later, were promised one third of the reward money.

However, this does not answer the question of why John came to India to find me. This is what I put together in the future as well.

It's important to know that with the exception of my lawyer Barry Hodges and later Harriet, nobody else knew that I had collected five million dollars tax free on Sophia's life insurance policy. In their search for me the DA speculated that I might be running out of funds, and perhaps I would apply for a physicians position somewhere. This was very good thinking, I might add. However, checking reference inquiries did not pan out until a bright assistant DA got the idea to contact Harvard to see if they had received and had replied to a reference request about me.

BINGO, they sure had. When the university responded to this request for information from the DA's office, the assistant passed their reply on to his boss with a note in the margin.

"Why do they indicate Freedom Hospital, Delhi, India? Is this an abbreviation for Indiana?

There was no Delhi, Indiana. The DA's office was completely dumbfounded that I could have reached India with my passport tucked safely in their security drawer. At this time they also committed an additional faux pas. They assumed that even if I were in India I must be traveling under a pseudo name. They did not move out of the box to consider that I might just have a duplicate passport.

John was also blindsided by this as well. He inquired about me at the hospital by my proper name because I used it to get the Harvard reference. However, he believed I must be living with a pseudo name. He also did not know Harriet was traveling with me, or even if there was a Harriet. John could have recalled that I had placed calls to Copenhagen early on. He could have done something the DA never did. He could have found out who was on the other end of the line, and then, could have taken a wild shot and searched all the hotels for Harriet Leeds. I point this out to show that there is only one Columbo, and he's working for CBS-TV!

I retrieved Gus Sherwood's list of countries that he had put together for me, although I knew them by heart.

"Here is our choice, Harriet, "Turkey or Morocco." I can grow my beard and mustache back and become part of the scenery again in either place."

"Turkey," she said.

So, Turkey it was.

CHAPTER 22

Turkey
May 7th-January 24th 1979

"**I**STANBUL WAS ONCE
Constantinople, New York was once
New Amsterdam and Beijing was once Peking," Harriet quipped trying to lighten
me up as we landed in Turkey. She then continued. "And now, my dear Charles, we
were once Indians and now we are about to become Turkeys!" Laughing out loud
she tapped me on my shoulders for a reaction. During the flight we had agreed that
we had to be more careful as the police net was now global, and we could not figure
out for sure how they traced us half way around the world. Harriet suggested that
we visit Istanbul as tourists for now, check out outlying areas as well and get a good
lay of the land. This made good sense to me also.

On our first day in Istanbul we thought that it would be a neat idea to witness
the city as it awakens in the morning. We managed to arrive at an open air teahouse
just before the sun came up. Rising above the horizon, the sun emulated the lifting
of a baton to start up a chorus of city noises. First, were the calls to prayer, followed
by a symphony of horns and whistles amid grinding ignition motors from stubborn
motorcycles. Then, began the cries of vendors hawking their wares and the clatter
of horses' hoofs on the cobblestone streets. Suddenly we heard the flapping sounds
of hundreds of pigeons taking flight when an ancient taxicab backfired. From our
vantage point we noticed a tinsmith beating his charcoal burning stove made out of
old tin cans. A blind beggar musician passed by singing what we assumed were folk
songs. I tossed a few coins into his cup.

Then there was the endless parade of men who carried "things" on their backs. The first to pass us was a man carrying ten plastic tricycles lashed together followed by a parade of others hauling crates of produce, sewing machines, refrigerators, sofas and various commodities of all sorts. One carrier needed more space then the others for a fifteen foot cypress tree strapped to his back.

"Let's sit here until we see a piano man," Harriet suggested.

We didn't see such a person but we continued to gawk at these men bent low to the ground with their heavy loads and clutching bills of lading between their teeth. I'm sure that they were happy to have trusted jobs. However, there were others making a living at less honest labor, men with boundless charm who operate on the fringes of the law. The first one we met was at the teahouse that morning. He was posing as a doctor. He approached us and introduced himself and said that I didn't look too well and suggested that I should have my blood pressure taken.

"How much?" I asked.

"Two liras," he replied.

"Fourteen cents," I whispered to Harriet.

"Go for it!" she urged.

The "doctor" retrieved the blood pressure machine from his black satchel bag, wrapped the band around my arm and started pumping. With only a cursory glance at the gauge he pronounced my health as "perfect" and then added:

"I only come here to do this when I am free to get away from my duties at the hospital."

He then went from table to table never once making any diagnosis other than "perfect health." This was even in the case of an old man who was gasping for breath.

"Chuckie, listen to me," Harriet exclaimed. "This is a terrific idea for you to supplement our income. Think about it, don't say no right away!"

I thought about her terrific idea for a second or two, and suggested that it was time to take a stroll. Swarms of people were moving in all directions spilling from the sidewalks onto the street and vice versa. This sea of humanity appeared to be never ending as it continued to bear down upon us. Well dressed women laden with bags of fashionable goods, tourists lugging cameras, couples in designer jeans holding hands all represented the prosperity of the city. Then, of course, there were the ever present beggars, street children and wandering people dressed in raggedy clothes. I saw an elderly Turk leaning on a building smoking a cigarette and watching the crowds go by. He was probably wondering what became of his city as he studied a huge movie poster featuring half naked women. This man would never understand that Istanbul is a city of many pasts now embracing the future.

We returned to our hotel where we had rented a ground floor suite which opened onto a private lawn where we could sit on Adirondack type chairs and watch the parade of ferries and freighters go by. The place only offered twelve accommodations, all were suites. If, by chance, John and his henchmen got wind that we were now in

Turkey, they would never think of checking out this out of the way hotel. We felt even more secure here then we did in India. Turkey had become an extra safe country against any call for extradition as the United States was now at serious odds with this country because of their recent invasion of Cyprus.

I had grown a new beard and moustache after discarding a similar growth in India in order to clear Turkish customs with a passport picture which looked like me. However, after my experience with John breathing down my neck, it was prudent to throw away my Yankee baseball hat for good. I purchased a new hat with Turkish writing not knowing what it meant. I had asked two nationals to interpret the wording for me and received two different answers. One said it read, "Allah is great." The other person said it read, "Allah was great." I asked the second person what the difference was and he replied, "plenty!" Anyway with my new facial hairs, Turkish cap, and sunglasses, all I can say is that I was not myself.

Our hotel only served breakfast and dinner and so Harriet and I would snack at different outdoor cafes during the afternoons as we watched the masses go by. Harriet was still looking for a piano man. We came upon an open air cafe where we had not been before. We were seated at a table next to two burly guys drinking beer right out of the bottle. Both of them had their arms tattooed from their wrists to their shoulders with out of the world designs. These included some menacing statements such as "mother forever," and "say thank you." After their gross tattoo shock, the next thing that we became aware of was their New York accents. Harriet squeezed my hand, grabbed her pocketbook and reached in for a pen. She wrote on a napkin, "don't talk!" They glanced at us but there seemed to be no recognition of any kind. She then scribbled, "It's them!"

John suddenly appeared walking out from the inside part of the cafe. He took a quick glance at us and sat down at the table with the two guys. His chair backed up to Harriet's and he excused himself when he bumped his chair into hers. Harriet just nodded OK without speaking.

Since we had not ordered anything yet it would be taking a chance to get up and leave. On the other hand, by staying we would have to talk to a waiter who happened to be heading in our direction at that moment. Harriet solved the problem by just pointing to a picture of a coke bottle on the menu and holding up two fingers. The waiter then asked me if we wanted glasses and straws. Harriet continued to prevent me from exposing my "you can't miss it, New York accent," by pointing to the coke bottle picture again repeatedly. The waiter just slipped away guessing no glasses, no straws. Since I was not recognized it became a great opportunity to eavesdrop upon their conversation.

"So boss, what's up?" one of the men asked John.

"I'm not sure," he replied. "I just spoke to my people back home and all they can tell me that conditions are serious."

"What exactly does that mean," the other thug chimed in.

"I don't know what it means for us," John responded.

"I don't mean for us," the guy shot back. "I mean for me and him, not us!"

It seemed to me that there was definitely some hostility in the air.

"Look you guys," John said in a raised voice, "if we beat the expected death, we are all OK. If not, we are not. That's all of us, not as you put it, me and him! It's plain and simple, get it! It's a pure legal issue, of which I have no control. Is all this too hard to understand, or what?"

Even though I didn't have a clue as to what John was talking about, I thought that he shouldn't be raising his voice to these guys who seemed agitated, nor should he tell them that they can't understand plain and simple things. For sure, John is a very tough son-of-a-bitch, and had the balls to go with it. I saw him as moving around a cage with two burly nasty bears and using his mouth as a whip.

"I'll tell you guys this," he continued. "As of now everything is the same, except we have to step up the damn search. We can begin with no beer drinking in the middle of the day."

The henchmen took another slug of beer from their bottles, offering John their replies. He ignored them and went on admonishing them.

"Time is money. We are racing the clock. Have you finished checking the hotel list I gave you yesterday?"

They did not answer his question. Their table was now quiet. I guessed that John was giving everything he had told them time to sink in. After a minute or two John sprung out of his chair and dropped some coins on the table paying for his buddies' beers. Harriet and I were stunned at what had just transpired as we watched them walk away. We then called the waiter back to order some real food and have our lunch while we contemplated or rather speculated upon what we had just overheard. Harriet turned over our paper menu to a blank side and began listing the things which we did not understand.

1. What condition is serious?
2. Why do the thugs think things are different for them?
3. What are these things?
4. Whose expected death do they have to beat?
5. What's the legal issue?
6. Why is everything OK for now?
7. How was I tracked from India to Turkey?

Neither of us could answer any of these questions. All we knew for certain was that they were here in Istanbul and they appeared to be up against an unknown timetable. However, we could ascertain a few things. One is that they had arrived very recently as they had just began to check hotels for me. It was also safe to believe that a death had more to do with the clock running out rather than money. It was also possible that they could have tracked me from India to Turkey by checking airline passenger lists. John had the credentials to get this information. Then again, it's just a guess.

We decided we would be better off waiting out the unknown in Turkey. Our only problem would be in not knowing when the coast was clear. However, it made more sense based on the conversation we overheard to think in terms of days or weeks rather than months. The only change in our personal plans was to delay moving from the hotel to a permanent residence for awhile. We would be more comfortable keeping the status-quo at least until after the summer when our kids would begin school here in the fall.

This was our first summer away on our little adventure. Harriet returned to Copenhagen to pick up the children as their school year was coming to an end. At first, the newness of this foreign land intrigued the kids. The weather turned extremely hot and so we spent our days around the hotel's pool. Boredom started creeping in on all of us. We realized that it was a mistake not to have the children come earlier while school was still in session here in order for them to have met youngsters their own age and make friends for the future.

The children began asking how long it would be until they returned home. This sort of conversation accelerated in earnest as the days went on. I even had a dream that I was driving with the children in the back seat asking over and over again "are we there yet?" We had not told them of our plans to register them here for the fall term. This was another mistake to have waited so long. The day Harriet gave them this news they cried and protested vigorously.

"What about all our friends back home?" they argued.

It was not going to work. Harriet told them if they wanted to return to Denmark for school they could. This relaxed them for the balance of the summer and they became much happier knowing the certainty of returning home. So, that took care of that, except Harriet became disheartened to contemplate having the kids away for an extended period of time again. She now realized that she could never have a normal life and relationship with them at least through their schooling years. When college time is added on, the period of time would be a decade or more. This real situation caused her to develop periods of depression. She even made it clear to me that the thought of calling Istanbul home for the rest of her life was a downer. I tried to assure her that we could move on at any time to somewhere else, to no avail.

"Where to?" she questioned. "Morocco, or Algiers, or some like country that affords some protection. I know now that these places are all the same. I miss real Western civilization. I miss the kids."

I was stunned to hear her talking this way, but understood fully, because deep down I felt the same way as well. I told her that it could mean a death sentence for me if I moved to Denmark. Of course, she understood, yet what I said was irrelevant to her growing feelings of despair. There was medication available here that might have helped her, but despite my urgings she would not see a doctor and my prescription writing days were behind me.

We all coasted along as best we could until the day arrived when Harriet and the children were to return home. The plan called for her to spend a month in Copenhagen receiving some medical care for her depression and then returning to Turkey. I had set up a PO Box in Istanbul for the purpose of managing the Swiss bank account. No name was required, only code numbers and that was the way Harriet would correspond with me. However, I could not contact her back in order to continue protecting myself to the fullest from being discovered here.

I received her first letter in ten days, a little later than I had expected. It spoke of cleaning up the apartment, paying overdue bills, and other mundane matters. The letter was just signed "Harriet." The "love" was noticeably missing. The next piece of correspondence arrived close to the time of her expected return. I tore open the envelope anticipating receiving airline information and so on, but instead the contents of the letter covered the same trivial matters as the first letter and was not signed at all.

I raced back to the hotel and my instincts were proven correct. Her jewelry box was hidden under a pile of shoes in the closet. I pulled it out. The box was locked. I jimmied the lock open with a knife and lifted the cover to see only a few cheap trinkets she had purchased to wear for fun. The good stuff was all gone. This did not bode well for her returning.

The weeks went on without hearing from her. It was more than a month when I received what was to become her final letter. It covered the same grounds as before. I thought of what she had said to me on the plane from India to Turkey to cheer me up. It was something about us having been Indians and now we will be Turkeys As it turned out, she became a Great Dane and I remained a real turkey in more ways then one.

Many months had gone by since we had seen John and his burly bears at the cafe and I generally stopped thinking about them altogether at this point. Surely they were gone by now. They seemed to be up against some timetable problems which they failed to meet because I'm still here safe and sound still watching the ships go by from the back lawn of the hotel. I tried to fill my days as best as I could, while minimizing my relationships with people I would meet in order to avoid explaining my presence in Turkey with untruths. For this same reason I joined a chess club where talk was held to a minimum because of the concentration factor required by the game. I would check my PO Box faithfully three times a week hoping against a probable lost cause that Harriet had written to me. It would not matter anymore if the news was trivial or not even good. Just to hear from her would be welcome. I know this may be hard to understand, but I felt that way anyway. I was so isolated.

Then, that fateful day for me arrived in November in the form of a letter, not from Harriet, but rather from Gus Sherwood, the lawyer. Since now and then he was involved with the management of my Swiss account, I realized that he could, if necessary, access the PO Box code. This made him the only other person in the world who could contact me this way, along with Harriet. Naturally, I was very curious as to the contents of the envelope, but waited to open it until I returned to my hotel where I could read it away from the noise and hustle and bustle of the post office. I saved the letter and here it is, verbatim:

November 16th 1978

Dear Charles,

I'm certain that you will be surprised to hear from me as you might say, "out of the blue!" However, let me assure you that I was just as surprised when I sought out the mailing address where the Swiss bank sends your statements. It turned out to be Istanbul, Turkey, my home town, so to speak. If I'd known earlier, I could have sent you to a hundred of my relatives who would have fed you handsomely. They are rich sons-of-bitches as I would have become if I had not chosen to become a starving lawyer in the United States.

All kidding aside, here is the real reason for my letter. It begins with a small three line ad I happened to come across in a local newspaper. I was attracted to it by your name. It was placed by a lawyer named Barry Hodges and included a telephone number. The ad simply inquired if anybody knew the whereabouts of Dr. Charles Feelgood, from Kennsington, Long Island, New York. If so, please call his law office.

I called the number out of curiosity and within an hour Mr. Hodges returned my call. I introduced myself, told him that I was an attorney. I volunteered that I had done some minor work for you in the past without giving him any details, of course. He did not ask for any as well. I let him know that I did not know where you were, which was true at the time, and added that perhaps I could be helpful in his search if I knew exactly what this was all about. I said this knowing that I might wet his interest, and it did. He went on to tell me as you might say, "the gonsa shpiel." (The whole story). To cut to the chase, I now am aware of all your troubles with the law and also understand the reason for opening the Swiss account and your need for "safe haven" countries. Mr. Hodges told me that he never gave up on your case, and has continued to develop it even in your absence to the point of now confidently going to trial for a successful outcome.

"I have all my ducks lined up and ready to move forward. All I need is the Doc," he stated to me.

I suggested that he send me his proposals and further information and I would be happy to try and locate you in my own way, but could not promise this. Mr. Hodges sounded like a savvy guy and realized my way was the only way for him and jumped at the chance. At this point I am waiting to hear from him. When I receive his correspondence, I'll pass it on to you. Then, it's all in your hands to determine if you have an interest or you choose to disregard it altogether.

Sincerely,
Gus Sherwood Esq.

I must have re-read the letter a half dozen times and kept coming back to the part where Barry told him that he had never given up on my case. I would have re-phrased it more honestly, saying that he had never given up on reaching into my deep pockets.

The letter gave me food for thought. Since Barry always has money accompany the weight of his work, he would have to agree to handle my case as a personal injury lawyer would . . . no fee unless he succeeds. This condition would be non-negotiable. I needed to study the details carefully.

I surprised myself that I would even consider laying out terms here. If Harriet were around things would be different. She would read the letter, toss it away and say, "Fuck it, you taught me about sure things!" It's true, I always told her that there was no such a thing as a sure thing except for those old standbys, death and taxes. I have since loosened up on these exceptions because I no longer pay taxes. Now all I have to solve is the death part. I now began thinking in terms of high and low risk, aware that there is no such thing as "no" risk.

A few days went by before Barry's letter reached me through Gus. As I had saved the letter from Gus, I also kept this one.

November 20th 1978

Dear Mr Sherwood,

In following up our telephone conversation the other day, I am directing this letter to my client Dr. Charles Feelgood in the hope that you can succeed in locating him.

Dear Dr. Feelgood,

The most important information to be aware of now is that technically you are not considered a fugitive for the following reasons.

1. On August 26th, 1977, a judge issued an order dismissing your case because of the failure of all parties to appear in court as scheduled on this date. The problem stemmed with the courts own failure to record a rescheduled date.

2. You assumed correctly that with your case dismissed there was no further obligation on your part to make yourself available and you left the community to change your life after a great tragedy.
3. Subsequently, the DA had a higher court reverse the dismissal order and a new date was scheduled. However, this happening was unknown to you. A warrant was issued for your arrest when you failed to appear in court that day.

Recently, the DA's office contacted me to seek my help in locating you for trial. I told them that I was no longer the attorney of record, but would jump back in under certain conditions. I sent them a memorandum of agreement which they signed. They only required that a second passport you might be holding be surrendered. Under Federal law they must claim it. Here is a summary of this agreement.

1. The charge of "unlawful flight to avoid prosecution" will be dismissed based on the courts own snafus in scheduling.
2. Bail money in the form of your primary residence will be acceptable.
3. A re-trial will not be sought by the state in the event of a hung jury.

I believe that this is as good a deal as you will ever get. I propose a flat legal fee of two hundred thousand dollars, with half due now and the other half placed in escrow now and payable upon completion of your trial.

Sincerely,
Barry Hodges, Esq

I searched carefully through Barry's letter looking for small print disguised as big print. There was one grey area of fact. Barry, indeed, had made me aware of the new September 9th date when I told him I was going away on vacation. So, I didn't really "leave the community" thinking everything was honky-dory. The truth was that I fled the country on August 24th. However, only Barry and I are aware of this. Barry must have put two and two together waiting for me on the courthouse steps, while I was drinking champagne in Hong Kong. I realized that if I did not accept his "new" timeline then I'd have to forget the whole thing. The saving grace for me was that the DA accepted it, agreeing to dismiss the unlawful flight charges.

All in all, Barry had made a favorable deal. The best part, in my opinion, was getting them to waive their right to a re-trial in the event of a hung jury. I never thought anything like that was possible. They were certainly eager to see me again. Those bastards always believed that they would be successful. However, I needed to read the actual wording of the agreement for myself. I was disappointed that Barry failed to lay out his strategy in detail indicating why he had such a high confidence level Yet, I fully understood that's what two hundred thousand dollars buys.

I could not argue with his boast that this was "as good a deal as you will ever get." However, no matter how tempting the opportunity appeared and while my heart is aching to return home, I'm still a free man now. Yes, I am also lonely, but it's something I can live with if it's to be replaced by incarceration or worse. If I do decide to return then I must hold Barry's feet to the fire on payment of his legal fees, for that's a critical measurement of my true confidence.

At this point in the negotiations I wrote a short memo to Barry through Gus.

TO: Barry Hodges, Esq December 2nd 1978
FROM: Dr. Charles Feelgood.

Agree to $200,000 for legal fees, payable in full, from an escrow account to be held by the law firm of Sherwood and Sherwood. This fee will be payable only after a permanent acquittal or dismissal of all charges. This is not negotiable. Also need a copy of the agreement with the DA.

Sincerely,

"Doc"

It took longer than expected before a reply came back through Gus. I guess Barry was tortured by my creative remuneration plan.

December 28th 1978

Dear Mr. Sherwood

If you agree to act as the escrow agent then I agree to Dr. Feelgood's proposed payment of legal fees. I would like to employ the services of your law firm as well to expedite his return to New York as quickly as possible. Enclosed is a copy of my agreement with the DA. Please note that it is dated November 7th 1978 and expires in ninety days on February 7th 1979. Thank you for all your good help in these matters.

Sincerely,

Barry Hodges-Esq

Gus enclosed a note saying that if I had the mind to return home, I should close up my affairs and purchase an airline ticket to New York. Since I was no longer incognito I should call his office directly with my arrival date in order for him to set up a meeting for me to get together with Barry at his office. He added that he was leaving for vacation on January 31st and to keep the February 7th deadline in mind.

I continued to ponder the decision over and over, perhaps, a hundred times. I came to the reality that I wasn't dealing with a "sure thing." Barry might say in his sports jargon it was "a slam dunk." Why wait? I'd just continue torturing myself maybe for years with those frustrating pro's and con's lists. I decided to return home.

The day of my decision was a Monday. It was a good day to begin a new kind of week. Until I boarded a flight to the United States I knew that I could change my mind, but, I was not about to. I sent a wire to my management company to open my house and do whatever it takes to have it ready for my arrival by the following weekend. The hotel porters began to pack the things I wanted to take back and prepare them for shipment. I purchased a one way ticket to JFK airport leaving on the upcoming Saturday afternoon, the 24th of January and notified Gus that I would be at his office the following Monday morning at nine o'clock. I didn't even consider if Barry would be able to make it, for no lawyer worth his salt misses a client date with a few hundred thousand bucks on the line for just some "slam dunk" work.

Now, that I was able to communicate freely, I placed a call to Harriet only to find out that her phone had been disconnected. Perhaps she had moved. I decided that when I was in the States I would write her at the old address and hope the post office would forward the letter.

With renewed energy I boarded my flight as scheduled. Upon my arrival in New York I rented a car on a month to month basis and drove to my home.

CHAPTER 23

January 26th

G US WAS HAPPY to see me Monday morning. He never gave me advice because he was ignorant of the facts. However, he felt the decision to come home was the right thing to do. Barry arrived shortly after I did and was equally glad to see me. I knew why, but I needed to stop thinking in these terms. I thanked him for his continuing support and he replied:

"You know, I never give up!"

Gus offered us a private room and asked Barry if there was anything he needed.

"No thanks," he answered, "I've got everything I need right here," tapping his briefcase.

As it turned out, and to no surprise, all he needed was a yellow writing pad and two sharpened pencils. Sometimes stupid images come to my mind at the wrong time, as at this moment. I imagined Barry telling St. Peter at the Pearly Gates, "I've got a pad and two number two sharpened pencils, I'm ready!"

Barry asked me lots of questions to fill in his own blanks. I related my experiences with John and his henchmen in India and Turkey. However, I did not tell him that Harriet had been with me and that she ultimately left me. I did not think this to be relative. In the process of crossing his T's and dotting his I's, Barry looked up at me and asked:

"Was your girlfriend with you?"

"Yes," I confessed.

He made a note of it, like if he hadn't, he might forget.

Our meeting took about an hour or so. Just as he was leaving he told me that he had informed the DA's office that I had already mailed my passport to them.

"I don't want you walking in there with it, so just drop it in the mail today," he sort of ordered.

I assured him that I would. He then suggested that there would be no need to get together until before the trial and that he would let me know of the date as soon as it was set by the court. I thanked him again, said goodbye, and returned to Gus's office where I signed papers for the escrow account and transferred the necessary funds. I thanked Gus again and left.

I walked out of the building and headed for my car. It was a typical January day in New York. I had not felt chilled breezes in the air for some time. Each gust of wind was like a present for me and I closed my eyes to savor the moment.

My management company had delivered a huge stack of mail which they had been collecting for me. They had the authority to open my mail when they recognized what might be a bill, so they could pay it. The mail in front of me was mostly third class, magazines and the like, so it was easy to sort out and disregard quickly. There were however about a hundred or so envelopes addressed to me, most forwarded from the hospital. It seems that in my absence an informal organization was formed and called, "The Committee To Defend Dr. Feelgood." The president was a woman named Ruth Schattner, a former patient of mine. As I began reading this mail I realized that each one came from a former patient. The theme of each letter was the same. First there was some statement of anger that the authorities would try to convict me of a crime they knew I couldn't possibly have committed, and then using similar words, each letter basically urged me to keep the faith. One larger envelope contained a copy of a petition of support with about five hundred signatures. I could have cried. A few people mentioned they were proud that the group had given five thousand dollars to my attorney, Mr. Barry Hodges, to help with my defense. This was something Barry "neglected" to mention to me earlier in the day, but something I would ask him about.

Several weeks had gone by before I heard from Barry. He finally called to inform me that the trial date was scheduled for April 19th.

"I'm all set. There is no need for us to get together again before then. Let's meet at the courthouse cafeteria for breakfast at eight o'clock on that day. I'll grab the check."

"Speaking of grabbing the check," I said, "did you receive any money from a group called "The Committee to defend Dr. Feelgood?"

"Oh yes," he answered without hesitating. "I meant to tell you but it slipped my mind. I'm using that money now as a slush fund for incidentals associated with your case."

I did not reply. The fact was that I was actually grabbing the bill using his hands. One day, pray to God, I will inform him that the $200,000 less $5,000 included all expenses.

When I arrived in the States I wrote Harriet telling her of my decision to return and little else. I just wanted to see if my letter would be received and awaited a reply. After many weeks passed, I figured that since I did not get my letter back it must have been received but not answered. Now, knowing the trial date, I wrote a detailed letter expressing my confidence about receiving an acquittal, hoping this would turn our situation around.

CHAPTER 24

April 19th

A SHAFT OF golden morning sunlight filtered through a window and beamed down onto the courtroom. I glanced over Barry's head to scan the crowd. There was an excited low pitched babble of voices, murmurs of expectancy. My two adult children were seated in the rear. I also noticed a few familiar faces from the hospital scattered about as well. As far as I was concerned, everyone else present were inquisitive nosey strangers. The media was recognizable by their ID cards hanging from a cord around their necks. Photographers were not allowed in the courtroom and it didn't matter much to them as at least a dozen cameras focused upon me as I approached the courthouse steps earlier.

Morning Session

"All rise," called out the officer of the court as he preceded the judge following him into the courtroom from a rear door. Everyone in the room scrambled to their feet. Then the jurors filed in. None of them made eye contact with me.

"You may be seated," instructed the judge.

The prosecutors were invited to make an opening statement.

"We will show that the evidence will prove the defendant's guilt beyond a reasonable doubt," the lead prosecutor proclaimed, plagiarizing a familiar line from Perry Mason.

He then presented a case which reflected the language of the indictment. 1. I had murdered my wife with an injection of Demerol. 2. The act was premeditated. 3. I covered up the crime with deceits and lies.

As for motive, he revealed that I had a secret mistress in Denmark, and had fathered two children with her. I was trying to prevent my wife from changing her will to eliminate or to dilute my inheritance, if she should die first. I was involved in a possible malpractice law suit without proper insurance and relied on my wife's money to pay off judgments, if necessary.

He promised that the State will present scientific evidence as well as witnesses to collaborate the facts.

"All the evidence will lead to a proof positive conviction," he promised the court.

This was their case in a nutshell. However, the prosecutor went back to expand each area. When what appeared to be a very damaging presentation finally ended, Barry leaned over to me and whispered in my ear:

"Promises, promises, promises. Is this all they have?"

I did not think that remark was funny at all, but I was now completely in Barry's hands and knew he was primed to overturn their case against me. It was after the noon hour already and a lunch break was called. Barry and I remained at our table in order to discuss the events of the morning in lieu of grabbing a quick lunch. The lunch would have given him of the chance of grabbing another notepad check scribbled upon by a waitress barking, "pay up front!"

Afternoon Session

When the trial resumed, the prosecutor called their first witness.

"State your name, please, and spell your last name for the record."

"My name is John LaGotta."

He slowly emphasized the capital "L" and the capital "G" and then repeated the name again as if this was a spelling bee contest.

"It's for the media, so they will get it right," Barry whispered into my ear.

"Please state your occupation."

"I'm a homicide detective working in Nassau County."

So far everything seemed to move normally. What's your name, what's your occupation, where do you work, and so on. Then only minutes into the questioning all hell broke loose.

"When did you first meet the defendant?"

"We met at his home the day his wife was murdered."

Barry, who had been resting his elbow on the table and rubbing his chin, shot out of his seat with such force that his chair tumbled at least three feet behind him.

"I object your honor. This was deliberate. As an officer of the court this witness should know better. I request that a determination be made to see if this was a rehearsed question and answer, and if it was to see your way clear to reprimand the parties in no uncertain terms and have them apologize to this jury."

"Objection sustained," ruled the judge. "I will give the witness an opportunity to re-answer the question in a correct and appropriate manner."

John looked up at the judge.

"Go on," ordered the judge, as he waved the back of his hand angrily at John.

"Yes your honor. I met the defendant for the first time at his home the day his wife was found dead."

Barry still standing tried to sit down, but couldn't find his chair right away which created some nervous laughter from the audience. The judge pounded his desk with his gavel.

The prosecutor then cut to the chase with the witness.

"What did Dr. Feelgood tell you about the drug Demerol?"

"He said that his wife suffered from severe back pains and Demerol was her medication to help reduce the pain."

"Did you notice a bottle of Demerol on the night table when you entered the bedroom?"

"Yes, I did."

"What happened then?"

"Well, Dr. Feelgood picked the bottle up, shook it upside down to show me that it was empty and handed me the bottle. No, change that to 'forced' the bottle on me, strongly suggesting that I take it back to the station house."

"Did you accept the bottle?"

"Yes and I asked him to drop it into the plastic ziplock bag I took out of my pocket."

"And then?"

"Then, nothing! Except, as I was leaving the room I just couldn't help myself. I admonished him for possibly destroying fingerprint evidence."

"What did he say?"

"He apologized, saying that he was sorry."

"What made you think that there would be a need for fingerprint evidence?"

"I wasn't certain about this, but you see I'm trained to be suspicious of things in this sort of situation. I didn't know what was actually happening. It was a normal knee jerk reaction for me. It had bothered me how he insisted I take the empty bottle back with me."

"I have no further questions of detective LaGotta, your honor."

The judge called a twenty minute recess which Barry requested in order to give more time to fine tune his cross examination. We reconvened and Barry stepped up to the plate.

"Good afternoon detective LaGotta. Is that a capital "L", capital "G"?

An undercurrent of laughter was heard throughout the courtroom. I looked at the jury. There was a faint smile on everybody's face. The judge was obviously not happy with Barry in his debut. He pounded his gavel repeatedly. The jury members wiped their smiles away quickly. John did not answer Barry's question, but Barry knew intuitively that the answer would bring on another wave of laughter, so he just moved on.

"Let me ask you sir . . ."

When he called him sir, it reminded me how John kept calling me sir at my house, and I called him officer in return.

"What would be the big deal if Dr. Feelgood's prints were on the bottle? Did you consider that since he was the one who left the Demerol on the table in the morning that his prints would be there in any event?"

John looked at the ceiling deep in thought for an answer.

Barry continued, "Maybe I'm not up to speed, but has criminal technology developed to gauge the difference between morning prints from evening prints?"

"No, of course not," he replied.

"So, why were you so upset with him?"

"Well, it wasn't only the fingerprints as much as an overall feeling that something smelled fishy."

"Can you tell the court what exactly was fishy?"

"My instincts. Nothing exactly."

Barry turned in the direction of the jury and repeated John's words backwards.

"Exactly nothing. Very interesting."

At this point Barry decided to switch direction.

"Is it a fact that you were assigned a role as the lead detective to further investigate the suicide?"

The witness hesitated to avoid saying that he was assigned to investigate a murder because of the earlier admonishment by the judge. He answered the question in a different way.

"I didn't know for sure if it was a suicide."

"OK then," Barry said, being equally as careful, "let me rephrase the question – were you assigned to further investigate this case?"

"Yes, I was."

"So, in time, you became aware that Dr. Feelgood was not available for questioning and court appearances because he was either on vacation or beginning a new life somewhere or whatever."

"More then whatever!" John asserted.

"Explain that?"

"Well, a warrant was issued for his arrest."

"Do you know why?"

"Yes, because he failed to keep a court date."

"You state this as a fact, but do you know why he failed to show up?"

"He just did."

"You say that he just did, but there is a reason for everything. Give me a moment to lay out the situation leading to his absence. Since you were involved on a daily basis please correct me if my time frame is in error."

John shook his head OK. The judge made him say OK for the record.

"The first indictment hearing was held on July 24th 1977. Is this correct? I see that you have a notepad with you. You can check me for accuracy."

"Yes, that's correct," he replied, flipping through the pages of his pad.

"We were both present that day. Is that correct?"

"Correct."

"This is what occurred. If I'm not describing it accurately let me know."

"OK!"

"The judge rejected the DA's indictment as inadequate, and sealed the arrest record. Let me quote from the court record. This is the judge speaking."

Barry took out a paper from a folder and offered it as evidence. The judge asked to look at it, and handed it back.

"You can just read from it, it doesn't have to be submitted."

"Thank you, your honor. I quote the judge addressing the DA's staff. Quote, 'I have to warn you again to avoid taking a premature reckless and irresponsible path towards justice.'"

"That's correct," said John, "but I'm not on the DA's staff."

"We know that, don't take it so personally."

"I'm not taking it personally. I only want the record to show my position here."

"Well, let's go on Detective LaGotta. Then the judge gave the DA time to re-present the indictment. A date was set about thirty days later, to be exact, on August 26, 1977. Please check your records to confirm this date."

"August 26th is correct."

"Thank you. Now at some point before this date the DA requested and received a two week extension. All parties were notified. True?"

"Yes, true."

"So, now we had another court date, is this right?"

"Yes," he answered, apparently getting bored with the slowness of the questioning.

"This new, new date was September 9, 1977. Can you verify this date as well?"

John looked at his pad again.

"That date is correct."

"Now let's spend a moment on this day, as it is very important and relative to the warrant for Dr. Feelgood's arrest. If you remember, I arrived early at the courthouse and you were already there. Dr. Feelgood had not arrived yet. We both walked into the courtroom and it was dark. You said something about people not starting their work on time. So far, so good, detective?"

"Yes, thanks for leaving out the curse words."

"You are welcome. The staff from the DA's office then walked in and we were all met by the clerk of the court. He advised all of us, very apologetically, that somehow there was a failure to record the extension. Now, here is the key part. The clerk went on to inform us that on August 26th, a new judge sitting on the court that day, waited for the case to be called. As nobody was there he simply dismissed the entire case and had some very harsh words against the DA's office. I need not read these from the transcript as there are too many women sitting in the courtroom today. Anything wrong with my characterization of what happened that day, Mr. LaGatta?"

"None at all."

"Now this was a snafu created by the court system, and no fault of the DA, you or I. A new date was now scheduled for October 3rd 1977. Can I refer to this date as the new, new, new, new, date?"

"If you want, but maybe one less new."

"Sure, why not!" Barry capitulated.

"Now I can get to a very critical point."

Barry was now directing himself to the jurors rather than to John.

"Dr. Feelgood, despondent over his wife's suicide . . ."

"I object," cried out the prosecutor.

"Look," barked back the judge, "we all have to stop this. The defense can call the death suicide, and you can call it murder. The jury won't be influenced either way. This is getting silly."

Barry continued:

"Dr. Feelgood, despondent over the death of his wife, and with the indictment dismissed, and having no reason to believe that he would be called back to court, decided to begin a new life and left the community. Yes, he did make a mistake by not requesting his passport back. Why, one may ask? The reason is easy to understand. He just did not want to deal with the authorities anymore They had damaged his life and caused him great anxiety. So, he simply got himself a duplicate passport. There was no pseudo name used, I might add. There was no need for it. This was an error in judgment for sure, but a misdemeanor at best. One also has to consider his law abiding life record. Did I mention that he did not jump bail either? There was no bail because he never was charged with any crime. And yes, he did have a mistress in Europe and fathered two children with her. He was also named in a malpractice law suit for the first time in his twenty year career. And yes, he did not carry the proper insurance as all other doctors do. Call all of this reckless, selfish, whatever you want to name it, but for God's sake don't call it murder."

Barry spun around back to John who had been listening intently.

"Right, detective LaGotta?"

"Objection your honor," cried out the prosecutor. "The witness cannot agree or disagree with this conclusion. He can only answer what he knows to be true or untrue."

"Objection sustained, go on counselor."

"Allow me now to finish up the sequence of events in order to make an extremely important point, your honor."

"You always entice me, Mr. Hodges," obliged the judge.

"So, after being advised on September 9th that the case had been dismissed on August 26th, I returned to my office to prepare a final legal bill for my client, Dr.

Feelgood. About ten days later I was notified by the court of a new October 3rd date. Mr. LaGatta I'm sure you became aware of this new date at the same time. Is that true?"

"Yes, that is correct," he replied.

"I attempted to reach Dr. Feelgood at home. His phone had been disconnected. The hospital could not help me locate him. Failing to reach him I sent a registered letter to the court indicating my surprise that the indictment which had been dismissed was now resurrected. I stated that I could not reach my client and also informed the court that I would no longer act as the attorney of record on this matter. I sent a copy to the DA's office as well."

Barry handed a copy of this letter to the clerk who announced that it would be marked exhibit number one for the defense. Barry then turned his attention back to John.

"Mr. LaGotta, you stated earlier that a warrant was issued for Dr. Feelgood's arrest because he failed to appear in court on October 3rd. When I asked you if you knew why he did not show up you said . . .

Barry shuffled through his notes, "you said, that he just did. Would you answer the same way now?"

"You mean because he didn't know of the date?"

"Exactly!"

John nervously thumbed through his note pad.

"Who knows, who can say for sure, who am I to say? If that's true, then that's true!"

Barry accepted this backhanded response. It was the best he could expect, for John would never eat crow.

"I might add here," Barry continued, "that the DA has dropped unlawful flight to avoid prosecution charges. Upon reviewing the facts, as you have just done, it was the correct action to take.

John did not respond and Barry quickly moved the questioning into another area.

"Sometime in late 1977 Dr. Feelgood's father-in-law offered a million dollar reward to anyone who could locate him and be instrumental in bringing him to justice, leading to a conviction of murder. Were you aware of such a reward?"

"Yes, I was!"

"Did you react personally to the reward?"

"Yes, I did."

"How?"

"Well, I saw the great injustice of not having Dr. Feelgood available to stand trial and defend his innocence, so I decided that it would be the right thing to do if I worked full time on the case."

"How did you accomplish this? Did you request this kind of assignment from your superiors?"

"No"

"So how?" Barry pressed on.

"Well, I took a no-pay leave of absence from my position to try and locate Dr. Feelgood."

"That's quite a noble thing to do. How could you afford to do this?"

"I depended on the reward money to defray my expenses, but I was taking a risk as well."

"Did you budget expenses?"

"Yes, I allowed myself $50,000."

"And so, if you were successful, you could realize $950,000 give or take a few bucks. I don't want to talk out of school, but since its public record, I can divulge that a detective's yearly salary in your category and years of service is $21,000. So, I'm thinking that a budget of $50,000 seems a bit much. Were there some investors in your project?"

"I wouldn't call this a project," he retorted. There were about a half dozen friends of mine who felt the same way as I did about Dr. Feelgood's returning to the justice system and so they lent me the money."

"Were they friends or investors?"

At this point the judge interrupted.

"OK, Mr. Hodges, move on, you made your purpose known."

John then spoke without being questioned because I guess he needed to explain this situation in a better light.

"Let me state in this regard that the money was secondary. We all felt, as law enforcement agents, that major crimes must be tried in a court of law!"

"What was the major crime here, detective LaGotta?"

Again, the judge broke in.

"And we don't want to go down that road either Mr. Hodges."

Barry walked along the jury box.

"So, the money was secondary," he stated to no one in particular. Then he shrugged, and looked up at the high courtroom ceiling and said, "Forgive me for not understanding, but I'm just a naive kid from Brooklyn."

The prosecutor sprang off his chair.

"I object!"

"Sustained! Counselor there will be no more poor boy from Brooklyn talk!"

The judge had now created his own monster. The audience and the jury could not contain themselves. Laughter resounded throughout the courtroom. The judge did not call for order but allowed the reaction to peter out naturally. I may have been wrong, but I could almost swear that the judge had a pleased look on his face.

Barry walked back to the witness chair.

"Now, for the million dollar question – did you find him?"

"I didn't find him, we located him in New Delhi, India."

"Who is we?"

"I had two friends with me."

"The same friends that lent you the money?"

"No, different friends."

"Different, you mean poorer friends?"

The judge broke in. "Stop that Mr. Hodges, and don't ask me what I mean!"

"Just out of curiosity, what were their occupations?"

"I don't know."

"Look," responded Barry angrily, "let's not get into the grey area of perjury. You're doing great so far."

"I object to that insinuation," piped up the prosecutor.

The judge did not rule on the objection but suggested that John may want another chance to answer the question.

"I believe that they were bounty hunters."

"You believe!" shot back Barry with raised eyebrows.

"OK, they were," John acquiesced, finally giving up.

"Thank you," replied Barry shaking his head. "I don't want to pull teeth. I'm a lawyer, not a dentist."

He used the same line I thought about when I questioned my maid Anna repeatedly about her meeting with the police.

"How did you and your companions know that Dr. Feelgood was living in India?"

"From a friend at the DA's office."

"You seem to have made great friends. So then, I assume that you left pronto for India. Is this correct?"

"Correct for having great friends, or leaving for India?"

"Answer just for India, we know about friends."

"Correct!"

"Thank You."

"You're welcome."

Things continued to heat up between Barry and John. At one point the judge stepped in by telling Barry to ask questions without inciting the witness, and told John to be more forthright, quicker.

"So, as I understand, after a time in India you became aware Dr. Feelgood was now in Turkey, correct?"

"Correct"

"How did you find out that he was in Turkey."

"Through airline passenger lists."

Well, that's one thing I guessed right about, I thought to myself.

"So, you and your friends followed to Turkey, correct?"

"Yes, sir."

This was the first time John called Barry sir, so I knew he was beginning to lose some confidence.

"Did you report to your superiors in New York that you had been hot on his trail in India and now knew that he was in Turkey?"

"No."

"No? Why not?" Was it because you didn't want New York detectives swarming around you and interfering with your investment?"

The prosecutor was on his feet again objecting to the inference. Barry did not give the judge a chance to rule.

"Your honor, I don't expect an answer. I remembered that the witness stated earlier that he was involved as a matter of justice, not money, so I'm going to accept his contention at face value."

The judge glanced at the jury. The smirks on their faces disappeared quickly.

"I understand, Mr. LaGotta, that while you were in Turkey Dr. Feelgoods father-in-law passed away. Were you aware of this?"

"Yes"

"You know, of course, that death voids all contracts of the deceased."

"Yes."

"So, there was no longer any reward money, correct?"

"Correct."

"So, what did you do?"

"I wired Dr. Feelgood's son in California, who with his sister, I imagined were in line to inherit their grandfather's estate. I asked him if he would reinstitute the reward money."

"Did he reply?"

"Yes he did."

"What did he say?"

"He said no, that's what the police get paid to do!"

"Did you then stop the search?"

"Yes, I had spent over $30,000 of my money already"

"Did this include payment to your traveling companions?"

"Some, I had only paid their expenses. They had contracted to receive one third of the reward money."

"Oh my, one third! I must apologize to you now. I had thrown out a net figure of $950,000 earlier without knowing all the financial facts. So, you were almost working for nothing, correct?"

"Mr. Hodges, this is going to be the last time that I will warn you to stay out of this area in this way" admonished the judge. "It's clear to everyone that Mr. LaGatta was driven by the reward and it's not necessary for you to keep harassing him over this."

Barry would pay half attention to the judge's order for it was time for the kill.

"Did you tell his son that his father was in Turkey?"

"No, I did not."

"Why not?"

"Well, I thought that since we were wiring each other from Turkey he'd figure out for himself that his father must be there, and tell the authorities himself since it was their job anyway."

"Sounds like sour grapes."

"I don't know what that means here," shot back John.

"Scratch that question, your honor."

The prosecutor sat down without having the chance to object to the remark, for Barry was too fast on the button.

"Just one last question detective LaGatta. You are a very experienced police witness. Don't you think it odd that the prosecution did not ask you one question about these bounty hunting days? Scratch that question as well, I'm finished with this witness."

Barry returned to the defense table, sat down and whispered into my ear "did you ever see a case of mincemeat like this in your life?"

CHAPTER 25

April 20th

Morning Session

D R. SAM KLEIN, Sophia's personal physician, was scheduled as the first witness when the trial went into its second day. The doctor was sworn in, and seated himself in the witness chair as the prosecutor approached him.

"Please state your name and occupation."

Just as an aside, he did not request that he spell his name as he had done with John, for prosecutors are fast learners.

"My name is Sam Klein and I am a physician," he responded.

"Were you Sophia's physician?"

"Yes"

"For how long of a period of time?"

"About sixteen years."

"Dr. Klein, can you tell this court for how long she had a back problem?"

"She never had a back problem!"

A hush of low voices developed throughout the courtroom. The jurors began to squirm in their chairs. The judge called for order. This moment had always been my worst nightmare.

"I have no further questions your honor."

The judge looked at Barry and asked him if he was ready to cross examine the witness or if he needed more time.

"Ready, your honor" replied Barry.

"Good morning, Dr. Klein"

"Good morning," he replied back, looking a little leery.

One could not blame him for he was present in the courtroom during Barry's cross examination of John LaGatta.

"Can you please tell us how serious Sophia's ulcer problem was?"

"She didn't have an ulcer problem!"

"Are you sure doctor?"

"Absolutely," he declared in no uncertain terms.

"Your honor I wish to place into evidence Dr. Feelgood's certified medical records covering the past ten years detailing the treatment of his wife's bleeding ulcers. I also wish to place into the record Sophia Feelgood's certified autopsy report indicating this exact same condition."

The judge directed the clerk to accept the documents and to number them two and three for the defense.

"Dr. Klein," Barry said sort of taking him out of a stupor.

"Yes, sir?" he replied, somewhat shaken.

"If you did not know about a ten year ulcer problem, would it be fair to say that you might not have known about the back problem as well?"

"Yes, that's possible."

"How often did she visit your office?"

"Maybe once or twice a year."

"Every year?"

"Not every year. Some years I did not see her at all."

"When you did see her, what did you treat her for?"

"Mainly upper respiratory infections."

"What is your medical specialty, doctor?"

"I am an eye, ear, nose, and throat specialist."

"So, if one has a problem above the neck they would seek you out. Is this correct?"

"You could put it that way."

"I just did, Doc!"

Barry now spoke more to the jury than to the witness.

"So, Sophia, with other medical problems below the neck, such as a bad back and bleeding ulcers opted for the services of a renowned, experienced internist and surgeon who not only happened to be her husband, but whose services were free. I have no more questions of this witness your honor."

As Barry walked back to our table and sat down it was my turn to compliment him. I whispered, "Another case of mincemeat!"

In their opening presentation the State promised the jury that they would show that I had two reasons to flee. One was the investigation into the death of my wife and the other the threat of a malpractice law suit where I was caught with my financial pants down. The hospital administrator was summoned as a witness to affirm the DA's contention that the financial problem added to my decision to flee. The State presented some background information surrounding the law suit, my role, and the hospitals defense and when they finished they invited Gary to take the stand.

"Has the state portrayed the facts of the law suit correctly?"

"Yes, factually correct," Gary replied.

"During your interviews with the DA you claimed that your office made numerous attempts to contact Dr. Feelgood after he failed to return to work when expected on or about September 9, 1977. Is this correct, sir?"

"Yes, it is."

"What did you think at the time?"

"Well, with his phone disconnected and all, we were sure that he must have left town in fear of the possible consequences of the suit."

"Do you still believe this today?"

"Yes, I do."

Thank you your honor, there are no more questions for this witness. The judge asked Barry if he could begin his cross examination now or if he required a short recess.

"I'm ready, your honor," Barry responded.

"Was there a time, sir, when the hospital board promised Dr. Feelgood they would, if necessary, cover him financially?"

"That's true, but only if there was an out of court settlement."

"So then, doesn't it make sense that Dr. Feelgood would have at least waited to see, if indeed, there might be a settlement?"

"Well, perhaps he believed that it would never happen."

"Perhaps, yes, perhaps, no," Barry shot back, "but nobody except the doctor knew for sure, true?"

"Yes, I guess that's true."

"And finding the phone disconnected did not mean that one and one made two, for sure either."

Gary did not respond and Barry didn't care if he got a reply or not.

"Don't you think the state prosecutor who asked you if he portrayed the nature of the suit accurately failed to ask about the outcome of the trial?"

"Objection!" popped up the prosecutor.

"I'll overrule," responded the judge, "the defense is going to ask the question anyway now, so let's hear it."

"Thank you your honor."

Barry moved close to the witness, flipped through his note book as if he was trying to locate the question and closed the pad.

"So, what was the outcome? You portray it now for the court!"

"The litigators refused to settle. We all went to court and they lost the case."

"Thank you for your succinct portrayal."

I knew Barry's ways in getting under the skin of the opposition. He was using the word portrayal to mock the prosecutor's use of the term.

Barry was now heading down the stretch with Gary.

"Wouldn't it be fair to say that Dr. Feelgood should not only have waited around for the possibility of a settlement, but also stuck around for the results of the court decision before deciding to flee?"

"Well, I see your point, so maybe he just disappeared because of the criminal investigation."

Barry shouted back angrily. "You were wrong about why he fled, and you are just as ill informed here. Besides, that issue is not your business and not for you to speculate about, particularly from the witness chair. Remember what the prosecutor has reminded everybody. Witnesses should only testify to what they know or do not know as being factual. No more questions of this witness, your honor, I've heard enough already."

Barry now addressed the judge.

"Your Honor, if I may, I would like to comment about the appearance of this last witness."

"Go ahead!" the judge replied.

"The State invited him to testify based upon their statement promising to prove a possible reason for my client leaving the community. This is a non-issue, your Honor. The State should never have gotten into this area in the first place. The DA dropped all charges of unlawful flight to avoid prosecution. What's going on here, your Honor, doesn't the right shoe know what the left shoe is doing?"

The judge called a sidebar conference of all parties, and then instructed the jury to disregard the appearance and testimony of the last witness. He added as a way of an explanation that the State failed to remove the witness from their witness list through an oversight and the prosecutor has apologized to the court.

The shmucks were heading further and further down a slippery slope and my friend Gary had his fifteen minutes of fame sucked out from under him. A recess was called as everybody needed a breather from what just transpired. Barry returned to the defense table, sat down and softly declared, "mincemeat, wouldn't you say?"

Barry often peppered his legalize with sports talk. So when the opposition was ready to call Howard Kanter, the pharmacist at the hospital, he whispered to me in the voice of a baseball announcer.

"Next, at bat, for the State of New York, is Howie Kanter. Kanter now batting zero!"

The witness stated his name and his position as a pharmacist at the hospital.

"Did you fill a prescription for Demerol on June 15th 1977 for Dr. Feelgood."

"Yes, I did."

"Do you have a record of this?"

"Yes, I do."

Mr. Kanter handed the clerk a copy of the pharmacy log for that day. It was entered as evidence number one for the prosecution.

"Did Dr. Feelgood, ever in the past, write a prescription for this drug?"

"Well sir, we responded to a request sometime ago from the DA's office for this information dating back two years and found no others."

"So, Mr. Kanter, if Dr. Feelgood had been treating his wife with Demerol for a long period of time he must have used an outside pharmacy or some other source to obtain this medication. Is this correct?"

"Objection, your Honor," snapped Barry as he bolted out of his chair. "This witness is being asked to give an answer to something he has absolutely no knowledge about."

"Objection sustained," ruled the judge.

Sustained or not, the prosecutor had done his job. The damaging question was left unanswered for the jury. At this point the witness was ready for cross examination.

"Mr. Kanter, you were just asked if you might know where Dr. Feelgood could have obtained Demerol tablets if not from the hospital. I objected to that question because, as you heard earlier this morning, witnesses can only speak to the facts as they believe them. However, this was a legitimate question nevertheless, and the jury deserves an answer, so I will give them one. Dr. Feelgood, as head of surgery, was the recipient and caretaker of thousands of drug samples supplied by most of the pharmaceutical companies. The Demerol he needed over the years came from this supply. The reason was not financial, for the doctor could certainly afford to purchase the drug. Rather, the reason was convenience for a very busy doctor. On June 15th, as the record verifies, he wrote a prescription for the drug simply because there were no more samples available. Yesterday, we sent a registered letter to the DA's office admitting what one may call, theft. We stated in no uncertain terms that it was wrong and unprofessional and had to be addressed. I have a copy of this letter which I will now hand over to the clerk of the court."

Barry then shifted his attention to the direction of the jury box.

"I must also point out that Dr. Feelgood admitted to this impropriety prior to today, not anticipating we were going to get into this area, but just to clear the air and his own conscience in this matter. Again, it was a mistake in judgment, but it was miles away from a charge of murder."

When Barry returned to the defense table he was completely washed out. After a moment in thought he leaned over to me and said, "it's a wash."

The lunch break came late. It was after one o'clock, and the judge limited the time to half an hour. Barry suggested that we stay put because he expected a short afternoon session as this was Friday and this court's tradition was to close up shop early for the weekend.

Barry told me he regretted not contacting the DA earlier about the Demerol tablet samples.

"Even though we beat them to the punch," he said, "it still appears that we were forced to do so at the last minute. If the letter was sent a week ago the pharmacist would never have been called."

"But, Barry," I reminded him, "this explanation was your brainchild which you only came up with two days ago."

He thought about what I said and replied:

"Oh well, whatever!"

Afternoon Session

The afternoon session was resumed. The jury had been dismissed at the break. There were only a handful of diehards seated in the front row, but the curtain was slowly beginning to drop on their show. There was a sidebar meeting discussing technical issues with the judge that lasted for thirty minutes. Then, the judge called it a day.

Barry reminded me, with a smile, to return Monday morning. Then he drifted into a sports talk mode again.

"Three strike outs and a passed ball. We can keep the starting pitcher in the game next week."

A pat on his own back!

CHAPTER 26

April 21-22

THE WEEK-END PAPERS reported on the trial and indicated that what had been considered an open and shut case for the DA had taken a turn in favor of the defense. The witnesses so far had "not driven the case into the beyond a reasonable doubt area." The reporting went on to remind the reader that the State had promised scientific evidence, and as the reporter put it:

"Without this evidence they are a dead duck! Stay tuned!"

Barry called me Saturday morning to let me know that the lab he had contracted to perform a Demerol property test had sent him the results. He had told me that he wanted to see the results of such a test directly rather than second hand from the DA's office.

"You can never trust those bastards," he reminded me again.

Barry did not volunteer what the result of the test was and I did not ask him for it either. I was not emotionally prepared to hear bad news or to get elated prematurely over a new favorable report.

He also informed me that the attorney, Ron Black, would be a final witness before the State presented its scientific evidence on Monday. Looking ahead, he guessed that Tuesday might be the last day of this phase of the trial because two original witnesses on the prosecutions witness list were scratched.

One was Anna, my former maid, who could have proven to be an effective witness. She had returned to her home somewhere deep in Eastern Europe. It seems that a cousin of hers, living in Queens, named the country as Molvania, or something close to that. Barry learned that the DA's office made attempts to find her, but, for openers, couldn't locate a country by or near that name on any map. Finally, they determined that Molvania was an obscure part of the Soviet Union.

"Fat chance," Barry asserted, "getting her out of there!" He was right. After all it was 1979.

Rene, whatever her last name was, the woman in charge of the safety boxes at the bank, was also scratched. Barry was told that when she was interviewed again in preparation for the trial, she had no meaningful testimony to offer. She also gabbed on and on about nothing, and was too eager to be a witness. I kind of felt sorry for her. She was a lonely gal, working at a lonely job, and was now robbed of her fifteen minutes of fame, just as Gary, the hospital administrator, had been.

"Well, at least that insurance agent never entered their radar screen," I said to Barry.

"Are you talking about that 'runt'? Is that the guy?"

"Yes, him," I confirmed.

"Let me tell you we will never have to worry about that guy."

"OK, tell me!"

Barry went on to relate how he read a case in a law journal just after I left the country. It was about an insurance agent from Queens whose name was familiar to Barry and figured out that he must be the "runt." It seems that he was convicted and sent to prison for "re-routing" homeowner's insurance premiums to himself and cashing them in. He would pay out small nuisance claims when absolutely necessary. He figured if the insurance companies that he represented took in more premium money than they paid out, then he could do the same thing. That was not a bad idea on the surface, we both agreed.

"So what happened, Barry?"

"What happened was that he began expanding his ruse. He started operating in the state of Florida and then a hurricane hit!"

"Say no more Barry."

CHAPTER 27

April 23rd

A S I APPROACHED the courthouse steps this Monday morning with Barry, we were met again by the same group of photographers screaming the same words at me, "Hey Doc, look this way." They snapped the exact same pictures as last week.

"Maybe, they all lost their used rolls of film from Friday," quipped Barry.

"All of them?" I questioned.

I immediately picked up upon his humor so I added that it couldn't be all of them.

"Maybe only some of them!"

Barry liked my retort, for I was learning to think like him.

Due to the broad publicity the trial was receiving, public interest had grown. We noticed a man handing out numbered tickets to would be spectators lining up near the courthouse.

"Don't worry, no numbers for us, our seats are guaranteed," Barry gleefully remarked.

"As long as our number isn't up," I joked back.

He didn't answer. Barry never wants to think about losing, even in the form of a joke.

Morning Session

When the proceedings began Ron Black was called to the stand as a motive witness. Basically, he would substantiate that I had a financial motive. He testified that in February of 1977, about four months before she died, Sophia came to his law office seeking his help in moving the bulk of her assets out of her estate and to the children directly. She also changed her will to reflect this action. When questioned about inheritance rules in New York State, he verified that surviving spouses are entitled to one third of the estate. So, this maneuvering by Sophia would effectively leave me with one third of almost nothing, in the event of her death.

Barry took over the questioning in cross examination.

"When did Dr. Feelgood learn that he was virtually eliminated from any inheritance?"

"I can't answer a question put in that context," he replied as the lawyer in him kicked in.

"OK then, I'll make it simple," Barry acquiesced. "Then, perhaps you can tell us when Dr. Feelgood found out that his wife executed a new will. Can you answer in this context?"

"At the reading of the will at my office."

"When did Mrs. Feelgood pass away?"

"I can't answer a question worded that way."

"Worded like what," shot back Barry.

"Like pass away."

"OK, let's try it this way. When did she suddenly die?"

"About two weeks before the reading of the will."

"Maybe I'm not adding the chain of events correctly, but if Dr. Feelgood found out about the new will two weeks after she died, then this timetable contradicts that he had a financial motive."

"Well, he suspected that she might do what she did."

"Really, who says?"

"Sophia told me that she had been threatening him for some time that she would take such action."

"Who else did she tell?"

"I don't know."

"So, there was no witness present when she told you this."

"Correct."

"Then you are asking us to accept your word alone on this important point."

"Well, I know, for example, that she must have told her father of these same plans."

"Well, great then," exclaimed Barry, "let's get him up here and clear this all up! 'For example,' is no proof!"

"Unfortunately, he is dead."

The crowded courtroom erupted into laughter. Some jurors held their hands over their lips. The judge hit his desk with the gavel calling for order. When the room quieted down Barry announced that he was finished with the witness, for he knew when to quit.

Having experienced their witnesses thrown against the ropes, as Barry would have termed it in sports jargon, the prosecutors opted not to call any lab technicians or other experts to the witness stand during their presentation. This phase of the trial now became very critical for them. Their new strategy was to allow the lab reports to speak for themselves. The lead prosecutor stood before the jury and spent about one hour with charts at his side explaining, first, the results of the coroner's tests with one verifying the other, and then, a confirming report by One Stop Labs used exclusively by the DA's office.

"Three tests, three reports, by reputable labs, all coming to the same conclusion ladies and gentlemen of the jury. That conclusion being that Mrs. Feelgood died from an overdose of liquid Demerol which could only be administered through injection. This is the evidence we promised you and now have delivered to you as well. This is indeed proof positive of what the truth is in this matter."

The guy must have used the words proof positive at least a half dozen times during his presentation. I noticed Barry jot down these words on his pad. No doubt, at some future point, the State's lawyer, yapping away like Clarence Darrow, will eat these words.

When the prosecutor finished he left the jurors with a glazed look on their faces, but I'm sure he didn't notice this at all. The judge canceled the afternoon session because of "impending court business," whatever that meant and told the parties that the trial will continue the following morning.

Barry winked at me and said:

"I didn't know that he played golf?"

As Barry had not scheduled any work for himself in the afternoon, he suggested that I return to his office to discuss some contingencies which I might be facing, even in spite of a not guilty verdict.

We entered his private office. Everything looked exactly as I had remembered it from my last visit. I eyed the lone chair in a corner of the room and pulled it over to Barry's desk.

"I am going to assume that, at the end of the road, you will be found not guilty. However, there will be two, maybe three problems we will have to address. They are all minor compared to the main charge, but they will need our attention as well."

My first thought was that Barry was looking for more money. However, at this point I just nodded my head ready to listen to what exactly he was talking about. I thought of one problem, was not certain of a second, and had no idea what a third one could be.

"I recommend that you plead guilty to two offenses. One is for a passport violation and the other is for stealing Demerol tablets from the hospital sample supply."

"But, Barry," I protested, "I never stole so much as an aspirin tablet!"

Barry just stared at me, to sort of wake me out of a slumber.

I thought for a moment and apologized.

"I'm sorry, you're right, I'm all confused."

"That's why I'm the lawyer, and you are the client," he reminded me. "I'm not certain about the class these offenses fall into, but I'll find out and try to get them reduced to misdemeanor if that becomes necessary."

He paused for a few seconds and boasted:

"I'm good at that, you know!"

"What are the penalties?"

"At the best you should get probation for perhaps a year or two. At the worst, you may be looking at up to a year or likely less in a Federal minimum security prison. They are not as bad as you might imagine. I'd describe it like a boy scout camp without the camaraderie of a camp fire."

All this didn't seem so bad considering the alternative.

"If I should get probation, could I still hold a passport?"

"I know what you mean. It's about seeing your family in Denmark, right?"

"Right," I answered quickly, so as not to give him any other ideas.

"The answer is no because the crime is a passport violation, and a serious one at that. However there would be no restrictions, of course, for them to visit you here. In time, after the penalties are satisfied, your passport will be restored."

I now asked him about a third legal problem.

"Well, it's civil in nature. It concerns the jewelry you took from the safety deposit box and from other places. These were all personal items left to your children in your wife's will. As far as the State is concerned, they have absolutely no interest here. After all, they are trying you for murder, not for a case of hide and seek."

Barry went on to explain that my children could sue me for their return within a three year Statute of Limitations period.

"Either hold onto the jewelry now or give them up."

"What do you think?"

"I say give them up, and I'll tell you why."

At that moment I remembered my father-in-laws more colorful advice, "Don't be a shnorrer," (cheap skate) he said.

"OK, tell me why. I'm listening, Barry."

Barry related that he had received a letter from Ron Black demanding the return of Sophia's jewelry to my children according to her wishes in her will. Barry believed this was a first step in preparing for a civil suit against me. He contacted Ron and requested a complete listing and description of each piece that he was seeking. Ron told him that he could not accurately supply this information. My children didn't know from shit what jewelry they were looking for and Ron Black was on a fishing expedition. However, he did tell Barry that there was one ring they could describe. It was an expensive fourteen carat blue diamond engagement ring which had belonged to Sophia's mother, given to her by her father when her mother died.

"What will happen if I don't return the ring?" I asked.

"Well, this is what I'm trying to tell you. They are getting ready to sue you."

"Do you know the value of the ring?"

"They claim a quarter of a million dollars. It's only a guess based on the fact that they are holding a bill of sale and an appraisal from the year 1935 when the ring was purchased by your father-in-law for $25,000. I think they are in line with today's value by multiplying this amount by ten."

"How the hell did he have that kind of money in the middle of the great depression?"

"Doc, I don't have a clue. I'm a lawyer, not an accountant. Maybe he juggled the books at the end of each month?"

I began to pace around the room thinking about my intentions. Barry watched me, but said nothing. I sat down, leaned my elbows on the desk, and told him how I felt.

"I bought all the jewelry in question. I may be off the mark legally, but as I see it, I own the whole kit and caboodle. However, the ring is different. I can't consider it mine. I'd be willing to return it under an agreement they waive claim to the rest of Sophia's jewelry, jewelry they can't even describe, or possibly, never even laid eyes upon."

Barry tore a piece of yellow paper off his legal pad and rolled one of his pencils across the desk in my direction.

"Here, write up an agreement. If you are comfortable with it, I'll present it to Ron Black for you."

I headed the paper in all caps with the best legalize I could create.

"AGREEMENT BETWEEN CHARLES FEELGOOD AND THE
ESTATE OF SOPHIA FEELGOOD"

I turned the paper around to seek Barry's approval.

"Is this OK?"

"Why not?" he answered.

I knew that I was on my own, so I continued writing.

"I, Charles Feelgood, agree to return a ring, approximately fourteen carats, alleged to have been Sophia's mother's engagement ring, and subsequently, given to Sophia by her father as a gift, after her mother's death. In return, the estate of Sophia Feelgood waives all claims to all other jewelry that may be in my possession or by other persons or institutions."

I placed lines where my son and daughter should sign and date. I told Barry that I wanted Ron to notarize their signatures.

"Sure," he replied, "whatever you say counselor!"

I turned around the paper again with the completed agreement so Barry could check it out.

"Couldn't have done better," he exclaimed. "I'll have it typed up and fax it over to Mr. Black. Since your children are in town for the trial perhaps we can get a signed agreement by tomorrow. If things go as planned, you should bring the ring with you in the morning and we can finalize a transfer of prisoners!"

CHAPTER 28

April 24th

F OR ME THIS was a do or die day. Barry put it in terms of a boxing match. "We're way ahead on points, now all we have to do is avoid getting knocked out in the 10th round!"

However, before the main event would reconvene, Barry had some minor business to attend to. There had been a decision by my children to sign the agreement as presented. Barry asked me for the ring in the same way a rabbi officiating at a wedding ceremony asks the best man for the ring before the deal is closed. I reached into the wrong pocket as jittery best men often do, followed by a slight panic attack, until I felt that circular shape in the opposite pocket.

Barry approached Ron Black, who returned to the courthouse today despite his poor performance yesterday, just for this occasion. Ron handed him the agreement, and Barry checked it over to insure there were no changes. There were none and so Barry handed over the ring. They shook hands as adversaries often do at surrender ceremonies. I caught my daughter slipping the ring on her finger with a broad smile on her face. I had not made her smile like this in years. Then again, on the other hand, I never had a fourteen carat sparkler to give away.

The judge pounded his gavel upon his desk calling for order. I played with my tie as Barry approached the jury box. I was somewhat apprehensive because Barry and I never discussed the results of the new Demerol test.

"Good morning, ladies and gentlemen of the jury."

About half the jurors mouthed good morning back. This was a good sign for me, that, at the least, I'd get a hung jury.

"We all agree that nothing in this world is certain except death and taxes. Even proof positive things are not certain. Let me explain that last remark by reading from a copy of a letter One Stop Medical Labs sent to the DA' office."

Barry entered the letter into evidence with the court clerk.

"It has come to our attention that on June 21st 1977, we completed and forwarded to your office our lab test report numbered DE12435 which confirmed the Nassau County's coroners own lab report findings which we understand they completed with two readings. The conclusion we supplied agreed that, when the chemical properties of the drug Demerol in tablet form were tested against the chemical properties of Demerol in fluid form used for injections, there were some minor differences. These would not be significant to the recipient, but differences, nevertheless."

"We recently accepted a work order from attorney Barry Hodges to redo the test. He asked that the test not be rushed. He requested this because your original instructions required quick results. Please note, we were required to reveal your June '77 work order under the Freedom of Information Act."

"We regret to advise you that we now believe that the chemical differences we had noted originally were very temporary and because of the short time frame that we were working under, we were unaware of this. Our re-testing indicates that after a period of seventy two hours we found that the differences no longer existed. It was a matter of allowing the different weights to settle down first."

"We regret if anybody has been inconvenienced by these new findings. Mr. Hodges had been notified of these results and has also been sent a copy of this letter."

Barry paced up and down in front of the jury box.

"Caused who any problems? The DA? What about poor Dr. Feelgood sitting over there. No wife, no career, no money, and no future. All he got was a murder indictment based on what now turns out to be an apology. So much for scientific evidence. So much for proof positive!"

Barry walked back to the defense table. The spectators were stunned, and the jury sat quietly as the judge announced a twenty minute recess.

When the trial resumed the prosecution requested a sidebar conference with the judge and Barry was invited to join in. After five minutes or so of this powwow Barry came back to our table while the prosecutors remained at the judge's desk.

"What's up?" I asked Barry

"Well, the prosecution wants to call another witness tomorrow. However this person was not on the final witness list submitted to the court before the trial began."

"So?" I replied.

"Well, I told them that I would have to check with my client first because they now need our permission."

"It's up to you, Barry," I responded.

"This is what I'm thinking. The judge is required to tell the jury what is going on."

Then Barry went into sports talk.

"As I see it now our case is a 'slam dunk' for sure. I'm afraid that if we refuse their request the jury might think that we have something to hide. I'm inclined to continue showing strength and let them call up whomever they want. Think about this, if they were not on the stand already, how important can they be now?"

"I'll go along with this thinking," I replied.

Then I added my own sports talk.

"Why take chances now by playing their game of hardball, for God's sake?"

Barry walked back to the bench and just shook his head OK. The judge proceeded to inform the jury of what had just transpired. The new witness was scheduled to appear in the courtroom the next day at two in the afternoon, giving that person some extra time to arrive because of the short notice.

As we were leaving for the day Barry continued to talk confidently.

"You know Doc, that rental car you are driving gets very expensive. Since we only had a half day why don't you spend the afternoon shopping around for a car."

CHAPTER 29

April 25th

BARRY AND I met for one of our famous informal lunches at the courthouse cafeteria. He had spent the morning at his office developing his final arguments. He showed me some of his notes. He would first go through the State's witness list one by one and remind the jury that none of these people left the stand showing any evidence of a smoking gun. Then, of course, he planned to make mincemeat of "proof positive scientific evidence." Finally, he would contend that the prosecution failed to prove "SPECIFIC INTENT," which is an essential element of the crime and must be proven beyond reasonable doubt.

Afternoon Session

The afternoon session began on time at two o'clock. The lead prosecutor walked slowly towards the empty witness chair.

"Your honor, I now call our final witness."

I heard the high squeaky doors in the rear of the courtroom swing open. At that moment I was intently engaged in reading a copy of Barry's closing arguments again. Barry glanced back to see who was coming down the aisle.

"Who the fuck is that?" he whispered.

A very attractive blond woman in her mid-thirties was making her way to the witness stand. She wore a short skirt with a tight halter top, high heeled shoes, and plenty of jewelry.

"Who the fuck is that?" Barry repeated.

"Harriet!" I answered.

"Your Harriet?"

"Yes!"

"For the prosecution?"

"Dammed if I know!"

This kind of back and forth bantering between us became audible to the judge and he tapped his gavel softly enough to get our attention. Harriet sat down in the witness chair and did not look at me. I scribbled a note to Barry asking him why he did not ask them yesterday who their witness was. He did not respond to my note. He was not infallible after all. I believe he was so cocky, successfully defending me, it was macho not to ask. This is hard to understand, but in this case, it's true.

I considered writing him a second note giving him back the words he often used on me.

"See, you can never trust those bastards!"

I decided against it. I knew, at this point, what Barry meant when he told me the points were in the bag but, to be careful of being knocked out in the 10th round. He himself fell for a left hook!

Harriet was sworn in, took her seat and the questioning began.

"Good afternoon, please state your name, where you reside and your relationship with the defendant."

"My name is Harriet Leeds, I am from Copenhagen, Denmark and Dr. Feelgood was, as you may say, my lover and the father of my two children."

"How long have you known him?"

"About ten years."

The prosecutor then addressed the judge.

"At this point Your Honor, we must reveal that this witness has been granted full immunity from prosecution on all matters related to this trial. Naturally there is no immunity against perjury. Miss Leeds has voluntarily agreed to come from Denmark to testify about her first hand knowledge surrounding the death of Sophia Feelgood in June of 1977."

He then returned his attention to the witness.

"Why did you come here to testify today?"

"It was something that I just had to do."

"Do you have a bone to pick with the defendant?"

"What does a bone to pick mean?"

"It means that something is bothering you, which may or may not be related to the trial itself, but you just want to vent your anger about it."

"No, nothing like that at all."

"OK, so tell the court specifically why you are here."

"Because the trial has brought new information to me that I was not aware of before. This began giving me great anxiety attacks which I never had before. I don't sleep well, and have become very nervous."

"Did all this start when Dr. Feelgood returned to the United States for this trial?"

"Exactly, because I always thought that it was euthanasia, not murder, and that he did not murder her but only caused her death. That's what he told me all along. Now, knowing otherwise I panicked that I could be implicated in this whole affair even though I was duped by him."

"Miss Leeds, I understand that under strict guidelines euthanasia is legal in Denmark. Is this correct?"

"That's right! A person must be near death or suffering from great pain and drugs do not alleviate it. Then, two disinterested doctors must agree independently from one another that the criteria have been reached."

"You know, of course, that we have no process such as you just described in the United States."

"Now, I'm aware of it! That's my problem. He told me that euthanasia here was just the same as in Denmark and his wife was a candidate."

I could not believe my ears. I grabbed the note pad and slashed across the paper with my pencil, "this is all bullshit," and shoved the paper under Barry's nose.

He wrote back, "Let's get through this and see what is really happening."

Barry had no intention of objecting to anything during the questioning, even if the witness was being led and giving personal opinions. He did not want the jury to think he was stymieing her story in any way. The judge, a little stunned himself, just sat back in his chair and did not interrupt the testimony, even if some rules were being violated.

"Did Dr. Feelgood tell you how he would cause his wife's death?"

"Yes, several times. He planned it for weeks. He told me that two doctors had given their approval, and because he was a doctor himself, he could be the one who could perform the act."

"Planned it for weeks?"

"Yes!"

"So it was premeditated?"

"What does that mean?"

"It means just what you said, that he planned it for weeks."

"Yes, of course."

"Can you tell us exactly how he planned to cause her death, and did he, in fact, tell you he did it as planned?"

"Just as planned. Yes, that way."

"What way, Miss Leeds?"

"It was an overdose injection of Demerol."

"Did you say injection?"

"Yes. Injection!"

"So, what do you know about the bottle of Demerol tablets found in the bedroom that day?"

"Well, he told me that while two doctors had given their OK, he became concerned that the unusually strict authorities, in reviewing this decision, may not agree that his wife was a fit candidate for euthanasia. He decided he would make her death look like a suicide. He ordered a bottle of Demerol tablets at the hospital. He did not use the tablets at all. He only needed the manufacturer's bottle. The tablets were flushed down the toilet in his office. At the time I thought nothing about this at all."

"Do you believe now, after you have had the time to put all these events together, that Dr. Feelgood, indeed, had murdered his wife?"

"Yes, I do. It's very clear to me now. That's why I'm here."

This answer would have normally sent Barry through the wall, but he just sat in his chair looking stoic.

"I have no further questions, Your Honor."

The judge called a sidebar meeting of the lawyers. Barry returned after a few minutes to our table and told me that the judge had given him overnight to prepare for Harriet's cross examination. The trial would resume in the morning. Barry picked up his papers and told me to ride with him to his office, and, as he put it, "to go over this mess!"

As we drove away from the courthouse, Barry asked himself out loud, "what's the motive, what's the motive?"

He glanced over at me and asked me what I thought. This was the very first time during our association that he asked me what I thought. I told him that I was still in shock and could not think clearly.

"Was it money? That's always a good starting point."

"Money? How money?" I answered.

"Where is the five million dollars from the insurance?"

"It's not five million anymore, but close to it. The money is in a Swiss bank account."

"Doc, I'm beginning to cringe even before I ask you the next question."

"What's that?"

"Is Harriet's name on that account?"

"Yes" I answered.

Barry almost sideswiped a passing car.

"Where else are you sharing the wealth?" he continued.

"Well, my home, but that's my bail money now, and two other properties."

At this point there was no need for Barry to consider any other motives. When we arrived at his office he told me that it's best that he spend the time alone preparing for the next day. He volunteered to have one of his lawyers working in his office drive me home.

"Can I get a ride back to my car instead?"

"I think, Doc, it would be better to go directly home. You're too upset to drive now."

"How will I get to court tomorrow?"

"I'll come around and pick you up at 8:30."

I waited in the reception area for a few minutes. A young man came in, introduced himself, and told me that he was the chosen one.

CHAPTER 30
April 26th

I AROSE EARLY this morning, having managed to catch some intermittent sleep during the night. As I peered out my bedroom window, I noticed the young lawyer's automobile parked off the driveway on a trail leading to a wooded area, hidden by shrubbery. But, not enough! It occurred to me that Barry might have thought after my experience in the courtroom yesterday, I might opt to take off again. So, he kept my car hostage at a lock-up garage and placed an overnight watch on me.

At about 8:25 the car's engine was turned on. The driver swung the vehicle out of its perch onto the driveway and rolled down the road. This was only minutes before Barry was scheduled to arrive. It looked like a well planned changing of the guard. As Barry and I drove off to the courthouse, I questioned him about the fellow who had spent the night in his car on my property.

"Did you think that I would disappear?"

He replied, "Who knows?"

We arrived at the courthouse before nine o'clock. There was twice the number of photographers huddled on the steps as before. The spectator line rattle snaked around the corner of the building. Now, two policemen were stationed at the front doors where none had been before. That feeling of faintness came over me again. I could have kicked myself for returning at Barry's urging, but the truth was that he had delivered what he promised, a first class defense. Who could have believed that Harriet would spoil everything now and place my future in jeopardy?

We had only one shot left to salvage our case and that was for Barry to discredit Harriet's testimony. However, this would be no small feat because she flaunted the truth and held no consideration or fear of perjury implications. There was still a chance for us. We hoped that at least one juror would not believe any of her testimony, and a hung jury was as good as a not guilty verdict.

Harriet's appearance this morning was not as dramatic as yesterdays. The judge had already placed her on the witness stand, and as soon as we took our seats at the defense table, he reminded her that she continued to be under oath until dismissed. To Harriet all this talk was a bunch of bullshit. The judge beckoned Barry to come forward with his finger. Harriet stiffened up in her chair. More often than not, Barry knew the answers to his questions from witnesses, for that is what makes a good defense lawyer. However, in this case, he would be somewhat in the dark facing a blatant liar when she chose to be. He was indeed treading in uncharted waters.

"Can you tell this court your occupation now Miss Leeds."

"I am a housewife," she replied back quickly.

"That's a very noble profession, but how do you sustain yourself and your family without an income?"

"Dr. Feelgood has supported us nicely. After all, the two children are his as well."

"And now?"

"Now, my children are getting older and I expect that I will need to find employment. I have worked before, so it's no problem and thank you for asking."

"Well, frankly, Miss Leeds, I was thinking more that perhaps you put enough aside for a rainy day."

"Why only on rainy days?" she provoked.

The audience began to chuckle. The judge tapped his gavel lightly. Barry did not respond to her for he had good instincts as to when someone was putting him on, and Harriet was an expert at that.

"Do you share any assets with Dr. Feelgood?"

"What does share mean?" she quizzed.

"It means whatever money or real or personal property he owns is yours as well," he explained.

"So, we do this with some things."

"With some things! Give me a few examples."

At this point, I believe Barry was beginning to think that he was becoming a dentist again.

"Like the house in Kensington," she offered.

"Give me another example."

"Another?"

"Yes, another!"

"Two other buildings. I think they are used for offices. I'm not sure. I never saw them."

"Is that it for real property?"

"Yes"

"Do you share anything else of value?"

"Not that I could think of. I have jewelry that he gave me, but they were presents. So, that doesn't count as share, right?"

"Right," Barry sighed audibly.

The time had arrived. Barry could no longer beat around the bush. The moment of truth or the moment of lies was upon him. He took a deep breath, looked her straight in the eyes and asked:

"Do you share a Swiss bank account with Dr. Feelgood?"

"I don't know anything about a Swiss bank account," she protested.

Her answer vibrated through my head. It was a sensation which I had never felt before. For the first time in my life I lost complete control of myself. I jumped out of my chair, pounded both fists on the table in front of me and screamed out from the top of my lungs:

"You God damn liar, you're a fucking liar."

I must have repeated these words at least a half dozen more times before two court guards caught unaware, reached me. One grabbed me behind the neck from the rear, while the other shoved a cloth into my mouth and then handcuffed me. They pulled me up the center aisle, dragging me along only with my heels touching the floor. I heard those large squeaky doors open up and figured I had more miles to travel. At the end of the trip I was propped up and led into a small room. Except for a long bench the place was completely empty. I guessed that this room was meant for such occasions. I also wondered how often the room had been used before. Was it every week? Every month? Once a year? I found out the answer by asking the guard after he removed the cloth from my mouth.

"It was in 1973, sir!"

My handcuffs were then taken off. The guards left the room, and I had nothing to do but just sit down to wait for whatever. About thirty minutes later Barry was let into the room.

"That was quite a rhubarb you instigated, Doc, but, at least, we found out for sure what her motive was!"

He went on to tell me that the judge canceled the trial until the following Monday.

"It's only mid morning," Barry said, checking his watch. "Now, what will I do?"

I didn't know how to answer him. I asked him how things were left in the courtroom.

"Well, I told the judge in front of the jury that he could dismiss Harriet because I couldn't deal with stonewalling and blatant perjury anymore."

"Did you really tell him that?"

"I said I did."

"What did he say to you?"

"He admonished me slightly. I believe he had to in his role."

At this point Barry asked if there was a way that I could confirm the balance in the Swiss account. I told him that I was able to do that, but I would need a phone to make a free call. Barry left the room for a few minutes and returned with a guard holding a phone in his hand who proceeded to plug the line into a wall jack. I placed the call. The toll free automated service was available as a perk for the $20,000 annual management fee required with the account. I listened intently to the recorded information, and then slumped down on the bench.

"The balance is zero. The account was closed by "why me" which was Harriet's chosen code words on the account. I, the fool, always thought those code words referred to why I chose to love her. So, for my new code, I selected "why us."

"When was it closed?"

"Three weeks ago, but what's the difference when,"

"How did she know that you were back in the United States and when the trial date was scheduled?"

"I wrote her two letters explaining what was happening."

"Wonderful, wonderful, author, author, take a bow"

We were both speechless. There were no more options to kick around.

"Where do we go from here, Barry?"

"I know where I am going, Doc, and I wish I knew where you were going. It's getting close to lunch time now and I've got to get back to my office. My staff will be going out for lunch soon, so I have to be there to answer the phone and take messages."

He spoke those very same words to me when I first called him way back, as I left the DA's office where I was advised to get an attorney. Now, those first words are the very last words I will ever hear from Barry, for I never saw or heard from him again.

When the trial resumed, I continued defending myself with a court appointed attorney, and was sentenced to twenty-five years to life for the murder of Sophia.

POSTSCRIPT

I N 1983, AFTER several unsuccessful attempts seeking an appeal trial, I finally won the right for one thanks to an attorney from the past, Gus Sherwood. I had written to him seeking his help, not knowing if he had any experience in the Appellate Court. I detailed all the happenings at my trial, including where the five million dollars came from and the fact that the insurance company did not question the cause of death. I included a transcript of the trial so he would see how close I came to a not guilty verdict and how Harriet spoiled everything at the eleventh hour.

He replied to my letter, suggesting that he had an idea that may prove helpful. He was trying to get permission to visit me in prison, which he did a few weeks later. At that time he told me that, while he was not an appeal attorney, he would be willing to testify as a witness on my behalf. He would testify that he set up the Swiss bank account and personally wired five million dollars into the bank, and would provide written documentation of proof. He would also let the court know that he added Harriet's name to the account about four months after it was opened.

"If we establish this as fact, which we can, it will prove Harriet lied about it under oath on the witness stand. Then your lawyer will then have a solid basis to support exposing other untruths she may have testified to as well."

Gus left with me a memorandum attesting to what he had just suggested to me.

"Here, take this. Use it as new discovery evidence when applying for an appeal with the courts."

It worked, for within four months I was granted the right to appeal my conviction. In preparing my case my new attorney, Richard Press, from the prisoners legal board, researched unanswered questions from the '79 trial. He relied heavily on the Freedom

Of Information Act because he had to prove new evidence which required digging up old dirt.

Question: Why did Harriet become a prosecution witness?

Well, for the most part we already knew why, but HOW turned out to be as enlightening. Richard Press developed the chain of events. It seemed that during the preparation for the trial Harriet wrote a letter to the Nassau County DA describing basically what she testified to in court. All about her nervousness, sleeplessness, and other nesses that she was experiencing because she had been fooled by me into believing that I caused Sophia's death in the name of euthanasia. She stated that she feared being accused as an accessory to a crime. Then, she was smart enough, or someone else behind the scenes was smart enough, to volunteer to testify against me only "with full immunity from prosecution."

In a way, the DA was elated to receive such a letter, yet suspicious, with the legality of the last five words. He decided to send an investigator from his office to Copenhagen to interview her before accepting her offer.

In addition to having access to Harriet's letter to the DA, my new lawyer was able to obtain a copy of the investigator's report as well. There were no positive or negative recommendations. The interview was described as a "mixed bag."

"Her contention of being stressed out was not evident. She is a first hand witness and offers an interesting and totally damaging story to tell. Her motives remain 'fuzzy' as she has never been accused of any involvement in the death of Dr. Feelgood's wife."

The DA had distributed this report amongst his legal staff for opinions. It seems that the consensus opinion sent to him in a memo was that the case had strong witnesses lined up as well as proof positive scientific evidence. Harriet's testimony was considered somewhat risky. Basically, it was felt that over-kill was not necessary.

As we know now, the State's witnesses either fell by the wayside or were made into mincemeat, thanks to Barry's skills. At the final stage of the trial all the DA had left were the testing results for Demerol. Knowing now how this turned out for the prosecutors got Harriet throwing in the bullpen! That's how Barry would have described it.

My lawyer, Richard Press, in preparing further for the appeal, took a deposition from One Stop Labs. He learned that the DA's office was one of their best clients. Yes, they did submit an accurate honest letter to the DA about the testing they did for Barry reversing the previous results. However, before the letter went out and right after the prosecution presented their test results to the jury, they notified the DA personally by phone and read the new report to him. This was not illegal, but in taking care of an important customer, it was a prudent thing to do.

Now the situation became a real problem for the opposition. The DA was contemplating a run for Governor of New York State, and did not want to lose a high profile case. At this point he didn't bother to ask his staff for opinions, but instead, issued a verbal order . . . "fly that Leeds woman over tonight!"

The Appeal

At the Court Of Appeals three judges were assigned to review my case. As he had promised, Gus Sherwood made himself available to testify on my behalf. He brought legal proof to the table showing that Harriet was named as an equal on the Swiss account, and thus, she obviously perjured herself as a witness, stating that she had no knowledge of its existence. This opened the question as to what other perjury she had committed.

One judge did all the questioning.

Judge: Since Dr. Feelgood has been convicted of murder and, if by chance, that decision is reversed in a new trial, the cause of death would revert to suicide. So, in either case, murder or suicide, neither Dr. Feelgood or Miss Leeds ever had rightful ownership to the life insurance money. As I see it, they both stole the money but, at different times. Is this the conclusion you would agree with Mr. Sherwood? Isn't it a case of Dr. Feelgood calling the kettle black?

Gus: Your Honor, I am a witness here, but if you are asking my opinion as an attorney, I would respectfully disagree.

Judge: Disagree, how?

Gus: Because, Your Honor, at the time Dr. Feelgood received the insurance money, there was no murder conviction and the insurance company accepted the coroner's cause of death as a poisoning overdose without further clarification. If the insurance company wants to reclaim the money now, by way of the murder conviction, they can and they should. The ball is in their court. If, as you speculated, the murder conviction is reversed in a new trial, the cause of death may revert to suicide where the insurance payment can also be recalled, or to accidental suicide where the insurance company should have paid double. So, you see, Your Honor, it's not all black or white.

The judge thought about what Gus had just said and did not reply, but ended the session promising a decision within three weeks. It was three weeks later when my court appointed attorney was notified to return to the court to hear the decision.

Unanimous agreement by all three judges was required. All three judges were in agreement that Harriet did, in fact, commit perjury by denying any knowledge of the account. However, the vote was only 2 to 1 to remand the case back to the lower court for retrial. The two judges ruled that I should have the opportunity to prove that Harriet's other testimony could have been flawed as well to conceal her real motive for testifying in the first place. The dissenting judge didn't quite see it that way. He said in his written decision:

"There was no proof presented of specific additional perjury. If there was, there would have been a more solid basis for a successful retrial of the murder conviction, not for financial mishap."

I sat in my cell waiting for my lawyer to return with the bad news, which deep in my gut I expected, but it was a good try anyway.

I began a new career as a medical aide to prison doctors. Many of them had lost their licenses for one reason or another. They were on probation, working gratis, under some community service agreement until their licenses would be reinstated. The State sure finds ways to circumvent anti-slavery laws!

One never knows in prison what the next day may bring. While it's usually much of the same old thing, sometimes it's not. One of these, "it's not days," came along for me when a prison guard delivered a registered letter, for which I had to sign. My first instinct was that it must be very important. Perhaps the judge, that prick, changed his mind and my appeal was granted. I was always thinking of getting out of this hole. Then I glanced at the sender's name. It was from my son of all people. I ripped open the envelope, curious as to its contents. He had written a two page letter.

Basically, it began as a saga in the continuing life of that damn engagement ring. It seems that he and my daughter were concerned with the high cost of insurance I'm sure they learned a lesson from me and never considered self insuring the ring. So, they stored the ring in a bank's safety deposit box, as their mother had, and peeked at it now and then. Now, it seems, that my daughter needed more funds to do what she does, which is bubkis, (nothing). She talked my son into selling it and he agreed because and I quote, "it was silly to have it languish in that dark box." I wondered if he felt as bad having his father languishing in a little dark cell. Here is the part of the letter where the shit hit the fan!

"What the fuck is going on?" He gently wrote. "The appraisal was a joke. The ring is glass, and worth only a few hundred bucks. What are you going to do about it?"

Well, I thought to myself, here I'm sitting in a six by nine jail cell in my fourth year of a twenty five to life sentence and I can't seem to come up with any good ideas for him. However I did understand his frustration as I was privy to what broadcaster Paul Harvey calls "the rest of the story."

At that manic moment in Bangkok when I added Harriet's name to the bank account, I also gave her the blue diamond ring and announced that we were officially engaged. I did not know its value, but imagined it was quite high. Harriet felt uncomfortable wearing the ring in public after we arrived in India. Her discomfort was not that it was so huge, but that it was so valuable. The only way to insure anything of great value in India was to hire a hit man!

There was a factory in New Delhi called, "Sparkling Imposters." They designed, copied, manufactured, and sold unbelievable jewelry fakes. One needed a telescope to ascertain the real from the not real. We brought the ring there, where they photographed it and two weeks later we picked up an exact zircon copy for which I paid six hundred dollars and well worth it. Just as an aside, my feelings were hurt when my son called the zircon glass.

Anyway, Harriet wore the ring all the time. When she went back to Denmark to bring the kids back for the holidays she deposited the original in a bank's safety deposit box in Copenhagen. When Harriet left me in Turkey the zircon was among the fun jewelry she left behind. I took it back to the States, and now you know the "rest of the story."

About every few months we had access to an attorney from the prisoner's legal bureau. At the next opportunity I requested a meeting. I showed my son's letter to a visiting lawyer and recreated on paper, to the best of my ability, my agreement with the estate. While I had no inclination to do anything, anyway, I was just curious as to the consequences of my silence. He asked about the date of the agreement. I knew exactly what it was.

"I don't know if you are aware of this. The Statute of Limitations has expired in a case such as this, except if fraud has been committed."

"I was told that it is three years, correct?"

"Correct, but not if fraud is involved."

I guess he was trained to emphasize this aspect because, after all, he was talking to prisoners every day.

"Well, the three years are up, so I guess I can just sit on it."

"Please take this as a joke, Doc, but just sitting on it now is your strongest suit!"

"Ha," I replied. "I can take a joke even if it cuts deep."

The lawyer pointed out that he noticed in the agreement that it does not mention the word diamond. It only refers to a fourteen carat ring. This was only a mute point now for him. However, for me, it was not only a foundation of a response to my son, but an opportunity to discredit my dear father-in-law, (may he rest in peace anyway), for putting a price on my head.

I thanked the attorney for his time and interest and began constructing a letter to my son.

July 2nd 1983

I received your letter and have been pondering its contents. You may be interested to know that I showed it an attorney and he advised me that the Statute of Limitations has expired. I hope that you don't think that I'm making this up. You can check it out for yourself. However, in any event, if you read on you will see it has no bearing upon anything, anyway.

First of all, if you re-read the agreement you will notice that I never mentioned a blue diamond ring. I agreed to return a fourteen carat ring. How would I know if it were a blue diamond ring? I'm a surgeon and a proctologist, not a gemologist!

Now this is the most important part to consider. Since your grandfather made part of his fortune applying phony designer labels onto his shmatus (rags), he was surely capable of coming up with a phony bill of sale and appraisal for a piece of glass which his wife would never have questioned. Think about this now. How come he never insured such a "valuable" ring when he insured his factories to the hilt?

I don't mean this to be a pun, but it's crystal clear to me what has happened. Let me end this letter with a piece of wisdom I picked up in my travels. There is an old Chinese saying which states, "happiness does not depend upon what you have, it depends upon what you think you have!"

P.S. You can pass this letter along to your sister as I am now giving up my last precious stamp."

I then turned my thoughts to the real stone laying somewhere in a dark safety deposit box in Copenhagen, or perhaps, on Harriet's finger. After all, I never officially broke off the engagement. Anyway, the ring is destined to be worn in the future by my daughter Susan in Denmark. Therefore, I named it "The Feelgood Diamond," because it will make her feel good one day.

My committee of former patients and friends disbanded after my appeal failed. I can't say that I blamed them. After all, they took responsibility for the effort, not the outcome. Only the group's founder, Ruth Schattner, continued to keep in touch with me on a regular basis through mutual correspondence, mostly about mundane every day living. She was on the outside, living in heaven, while I was on the inside, rotting in hell.

However, I must admit that when one's expectations are at times reduced to zero, one really appreciates everything one does have, including the postage stamps included with Ruth's letters. I appreciated her contacting some new attorneys who I thought might take an interest in my case. They took their sweet time answering my letters. I also appreciated being alive, as well, while witnessing the daily deaths from medical neglect, stabbings, beatings, and then came along, the dreadful AIDS.

I became kosher again, not so much through a reawakening of my religious traditions, but rather, in order to upgrade my meals to a palpable level. Muslim prisoners followed suit probably for the same reason. I must confess, however, that I do miss my McDonald's lunches, particularly the fries.

Ruth Schattner suggested that I might consider requesting a clemency hearing. She even volunteered to write to the Governor directly and recount the strong community support I had received and other good things. I told her to go ahead and that I would put in my request at the prison. Fortunately, I could accomplish this without a lawyer as the prison supplied the necessary forms. The process took almost a half a year. I finally received a one word reply ... DENIED. Ruth was more fortunate because, I guess, she could vote and influence others. The Governor's office saw fit to thank her for "a well drafted letter," and proceeded to explain the Governor's criteria for clemency consideration which she passed onto me.

"The Governor views clemency as the act of forgiving a person the criminal liability of his acts, because of extenuating circumstances, and/or consideration of fairness in particular cases. The record indicates that Dr. Feelgood has never acknowledged his guilt of the crime for which he was convicted. Thus, making any consideration of his petition a mute request."

I was not surprised at the decision for two reasons. Firstly the State of New York is expert at creating catch twenty two situations. Ask any taxpayer. Secondly, the Governor at the time, was Dennis Dillard, the former DA, who succeeded in putting me here in the first place.

Ruth added thoughts about asking for things through prayer. She finally realized, more than I would admit, that this avenue was becoming more practicable than asking for things through the justice system.

Ruth became my only contact now with the outside world. Then, suddenly and surprisingly, her regular letters ceased to arrive. I wrote a letter to her to find out if everything was all right. I received a letter from her niece, Adele. She had just learned of our relationship. She informed me that her aunt had passed away from a heart attack, and had just found all my letters neatly stored in a cigar box among her effects.

Adele's letter included an intuitive and comforting thought suggesting that the loss of her aunt was almost as great, or perhaps greater, to me then it was to her. No doubt she came out of the same mold as Ruth, yet more realistic and honest in her perception of my situation. She spoke, not about faith, belief, and hope, but rather, about failure, mistakes, responsibility, and forgiveness. I have saved her letter and continue to ponder upon its contents from time to time, but could never draw upon the courage to succumb to its advice.

"Everyone makes mistakes and has failures," she wrote, "but it is only an error in judgment to make a mistake. However, it shows a defect of character to adhere to it when discovered. The man who can own up to his error is greater than the man who merely knows how to avoid making it. To receive forgiveness for a mistake is the most beautiful form of love. In return you will receive untold peace and happiness."

Every dog has its day

I conclude my postscript under the above heading. I came across a news article in one of the local newspapers available in the prison library. The headline caught my eye, "REPORTING FRAUD ALMOST PAYS OFF." No names were given, but there was enough detail to know that it was about me and the person who reported the fraud. That person was described as the whistle blower and former insurance agent, better known to me as "that runt."

The story first explained that it is standard practice for most insurance companies to offer rewards to those that report fraudulent claims that had been paid, leading to the prosecution and conviction of the guilty parties. The reward is usually 10% of the recovery value.

It seems that "the runt" must have become aware, through media coverage, of my appeal efforts. My unusual last name must have jostled his memory that our paths had crossed before. At the time of my trial in '79 he had been in jail for insurance fraud, so he must have been unaware of my situation until now. He probably remembered the five million dollar policy being a little above average in value and our discussion when I told him that my wife committed suicide.

I can only speculate that "the runt," knowing his way around in insurance circles, checked out old death benefits and found out that I had collected in full. Bingo! The light must have gone on in his head. He must have taken a shit thinking about the $500,000 windfall. I'm sure he felt that this was far better than cashing $100 insurance premium checks and legal to boot!

The article went on to report that the recipient of a five million dollar life insurance policy deposited the money in a Swiss bank in 1977, and a co-owner transferred the balance to another account in April of 1979. According to investigators, approximately three million was found intact and frozen under an international court order dealing with fraud.

I knew that I had spent and lost close to a half million dollars from the time I fled the United States until the time of my trial. I know now that Harriet's four year party was worth another million and a half, and now "the runt" expected a 10% or $300,000 reward. However, the article reports that the insurance company refused his claim on the basis that he had, at the time he was working for them, a fiduciary obligation to have notified them that I reported my wife's death to him as a suicide.

Indeed, every dog has his day, and as I finished reading the story I knew that today I was that dog. So, I yelped out loud twice, "woof, woof," once for "the runt" and again for Harriet. Now poor Harriet had to find work for real. This would not be difficult for her. She was literally working her ass off when we first met. I was a physician looking for a good time while at a convention in Copenhagen, and she was a prostitute in the Red Light District.